This is one of those books that can be consider── nuisance, if you are not the one reading it. Chuckles and hoots issuing from the next seat, deckchair, or bed maybe, can be so tiresome. I sincerely hope I am to blame – for writing *Five Times as Funny*!

Peter James's comment was, 'A marvellously funny read!'
From Boris Johnson came 'Very funny!'
Willie Rushton 'loved it' and so did Alan Coren.
Spike Milligan wrote of the first book, 'I am in very great company indeed!'

My own acknowledgements go to

WODEHOUSE
RUNYON
MILLIGAN
THURBER

– all of whose influence might, I hope, be detected here and there.

Hilaire Belloc famously said

'...There's nothing worth the wear of winning,
But laughter and the love of friends.'

If these pages of humour lead my readers in that direction, my own enjoyment in writing them will have been doubly rewarded.

Bernard

FIVE TIMES AS FUNNY

Bernard Bush

The Book Guild Ltd
Sussex, England

First published in Great Britain in 2003 by
The Book Guild Ltd
25 High Street
Lewes, East Sussex
BN7 2LU

Typesetting in Palatino by
Keyboard Services, Luton, Bedfordshire

Printed in Great Britain by
Athenaeum Press Ltd, Gateshead

A catalogue record for this book is available from
The British Library

ISBN 1 85776 732 2

CONTENTS

THE POT THICKENS

The Life and Loves of Lord Limpet

MR RUTUMUTU

1

M'Bongabonga

The Reverend Bruce Featherstone-Phipps stood up to his armpits in water in the ceremonial tribal cooking-pot contemplating his predicament.

There seemed to be no explanation for it, and he sought guidance from above. He was satisfied that the N'Chuyu tribe were his good friends, and he was especially fond of the Witch Doctor himself – on Christian name terms in fact, with him and his several attractive wives. The latest wife he had found particularly fascinating, and her ready interest in the biblical stories and her quick grasp of the English language had encouraged him to devote many hours to her private tuition at the Mission, sometimes late into the night.

Chief Tumtumroli (affectionately known to him as Fred) also had good reason to show his appreciation for the special attention he had paid to the religious

3

development of his handsome youngest son, and the progress being made on the concept of 'turning the other cheek'.

Life is so strange. What would his dear wife Sybil have thought of this extraordinary situation? It was just three years since she had passed away and thereby denied him that devoted comfort and guidance he always felt was heaven sent.

He could feel the heat of the fire now and the water beginning to warm up around his feet. He searched his mind for a prayer or hymn appropriate to the occasion, a talent he prided himself on, but he could remember no references in any ecclesiastical manuals or lecture notes on this subject. In any case, his congregation did not appear to be in the mood to join him in prayer or hymn singing at that particular time; indeed, they seemed to be singularly uninterested, assuming of course that they were all aware of what, to coin a phrase, was cooking.

No men were to be seen, but the women were busy with their normal morning chores, sweeping out the kraal, carrying small babies on their backs and cuffing and cursing the others as they played and fought with each other in the dusty spaces between the forty-odd mud huts that constituted the village of M'Bongabonga. Such a charming little community, thought the Rev. B.F. (as he had always been known at home). So kind and welcoming to him on his frequent visits to bring the holy bread and wine from the Mission to the open-air services. It was such a pity that due to the directive received last week from London, he had had to announce that this tradition would have to stop. He conceded that perhaps the provision of wines had become a little excessive at several crates a week, but the congregation had grown so rapidly and they did seem to enjoy the

FRED

services so much. Clearly, they had been disappointed at the news, and here he was.

Two of the women came over just then to put some more branches on the fire and gave him a friendly little wave as they did so. He recognised them as the senior wives of the Chief and the Witch Doctor and acknowledged them with a nod, that being the limit of his freedom to proffer the common courtesies natural to his upbringing, such as raising his hat.

He missed his clothes. Naturally he could quite understand that it would hardly be sensible, in any society, to prepare a meal which included a straw hat or a suit-length of barathea, but there remained a degree of indignity in complete nudity even when it was concealed by a three-quarter-length pot. He began to muse on the likely wearers of each piece of his attire, and was pleased and relieved to know that his underclothes were clean on that morning. It would have been such a comfort to Sybil.

It was at this moment that he noticed what was happening to his beloved bicycle. The basket had been removed from the front of the handlebars and was being worn as a headdress by a nubile young female who was not otherwise wearing very much, except for the cycle-chain around her neck and the bell cover in the loop of her ear lobe. Even in the heat of the present moment, so to speak, the Rev. B.F., wearing rather less, could not but admire the beauty of this vision and wonder at the breathtaking works of nature bestowed on us by the good Lord.

Meanwhile, the group of youths who had taken charge of the bicycle had now discovered that with the machine lying on the ground they could spin the wheels, and using an old shin-bone on the spokes, produce sounds much in advance of the usual jungle drums, plus some far more interesting noises from the smaller children as they took it in turns to try sticking their fingers into the spokes at the same time.

Reminiscing, he recalled his delight when Sybil had bought him this Raleigh bicycle on the occasion of his thirtieth birthday, having sent away to Harrods for its special delivery. And how, bless her, she had insisted that he lose no time and should set off there and then into the jungle to master the riding of it, quite regardless of the impending storm, and of those rumours of a man-eating leopard in the neighbourhood. She was such a brave woman, and so outgoing in her nature. It was in fact that very generosity that had apparently led to her sad and untimely demise. She had not needed to...

At that moment his thoughts were interrupted by a sudden call of nature. He wished to break wind. So embarrassing at such a time, and much against all the etiquette instilled in him by his mother, especially at meal times. Would there be a noise, and if so, would it reverberate via the pot? And what of the bubbles? Should one in the circumstances apologise, or would it be possible to feign innocence?

He blamed it on the beans and Brussels sprouts he had so carefully nurtured in the Mission garden, and he remembered a word of warning on the subject from dear Sybil. Oh dear, such indignity he was about to inflict on the church he had represented and worked all his life for. Until, say, about six thirty or so this evening that is, after which there would be nothing more he could do about it.

He considered the time factor a little further. He realised, quite simply, that he had time on his hands (which in fact were tied behind his back with a secure binding of creeper) and tried to remember the formula so often quoted by Sybil regarding cooking time per

CARSTAIRS

pound when producing one of her excellent Irish stews. Momentarily, his mouth watered at the memory. It had been so long since he had enjoyed such delicious meals, particularly her roasts. He had to admit he preferred roast to boiled, when the chips are down, as the saying goes. She had so loved entertaining.

That side of her nature had never been better illustrated than in her concern for Carstairs. Roger Carstairs was a colonial administrator stationed some ten miles down river, a pleasant lonely man who became a frequent visitor after a while, attracted no doubt by dear Sybil's skill in the kitchen.

This seemed to be improved by his visits, probably as a result of the many hours they spent together discussing culinary matters while Bruce was out and about spreading the word in the far-flung depths of his vast parish, which could take him many days to traverse on his bicycle. It had been a great comfort to him to know that his dear wife would probably not be lonely for the entire time, and could invariably rely on a passing visit from Carstairs when Bruce was known to be on his travels.

And that, unfortunately, was how the tragedy had occurred. How she had known that Roger was so desperately ill and in need of her help he never really understood, but it seems that on that stormy night she had thrown caution to the winds and, with her customary generosity of spirit, packed a few essentials in the canoe and set out to paddle down river to his assistance, leaving a short note propped up on the pulpit in the Mission. She was never seen again.

That was the story, as Carstairs, who made an excellent and speedy recovery from his illness, had tearfully explained in considerable detail, whilst taking what comfort he could get from several large doses of Johnnie Walker.

Once again, he felt great pity for Carstairs at so unwittingly having been the cause of his sad loss, as he affectionately called to mind that last heart-rending communication from his beloved wife which he had framed and fixed on the wall over his bed.

Dear Bru-Bru,

I have to go to poor dear Roger. Clean laundry is on the line. Avoid beans and brussels sprouts.

Sybikins

Sometimes life does seem to move in the most mysterious way, he thought, forever trying and testing one's faith to the limit.

Moving uncomfortably from one foot to the other, he viewed his present circumstances as one of those occasions.

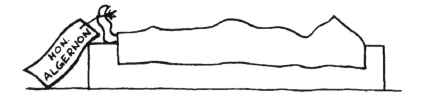

2

Algernon

He was presently aroused from his reverie by a plop in the water in front of his nose, followed by a series of small missiles falling at random on or about his head. Without his spectacles (which he now noticed were being worn with great pride by a sweet old lady at the centre of a large family group), he could not immediately identify anything so close to his face. But the smell soon gave him a clue and so did the occupation of the tribeswomen, in which he now took a much closer interest.

A variety of vegetables, leaves, flowers and roots were being chopped and pounded in the entrances of all the nearby huts, producing a strange and quite unfamiliar range of the most succulent and appetising smells. This aroma was stimulated as the ingredients suffused into the water, so that even the gastric juices of the Rev. B.F.

himself were aroused. If only he could have communicated some of these culinary secrets to poor dear Sybil, how excited she would have been. She so loved to experiment with new exotic herbs and flavours, and he remembered well the many occasions when she had welcomed him home with some new novelty boiling away in the stockpot.

'Bru-bru,' she would say, 'you really must try my latest recipe, a little something I've just cooked up,' after consultation with some passing native or the discovery of a new root or fungus. Poor dear, her constitution was such that she simply could not enjoy stews of this kind, and relied entirely on his judgement before entering them into her ever-growing cookbook – a work she said she hoped to publish when they returned to civilisation in due course.

Inevitably, they were not all successful, and there were times, quite a number of them as he now recalled, when they could result in the most unpleasant reaction. Indeed, on two occasions he was saved from an early grave only by the fortuitous appearance on his periodic rounds of the region by dear old Percy Littlejohn, the colonial medic, complete with his stomach pump.

Sybikins was so upset that he had the utmost difficulty in consoling her, and Percy Littlejohn declared he had never seen such grief and devotion in a woman, as she took careful note of his itinerary for future reference. No man ever had a more considerate and far-sighted spouse.

Their marriage had in fact owed much to this out-standing facet of her multi-talented character. He remembered as if it was yesterday their first meeting, and that formal introduction at a house party at her family seat, very shortly after the announcement in *The Times* of the untimely death of his elder brother, Algernon. Reportedly, it had taken the staff three weeks to discover the well-preserved body in the vast cellars of Cawkwell Hall.

DR PERCY LITTLEJOHN

This sad event, to his dismay, had put him in line to succeed to the Barony and all the responsibilities of the family estates. It was a prospect which filled him with the desperate fear that, fresh from his ordination, his ambition to spread the gospel as a missionary might well be thwarted.

Sybil and her beloved mamma had been both sympathetic and supportive in regard to his bereavement, inviting him to share the burden of his grief with them by staying overnight, which, after the departure of the other guests and the unaccountable failure of his driver to collect him, he was pleased to accept. Looking back, he realised what a lucky coincidence it had been that two

AUGUSTINE   SYBIL

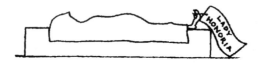

of the wheels of the Daimler-Benz had disappeared from where it had been parked in the grounds awaiting his return journey. Such a blessing in such a disguise, for which he again thanked the good Lord as he had so often done before.

Within a few days, by which time the wheels had been traced and refitted, they found themselves on the most intimate terms, using Christian names and from time to time holding hands, so that he had little difficulty in persuading the fascinating Sybil to pay him a return visit to the baronial hall. Their engagement and marriage followed almost as though predestined, with the minimum of delay befitting such an important alliance.

Management and finance not being his forte, the Rev. B.F. was delighted to discover that his new life partner was particularly talented in this regard, and was happy to leave mundane matters of this kind in her very capable hands. Thus it was that the Old Manor House, her family seat, was sold (or as she explained, set against the family mortgage) and her charming mother Augustine moved in to join them at the Hall. Such a sensible arrangement, and one which his aging father, old Lord Limpet, viewed with an open, and generally absent, mind.

Ever since the demise of the late Lady Honoria Limpet in that unfortunate incident with the hounds, the noble lord had pottered happily through life with enviable carefree abandon, once he had recovered from mourning the loss of the dogs that had to be put down.

3

Cawkwell Hall

A sudden commotion in the village compound brought him back to an acute awareness of the matter in hand. His erstwhile friend Mr Rutumutu, the Witch Doctor, had returned with some other members of the tribe from what apparently had been an unsuccessful hunting expedition. He seemed at that moment to be berating some of the womenfolk for allowing the fire under the pot to die down somewhat, and indeed the Rev. noticed now that the temperature had remained at a comfortable level – he estimated 70°F or so, give or take 5°. He did not regard himself as expert in such matters, and once again wished he had paid more attention to the expertise of his dearly departed – she would have been specific to within 1°.

Whatever it was, Mr Rutumutu was certainly unhappy about it, dipping his finger in the water and eyeing the

Rev. in a rather less companionable fashion than had been the case in the past.

'*M'bunga mugubangochomchom zumpampapa zumchuchu rutumbubu n'chukshuk bogo m'bingo,*' he said, or words to that effect, as he tasted the flavouring on his finger.

For the benefit of any readers unfamiliar with the language, this was an order for more of one particularly pungent root to be prepared and introduced. The older children were sent flying with a whack from the flat of his assegai to collect more tinder and to cut logs, and a large pile soon started to build up ready for use by the womenfolk.

Not a very hopeful prospect, thought the Rev., trying without success to catch the eye of the Witch Doctor and engage him in polite conversation. Mr Rutumutu seemed for the moment too deeply engrossed in the business of painting his face, adjusting the bone through his nose, preening his ceremonial headdress and untangling his tooth necklace, to respond. There, in the mind's eye of the Rev. B.F. stood his mother-in-law, Augustine. For her, the procedure of making-up, the selection of hairpieces and wigs, and the application of eyelashes, teeth and bosoms were an accomplished art form which would have been the envy of Mr Rutumutu. Much as 'Brucy darling' loved her, as he knew he should, he could not help wishing that she would remain a little plainer and more wholesome, and that she could be persuaded to use his simple Christian name; neither of which prayers were ever answered.

His father, on the other hand, found her more attractive than his son would have preferred, and it was but a few short weeks before it became apparent that, God willing, Lord Limpet would lead his second bride to the altar. There developed, sad to say, a distinct chilliness in the relationship of dear Sybil to her mother – perhaps frigidity would be more accurate. Indeed, by the time

LORD LIMPET

the marriage took place and the centre of authority changed hands, it became apparent that, large as the baronial hall was (and there were some thirty bedrooms, fully en suite, with all the most up-to-date plumbing and thirty staff), there was no longer room in it for both mother and daughter.

The problem was solved quite simply and to the complete satisfaction of the Rev. B.F., whose dreams came true. The influence of the noble lord was, at the persuasion of his new bride, brought to bear on the elders of the Church Council. In no time at all his son was given his wish and granted the post of Missionary to a vast area somewhere in central Africa, a region which the elders in their wisdom made no attempt to identify exactly.

It would be difficult to put into words the views of Sybil on this turn of events. The Rev. could not escape the feeling that her heart and soul were not in the project, though she did say, and he loved her for it, that she would go to the ends of the earth to make sure that she took good care of him.

With tears of love for his lost spouse in his eyes, he looked up and beyond Mr R. to where, emerging from a jungle path, he saw a group of tribal warriors led by Fred, and in their midst there appeared to be a captive. The entire village seemed to gather round and murmurs of admiration were mixed with chants as the stories of their dangerous adventures were told and the next tribal meal was examined.

Finally the captive was led into the open, and their eyes met.

'Pimples!'

'Phippsy!'

'Good lord.'

'Amazing.'

'How are you after all these years?'

'Wizard. And you?'

'Keep pretty fit, y'know.'

'How long has it been now?'

'Seems like a lifetime.'

'What are you doing in there?'

Before 'Phippsy' could think of a suitable reply they were rudely interrupted by Fred. Orders were being given to the women, and the elders were being called together for an *ad hoc* meeting on the subject of this addition to the menu. It appeared to 'Phippsy' that his

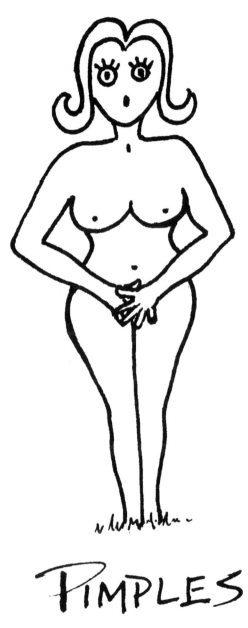

PIMPLES

old school and college friend was also being prepared for the pot. She was attractively buxom, which he found a pleasant change from the angularity of Sybil, and whilst he felt it right and proper that he should avert his eyes as items of her underwear were removed, he simply found it impossible not to take a quick peep now and then. She had developed a lot since their school days, and what he saw he liked.

Piece by piece her garments were stripped off and distributed, and he sympathised with her distress at the inconsiderate treatment given to her highly fashionable (and very expensive) dress and jacket. Her sheer silk stockings were quite thoughtlessly laddered in removal, and as for her lace panties – it was so sad to see. Her hat became the property of the Witch Doctor, as he wanted the feather in it for his headdress.

With her hands tied behind her, 'Pimples' was now considered 'oven-ready'.

'Surely,' thought the Rev., 'they will save one of us for a rainy day.' But no, it seemed that the deliberations of the committee had come down in favour of a 'joint venture', a decision he had guessed when he saw that the casting vote fell to Fred, who could eat like three men, and sometimes did.

Pimples was calm and exhibiting true British phlegm. 'Stiff upper lip' might not be quite correct, as there was a slight quiver noticeable to Phippsy as he surveyed the lady who was, it seemed, about to join him for dinner. Was there room for two, or would it be a case of 'one for the pot? (He must remember to tell her that.)

He was carried back to those happy school days when he had pulled her pigtails and she had kicked his shins. Such jolly times, and he wondered why they had not bothered to keep in touch. That would literally be corrected very shortly.

21

Her thoughts were, at that moment, more mundane. So nice to meet up with old Phippsy again, but hardly in the ideal circumstances. Why on earth, she asked herself, had she accepted that mad invitation to go on a safari, especially with that idiot Sidney Sidebottom? Pity about the waterfall incident, but truth to tell, she wouldn't really miss him terribly. Even if there was time to.

She viewed the prospect of a dinner date with Phippsy as quite an attractive one, given a more romantic setting. They'd always got on rather well together, and she had read of his marriage six years ago with just a little sadness and just a touch of envy. Her mother had been at pains to point out how close she might have come to a title, and to the stewardship of a baronial hall which, she had heard say, had some thirty-odd bedrooms fully en suite, with all the latest plumbing and thirty staff. Mumsie wouldn't understand, of course, that Pimples (Cynthia to mumsie) had no such ambitions. The grand lifestyle would be a bore, and her real interest was in travel and in the study of primitive life and conditions.

It seemed that she was about to experience a surfeit of fulfilment.

SIDNEY SIDEBOTTOM

4

Thongs at Twilight

The compound of the M'Bongabonga village was a hive of activity. With a generous feast in prospect, many eyes had been surveying the main course in some detail, with a view to getting at least a small share of the more succulent and tender portions. Inevitably, this concentrated all attention on Pimples, not only because she was at present fully exposed but also because of the obvious preference of any sensible diner for the chump little lady over the rake-like minister. Arguments broke out on the subject of timing. Clearly it would be advisable to leave Pimples in rather longer, yet there were technical difficulties involved in taking one out before the other. Two pots would certainly be the correct answer but unfortunately their spare communal pot had been badly cracked only last week in an undignified scramble by the youngsters hacking out the remains of the last jumbo meal.

So setting the problem on one side for the moment, Miss Cynthia Pinkerton-Smythe was duly hoisted up and gently lowered into the water, carefully avoiding any unnecessary bruising. To achieve this via the limited space available in the neck of the pot, considerable personal contact with the Reverend Father was unavoidable, and while he could not but enjoy a certain thrill resulting from this procedure, he did make commendable efforts to make her feel welcome, and to create the minimum of embarrassment for her by compressing himself against the side and by turning his face away as the more intimate parts went by. Nevertheless, very little was left to his imagination, and a great deal went through his mind, not all of it true to the cloth.

He thought a word of welcome would be in order, if only to break the ice.

'What ho!' he said. It seemed inadequate. 'So nice to see something of you again.'

Not quite right. He thought hard.

'Come in, the water's lovely.' No, 'Welcome to my humble abode.' Hardly. Broaden the conversation perhaps.

'Whatever became of young Binstead Minor?' he said.

'Went to the Punjab,' she replied. 'Went to pot.' And on second thoughts, 'Sorry about that.'

There was a sort of conversational void.

'What are you doing in these parts?' she finally came out with.

'Converting the natives.'

'Oh.'

A silence.

'Anything I can do to help?' she volunteered.

'Not right now,' was all he could manage.

All these diversions had resulted in a lack of attention to the fire again, and now the men gave assistance and a few bruises to the women in charge of that duty.

They fanned the embers and with the aid of some dry brushwood, that soon got a really cheerful fire going. A good deal of smoke was created, for which Phippsy felt obliged to apologise, it being his pot and his congregation.

'Can't blame you, Phippsy.'

'S'pose not,' he said. 'But I do abhor smoking.'

'So do I,' she replied. 'Especially before the Loyal Toast.'

At this point the Reverend Father experienced a rather embarrassing sensation. Cramp. The big toe on his right foot had quite seized up and was agonising.

'Pimples,' he said, 'please excuse me, but I suddenly have a most embarrassing sensation.'

'Oh Phippsy, my dear, not here surely.'

'I'm afraid so, and I'm going to need your help to deal with it.'

'What exactly would you like me to do? The space is very limited.'

'Pimples, do you think you could possibly ... no, I don't like to ask.'

'Try, Phippsy darling,' she said.

He noted that welcome endearment, but was in too much pain to respond adequately.

'It's my big toe,' he said. 'On my right foot – I need you to tread on it.'

There was a distinct note of disappointment in her reply.

'Certainly,' she said, and gave a hefty stamp that failed to cure the actual problem, but at least diverted his attention to another more painful one.

At that very moment a fly landed on the end of his nose. 'Pimples, my dear...'

But by this time she was rather pointedly looking the other way. This directed her gaze eye to eye with Fred, who immediately began to drool. She quickly turned back to Phippsy.

'Yes, darling?'

'Pimples, my sweet, could you please do anything about this wretched fly?' It had by this time made a move, only to alight again on his upper lip.

'With pleasure,' she whispered, and on tip-toe gave him the most pleasurable kiss of his life.

'Phippsy,' she cooed, 'I have an itch, but I daren't tell you where.'

They laughed happily, causing great consternation to the villagers, who felt that the ceremony was not being taken as seriously as it should be. They threw on a few more logs.

As things began to warm up and the day wore on, it became noticeable that one by one the villagers retired to their huts, first for a siesta, and then to dress for dinner and indulge in a drink or two beforehand. Feast days were there to be enjoyed, and luckily they still had a few crates of the good preacher's wine left for the celebration.

It seemed to be getting dark a little earlier than usual today, and the glow of the fire was intensified. The drummers had started, with a few gentle rhythms to begin with, and excitement was in the air.

Pimples had been thinking. Finally she whispered, 'Phippsy darling.'

'Pimples, my pet, what is it?'

'Phippsy darling, I've been thinking.'

As a matter of fact, so had the Rev. Featherstone-Phipps, but to little avail. It was not his forte.

'Phippsy dear, don't think me rude or stand-offish, will you.'

'My dear, how could I?'

'What I mean is, wouldn't it be a good idea for us to stand back to back.'

With the heat affecting him as it now was, he could think of at least one reason to do so, though he found he really was enjoying her company and didn't wish to give the wrong impression.

'If you wish to, my pet,' he said.

'It seems to me,' she went on, 'that we might then be able to hold hands...'

'What a touching thought,' he said, quite unwittingly.

'...and then maybe we could release each other's thongs.'

The Rev. recognised immediately how the hand of the Lord was showing itself, through the humble medium of this blessed little woman.

Putting the plan into action did create two or three physical problems, two of them were hers certainly, but gently jostling each other they managed the manoeuvre, and began to feel around for each other's thongs. The exploration was quite an exciting experience for both of them, but they made it, and found the release of the bindings to be not too difficult.

The freeing of hands could hardly be said to solve their basic problem, but they could at least offer great comfort to each other, passing the time with little games learnt in the nursery such as 'this little piggy...' and 'one two, buckle my shoe', etc.

With their attention otherwise engaged, they had not noticed how very dark it was now getting, but a flash of lightning followed closely by a peal of thunder, which they had hitherto attributed to distant drums, now sent all the villagers running for cover, having only one party dress each to their names. When the rain came, it pelted down. Smoke billowed from the fire as the water doused the flames, and the pot filled up rapidly. By the time it had started to overflow, the weight became too much for the supporting bough; it snapped, and the pot rolled away, disgorging its contents into the jungle *en route...*

5

While Stocks Last

The announcement in *The Times* of the passing of
Lord Limpet gave very few details of his lifetime
achievements. There were but a couple of lines to credit
him with his successful development of his enlarged
ear-trumpet, and a brief word or two on his research
into gout and its causes (which, incidentally, was later
abandoned when it led in the direction of port and
sherry intake). Lady Augustine Limpet was described as
devastated and speechless with grief, although there
were those in the servants' hall who attributed her
condition to other causes, gin being but one of them.

Lady Limpet had over the last few years born the loss
of communication with her daughter and son-in-law
with admirable fortitude. She carried the responsibilities
of running the estates and controlling the family fortunes
without complaint, and had sensibly taken care to ensure

the security of much of the wealth of the family by wearing it on her fingers and hanging it round her neck.

The problem now was succession. Somewhere in the depths of the African jungle there was, presumably, the new Lord Limpet, last known and seen off as the Reverend Bruce Featherstone-Phipps, with his dear wife Sybil. There was no dire urgency to bring them back 'while stocks last', but the cellars were finite and subject to heavy demands from both above and below stairs. Moreover, the family solicitor, Eustace Pratt, insisted that what remained of the Limpet fortune, which was still sufficiently sizeable to ensure that his substantial fees were well covered, must remain frozen pending the return of His (new) Lordship.

Something had to be done, and enquiries through the Church Council produced the most vague replies. The last communication seemed to have been one directed to the Mission, cutting off supplies of holy wine, which had reached proportions not dissimilar to the standing order supplied to His Lordship's cellar. Like father, like son, was the un-Christian judgement of Lady Augustine. She decided to take drastic action, before it became necessary to convert back into sterling any of the security she had so carefully accumulated.

As it was, one diamond tiara had to be sacrificed – a ghastly ornament she never wore, given to her as an engagement present by the late noble lord. This covered the expense of luxury travel to Africa, together with a suitable wardrobe. Less than two months later, she had reached the shores of the dark continent and set off into the jungle in the general direction of the Mission, as vaguely directed by the Church Council. Her cases and trunks were borne by twelve native porters and for much of the time, she was borne by two more.

Her knowledge of the African continent was limited. She knew it to be big, triangular in shape, and with a lot of trees, which was entirely correct as far as it went, and she had never had occasion to go into further detail. Navigation was therefore one problem, language and communication another, and the only clue she had, in the one and only letter she had ever received, was the name of the tribe, N'Chuyu, and of the kraal, M'Bongabonga. She soon discovered, however, that sign-posts *en route* were in short supply, and it was both monotonous and unrewarding to walk through mile after mile of jungle repeating the cry *'M'Bongabonga N'Chuyu.'*

The good Lord, as her son-in-law would have advised her, moves in a mysterious way, his wonders to perform. Especially, as the Rev. had by now discovered, in Africa. Her chance meeting with the remains of a safari party on a river bank in the very depths of the continent ranks as a coincidence on a par with that of Stanley and Livingstone, and not that far away from the same location, give or take five hundred miles.

The safari party, led by a one-legged red-haired Scot by the name of McTavish and known as 'Blinder', were still mourning the sad loss of two of their party. Blinder had led them in a flotilla of canoes to study the habits

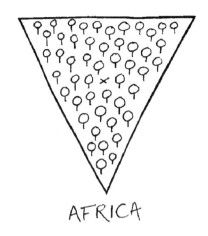

AFRICA

EUSTACE PRATT

and family life of the local crocodile, an adventure that resulted in some successes and some failures. Apart from the unfortunate loss of her right arm by one rather careless young lady in the party, the study was a great success, and a lot was learned about the creatures, especially by the young lady herself. Blinder sympathised with the young lady, 'Lofty' Shorthouse, about the crocodile business, as it was in this very location three years before that he had lost his left foot in somewhat similar circumstances.

The failure, on this occasion, was the total loss of one canoe, together with a young man called Sidney Sidebottom (known to the party as 'Bumsy'), and his companion, an attractively buxom young lady called Cynthia something-or-other. Bumsy, it seems, had fancied exploring further down the river, but as Cynthia well knew what sort of exploring he had in mind, she had tended to paddle in the opposite direction, so that as the tide race accelerated towards the waterfall, they were already in a spin. There was a parting of the ways at a point roughly half way down the hundred-foot fall, without any opportunity to say farewell or to make any plans for the future. Indeed Cynthia, who was lucky enough to find herself caught up on a ledge, had grave doubts if there was any future at all for Bumsy.

Blinder was upset at the loss of a canoe and of two party members, with a third one injured, as it necessitated a lot of readjustment to his schedules and would result in more paperwork than ever on his return. He hated paperwork, but he was philosophical in face of these setbacks and comforted by the knowledge that an all-in price had been paid in advance.

The arrival at his camp by the river of the dowager Lady Augustine Limpet and her entourage was a complication he could have done without. It was natural to

BLINDER McTAVISH

LOFTY SHORTHOUSE

her to immediately take charge, and it was not long before Blinder retired to sulk in the corner of his little tent. The lady could not allow this to happen for very long. She saw in Blinder an opportunity to find out where she was, little knowing that it would be a simple case, as one of the wags in the party later commented, of the Blinder leading the blind. So she prepared herself to sacrifice one of her precious bottles of scotch (she had recognised his accent). She selected the blondest of her wigs, spent half an hour longer than usual making-up and then, preceded by a penetrating waft of *Nuits de Paris*, burst into his tent and gave him a hearty kiss and a large slug of scotch.

Such was the welcome effect of the scotch and the sight of the bottle that Blinder found he could forgive the familiarity, and by the time the bottle was put to rest, even welcomed it.

So began an unlikely alliance which, as in the case of Stanley and Livingstone, was to lead to greater things.

6

Pot Luck

The N'Chuyu tribe was hungry. When that sudden devastating rainstorm had passed over, and in the light of early dawn, they discovered to their dismay that their entire feast complete with the pot itself had disappeared. While the hunting party, to be led by Fred himself, was putting on its war paint and adjusting its loin cloths, the children, who were reduced to searching in the forest for the odd berry and the occasional slug for their breakfast, came clamouring back with the news that the tribal pot was to be found washed into a small ravine just an assegai's throw from the boundary of the village. Empty.

The search party set off from that point without any breakfast, led by their number one tracker, M'Pupu, a large-nosed bulbous-eyed little man whose prowess was of a very high order, if judged by the stories he was famous for telling around the camp fire. This was to be

M'PuPu

one of his more difficult cases. The heavy rain had not only washed the pot away complete with its contents, but also any clues as to the direction taken by their supper. Except, that is, for a faint lingering aroma from the gravy.

M'Pupu's nostrils flared, and with his head down very close to the ground in a most undignified posture, he headed off on all fours into the jungle in the general direction of the river. As the scent became ever more faint he was obliged to stop more often to snuffle around before giving a little cry and heading off again, followed by Fred and his warriors, who were by this time ravenous and inclined to be short tempered, to the point of giving him a little prod with their spears when the delays became unbearable.

The Rev. B.F. and Pimples watched them go by from their hide-out in the bushes, and followed at a decent distance on the assumption that the locals would have a better idea where they were going than they did, and might be expected to clear the way from any itinerant lions, leopards or the like. Fortunately the magnetic attraction of the gravy had by now worn off them, but their total exposure to the eye of any such beast remained a real danger.

On reaching the river the party needed to rest for a moment, to have a drink, and to ablute. The decision to turn up river at that point was a pure fluke, whatever M'Pupu the tracker might claim at a later date. Rounding a river bend a mile or two further on, they were greeted by what can best be described as a sight for sore, and hungry, eyes.

On the opposite river bank a small camp fire was burning, a group of campers were happily frying eggs and bacon, and a line of five canoes was drawn up on the mud. As they watched, one of the couples came down to the water's edge, launched a canoe, and climbed in. As it came nearer they could make out that the red-haired man was wearing a sort of plaid skirt and carrying a bottle, and the lady, hugging to her bosom a large handbag, had the most beautiful blonde hair they had ever seen. The man lowered a fishing line into the river while the lady lay back and trailed her bright red fingernails through the cool water.

This, as it turned out, was a mistake.

The idea of a little gentle fishing had appealed to both of them after what had been a very heavy night, and the dowager Lady Augustine was feeling particularly relaxed and just a little brittle. What she was not aware of, with her knowledge of the dark continent still incomplete, was the presence in the neighbourhood of the odd hippopotamus. So when her long fingernails touched on the nose of one, she made to grab what she thought to be a fish, to thereby go one up on Blinder. The submerged hippo, who was enjoying a perfectly normal snooze, was irritated and suddenly surfaced to see what the hell was going on, throwing the startled couple several feet into the air and well away from the canoe.

Surviving in this emergency caused both Her Ladyship and Blinder to discover hidden talents by swimming at Olympic pace to the far shore.

The disaster had been witnessed not only by Fred and Co. with relish, but also by Phippsy and Pimples with utter amazement, from their vantage point further downstream.

'I know that man,' said Pimples. 'It's Blinder, the leader of my safari.'

'I know that woman,' said Phippsy. 'It's my mother-in-law.'

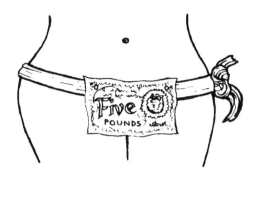

7

Money Belt

The canoe so spectacularly abandoned by Blinder and his new lady friend continued downstream only a short distance before drifting into an eddy at the bend in the river and settling in the mud of the shallows precisely below the bushes currently occupied by Phippsy and Pimples. On examination they were disappointed to find no paddles, but there was a bulging handbag trapped under the coaming.

Phippsy thought it quite improper to look inside what was clearly 'lost property' before handing it in to the proper authorities, but was persuaded by Pimples that these were exceptional circumstances, that there were no proper authorities within a thousand miles that they knew of, and that it was, after all, in the family. Its bulkiness was soon accounted for by a bottle of gin wrapped in a silk scarf, beside a bottle of scotch whisky wrapped in several silk handkerchiefs, resting on a large blonde hairpiece and a bed of exquisite jewels and wads of money, together with a large comprehensive make-up case.

Without hesitation they both plunged their hands into the bag, Pimples being the quickest off the mark and triumphantly grabbing the silk scarf and the handkerchiefs, leaving Phippsy the blonde wig.

Clothes at last!

The next half-hour was spent happily designing such creations as were possible from the available material and they became more and more excited at the novel prospect of seeing each other clothed, for the first time in ten years. Pimples' outfit was most becoming, the colourful scarf being draped decorously over her ample bosoms and tied neatly at the back, and three handkerchiefs knotted together loosely round her waist carried a large white five pound note suspended by two split-pin paper clips in a strategic position.

Lady Limpet's spare wig had, quite literally, gone down in the world. The cup that it formed when inverted not only fitted perfectly at the noble lord's crutch but was also very comfortable indeed. He found it a simple matter to knot the long tresses around his waist, and the effect, according to Pimples, was stunning.

Now decently clad, they felt better able to take notice of the world about them, and up river a lot was going on. Fred and Co., hungrier than ever, had given Blinder and Her Ladyship the usual initiation, stripping them off for a quick examination and then leading them away into the bush with hands tied in the customary manner. The absence of half a limb on the part of Blinder caused some disappointment, but there were some compensations evident on his companion. In the case of Her Ladyship it was quickly found that a binding round the mouth was also necessary.

Across the river there was even more ado. Now leaderless, the band of eight adventurers plus Augustine's fourteen porters, desperately needed to make some decisions, and it fell to Miss Lavinia Shorthouse to take the initiative. At 6 feet 3 inches in her stockings she was unfortunately named, and inevitably dubbed 'Lofty' by everybody. She it was who while studying the mating habits of the tsetse fly down by the water's edge had watched with fascination the post-mating habits of her two leaders and their unaccountable somersaults into the river. Their reception on the far side by a native tribe wearing war paint and carrying spears bothered her.

So far as the fourteen native porters were concerned, there was no problem. They also had witnessed the same events and had immediately disappeared without trace, but with most of the rations. So under Lofty's leadership the eight intrepid explorers set forth across the river in the four canoes. Without the guiding hand of Blinder they naturally failed to make allowance for the tide, and were carried off course to a point downstream on the opposite bank exactly where their fifth canoe was lying in the mud.

They were greeted ashore by a charming English gentleman dressed only in a rather flashy swimsuit, and a plumpish young lady in a quite original twopiece. Lofty Shorthouse, who was a second year student in dress design, took note.

Not literally, of course.

Introductions were made, Lofty apologised for shaking hands with her left hand, and Phippsy was amused to find that Pimples was better known to the party as Podge.

A small committee was elected and given the problem of what to do next. The Rev. held a service of thanksgiving, and then Pimples in a fit of hospitality produced the whisky and gin. Very soon a party spirit took hold and many bold and courageous plans were laid. In less than three-and-a-half hours and armed only with their paddles and two empty bottles, they set a zig-zag course for the village of M'Bongabonga under the nominal leadership of the Rev. Bruce Featherstone-Phipps, now, if he only knew it, Lord Limpet.

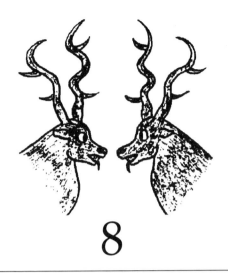

8

Good Gnus

When the tribal posse had set off from the village in search of their dinner on that fateful morning under the leadership of Fred and the guidance of M'Pupu, seniority and authority in the village fell to Mr Rutumutu the Witch Doctor. He too was extremely peckish and bad-tempered, and he put everybody to work with a will and with the flat of his ceremonial spear. In the fervent hope that his warriors would be successful, the centre of the compound was cleared of all the mess, any old skulls and bones were put into a neat pile along with fresh dry brushwood and an ample supply of branches and logs.

The women set to again, chopping, whittling, peeling and crushing every available fruit and vegetable, root and fungus that the children could bring in, until all the ingredients for a top class feast were on hand. All, that is, except for any beans or brussels sprouts, and, regrettably, the main course.

The N'Chuyu tribe had not always had a great deal of luck, as the costly storm of the night before demonstrated, so it was perhaps no more than simple justice that their turn should come for a minor miracle. It came, as such phenomena often do, heavily disguised. That is to say, nobody present in the village saw the entry of a ferocious male gnu with the most fearsome horns into the centre stage as a 'good thing', and neither was the entry of a second similar beast from stage left seen in that light either.

Mutual distrust was apparent in both of the creatures as they eyed each other in a most unfriendly way and started to circle the arena, forcing back their dumbfounded audience into the trees and pawing the ground. When they finally locked horns and got down to some serious fighting, the audience was able to move back in, and there followed a matinee of enthralling entertainment, with ever-mounting tension as the audience became emotionally involved to the extent of shouting, booing and clapping as the mood took them. Mr Rutumutu made a brief attempt in the background to open a book and offered very attractive odds, but the excitement was too intense for much business to be done. It would in any case have been a wasted effort, because the result was a draw, and both animals died, falling conveniently at the very spot allocated for the new fire.

The villagers wasted no time in getting a really good blaze going, and a magnificent roast was now in prospect to round off a highly entertaining afternoon. From a distance of some three or four miles away the smoke could be seen by Fred and Co. as they dragged their tired feet, their hungry bodies, and their disgruntled captives homeward. M'Pupu the tracker lifted his head, his powerful nostrils twitched, and he made a most welcome announcement.

'Roast,' he said. 'I smell roast.'

It is sad to say that discipline broke down completely at this revelation. The warriors broke ranks and finding fresh energy from somewhere they set off at a trot and then a run, and the captives, driven by hunger and without giving the situation any serious thought, actually did the same.

The sight that greeted them when they staggered into the compound was quite unbelievable. A fantastic party was going on, headed of course by Rutumutu, with much dancing and casting of spells. There was food galore – quite enough to last the tribe into the next full moon – and they joined the diners without even stopping to wash their hands.

Good humour and bonhomie were in the air, and being basically of a generous disposition the tribe were pleased to invite their guests to join them, though it has to be said that it was at least half an hour before they remembered to remove the bindings from their hands and another hour before Her Ladyship's gag was taken off.

So great was the *entente cordiale* that Fred went so far as to disclose another cache of holy wine, and they were on the point of opening it when yet another commotion interrupted the proceedings.

It seemed that ten more guests had arrived, and sensing the air of good fellowship throughout the tribe, Phippsy, Pimples, Lofty and company joined the happy gathering and moved in on the abundant food, pausing only briefly to pass the time of day with Fred and Mr Rutumutu and make the formal introductions.

Fred and his fellow cannibals were by no means mean-spirited when food was plentiful, and were well aware that, taking the long view, it could be counter-productive to starve one's guests. There was, however, a matter of pride and honour 'at stake' here in respect of the two captives his brave warriors had brought back. The pot was no longer serviceable and food was in abundance for the foreseeable future, so it was simply a matter of making an honourable deal. Once again it was Pimples who provided the answer, a most satisfactory one in the eyes of everyone except the dowager Lady Augustine Limpet.

Taking from her new found handbag a large handful of the most exquisite necklaces, bangles, brooches and rings, Pimples proceeded to move among the womenfolk of the village, starting of course with all the Chief's wives, distributing a little jewel here, a little necklace there, to each one in turn until everyone had something and the bag was empty. They were quick to bedeck themselves, though those with brooches had some difficulty in this respect.

Under the mellowing influence of the red wine much dancing and merriment filled the night air, and consequently the sun was high in the sky when, on the following day, the entire party set out in the general direction of England under the joint leadership of His Lordship and Blinder, with navigational advice from the mother-in-law of one and the bride-to-be of the other.

'CUDDLES'
BUCKMASTER

9

A Visit to Harrods

When it became known to society in general and to
Eustace Pratt in particular that the Dowager Lady
Augustine had so boldly made a personal mission to
Africa in search of the new Lord Limpet, and when
many months went by without any news, it was felt that
something should be done.

No news is not good news in the eyes of a loyal professional family solicitor whose fees are well overdue.
He therefore caused the following advertisement to
appear in *The Times*:

> *Wanted. A leader and volunteers for rescue expedition to*
> *Central Africa. Moderate expenses paid. Overseas travel*
> *experience an advantage. Apply E. Pratt, etc.*

A response was received in the post the following day.

Dear Pratt,

Shall arrive at your office 12 noon tomorrow to take over expedition. Have all details available. Never been known to dilly-dally. Can't stand any nonsense.

> *Lt. Colonel Sir Ferdinand Buckmaster,*
> *OBE (retired)*

It was as obvious to Eustace Pratt as it is to you, dear reader, that the Colonel, when he arrived, would have a large red face, watery eyes, an enormous white moustache and a tigerish expression, preceded by a very large nose tinged a delicate shade of blueish purple. And how right you all were, even to the well-rounded figure and the touch of gout.

He arrived at five minutes to twelve and by twelve fifteen had taken full charge of Mr Pratt, his staff, and the whole operation. In the time available Eustace Pratt did well to establish that the Colonel had indeed served for many years in His Majesty's forces, and while he personally had not ventured a lot further than Aldershot and London, his regiment had actually served with distinction on the North-West Frontier, and had provided him with a great deal of background information in regard to travel abroad.

'The Bull', as Sir Ferdinand was always known in the regiment, had already put together his party, which consisted of his batman, Chalky White and a Miss Gloria Bumpkin, whose connection and duties were unclear, and who was described as a good friend. Lady Buckmaster's name did not appear on the list.

Ten days later they were in first class accommodation aboard the *Arcadia* out of Southampton, and eleven days later sizeable charge accounts from the P. and O. Line and from Harrods were received by Eustace Pratt without enthusiasm.

GLORIA BUMPKIN

Harrods detailed the Bull's shopping list as follows:

Maps, Africa,	1
Compasses, navigational,	1
Hampers, picnic, large, fully stocked,	100
Whisky, malt, Whyte and Mackay, crates,	20
Claret, Mouton-Rothschild, Premier Cru, crates,	20
Sherry, Tio Pepe, crates,	20
Port, Warres vintage, crates,	20
Cigars, Havana, large, boxes,	20
Suits, tropical,	5
Helmets, pith,	3
Underwear, sets,	100
Guns, elephant,	1
Ammunition, guns, elephant, rounds,	100
Tents, bell,	2
Beds, camp, double, large,	1
Beds, camp, single, small,	1
Negligees, silk, sheer, black,	1
Stockings, silk, pairs,	50
Lingerie, assorted.	
Delivered Africa, 3 weeks.	

The Colonel's planning of the journey and the navigation of Africa was a substantial improvement on that of the Lady Augustine. He went into a good deal more detail, such as buying a map, and establishing that as well as a lot of trees, the dark continent also contained several rivers and one or two deserts. As a result of this research he had wisely sent orders ahead for a river gun-boat to be available, together with at least three camels. He had heard of the Nile river in the Mess, so he started there, and within a further four weeks was aboard his gun-boat, complete with his stores, his party and a dozen native porters, heading south.

10

The Enterprise

The first call for the party of twelve now heading for England was the Mission, and the purpose was three-fold. One was to clothe the Rev. Father, his fiancée, his mother-in-law, and Blinder. This was no problem for His Reverence as some of the laundry was still on the line and his second Sunday suit was neatly folded away in moth-balls. For Pimples it was not quite so easy turning the long narrow dresses left by Sybil into shorter fatter ones, but she soon realised that what came off the bottoms could be let into the sides, and in this matter Lofty Shorthouse lent a left hand.

Lady Augustine had come to terms with the sad loss of her daughter remarkably well and soon found that having lost a lot of weight in the course of her travels, she could easily slip into some of her daughter's things and was able to show proper respect for convention by finding a black dress to wear with her black underwear for a day or two. Blinder fitted well enough into the vicar's clothes with the exception of the dog-collar.

The second objective was to gather some stores for the journey, and this they did with a will, including a new Bible each and, regretfully, a large quantity of beans and brussels sprouts.

Thirdly, to collect the mail. Not surprisingly, there wasn't any, apart from the recent invitation to the tribal feast, dress optional (RSVP), which the Rev. Father had so unwisely accepted just three days ago.

Everybody knew from their schooldays (with the possible exception of Augustine) that England was to the north. With the Rev. B.F. looking to heaven for guidance and being blessed with an abundance of stars to follow, with Blinder following his instincts, and with Pimples having a more practical reliance on the sun, they headed in that general direction, following any track or river-bank that seemed to lead that way. As most of Africa was in the Rev. Bruce's parish, he found it a wonderful opportunity to try to spread the gospel in regions he had never before had a chance to visit.

His reception in most villages can best be described as mixed. After a short service followed by hymn singing, each member of the party in turn would unselfishly donate a Bible to the villagers, and in return for such a generous gift, they would often make a present of a goat or the odd female child, which Blinder always traded back for a few pouchfuls of their beer. It was only when one of the party used the village chief's latrine that they discovered what a very pragmatic and hygienic use was being made of their gift to the village.

Their journey over the next month or two was comparatively uneventful, save for the occasional encounter with an elephant herd, the tangle with the lion family, and the unfortunate business with the python in which the Lady Augustine became so enwrapped. In each case it was clearly a combination of the power of prayer offered up by the Rev. Father, Blinder's vicious use of his left stump, and Her Ladyship's powerful screams that saved the day.

Now, here they were, encamped on the bank of the biggest river they had ever seen and faced with the problem of crossing it. Lofty Shorthouse took the trouble to point out in the most convincing manner possible that she had no intention of attempting the swim for two very good reasons. One was that in the absence of one limb she was unable to swim breaststroke in a straight line, and the other was the fear that she might bump into an old acquaintance she was trying to avoid.

When put to the vote, the proposition of leaving her behind was lost by the Chairman's casting vote, on the grounds that she was so useful when finding their way through elephant grass.

The solution came when Pimples spotted what she first thought to be that old acquaintance of Lofty's drifting down river on the tide. It turned out to be a large tree trunk, closely followed by several more that rather conveniently built up into a logjam in the reeds close to their camp. All thanks, no doubt, to the heavy storm up river which had once before been helpful to them. Obviously a raft was in the making, and in about the same time as it took the Almighty to create the world about them, they created the means of further progress, a massive raft.

After loading on board what stores were left, there remained only the formalities of the blessing and the launching ceremony to be carried out. A short service followed by a vigorous rendering of *For those in peril on the sea* took care of the blessing, after which the dowager

Lady Limpet was called upon to complete the proceedings by breaking an empty bottle of *Nuits de Paris* on the leading trunk and naming the vessel the good ship *Enterprise*. Thereupon they all leapt aboard and pushed off, drifting gently to the middle of the river.

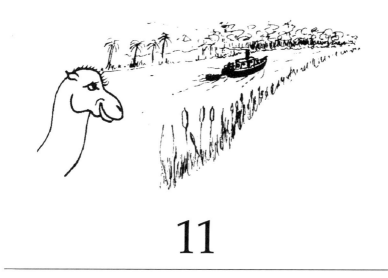

11

Lady Luck

The owner and Captain of the small river gun-boat *Lady Luck* was a well-worn mercenary, a hairy little Irishman by the name of McGinty. Rusty McGinty was not best known for his patience or his tolerance, and from their very first encounter it was obvious that the Captain and the Bull were not made for each other.

The stores, when he examined them in detail, he welcomed on board. The Colonel and his party he was obliged to accept, and the porters he found space for on deck, but he drew the line at the camels, and here was the first trial of strength. It ended when there was a call to 'Cuddles' (the Colonel) from Miss Bumpkin, who wished to complain about the size of her cabin compared with what she was used to on the *Arcadia*. And while Cuddles was engaged in consoling her, which took the rest of the day and the entire night, the Captain and

RUSTY McGINTY

CHALKY WHITE + CHARLIE PERKINS

his crew, Charlie Perkins, cast off and left the camels to look after themselves.

From the camels' point of view this was no bad thing. They had all been eyeing the Colonel with some trepidation and mentally casting lots as to who would draw the short straw, the one popularly believed to break one's back. They watched the *Lady Luck* disappear up the river without regret.

Meanwhile, leaving Charlie Perkins at the wheel, the Captain thought it his duty to make a further check on the cargo, particularly the crate marked 'Whyte and Mackay Export Special', just in case it was not the genuine article. He was able to confirm from long experience that it was, and did not reappear for twenty-four hours.

Charlie Perkins and Chalky White hit it off right away, both having their roots well within earshot of Bow Bells. So when after six hours Charlie needed relief at the wheel, he handed over to Chalky with a few clear words of instruction – 'Clockwise is to the right and don't forget to stoke the boiler.'

Having guessed where his Captain was to be found Charlie knew it was his duty to make sure he was alright. Finding him flat on his back in the hold, he took it upon himself to test what his Captain had been drinking, very very thoroughly. It was not therefore surprising that the progress of *Lady Luck* was erratic to say the least, and it is a good job that the mighty Nile is extremely wide at that point. They used it all.

There followed several weeks of travel in which the stock of goodwill on board, small to start with, was used up almost as quickly as the stocks of Whyte and Mackay. The Daily Routine Orders issued without fail at 8 a.m. every morning by the Colonel were the crux of the problem, and it was after the demise of the last bottle of scotch that the real unpleasantness broke out.

The trussing up of the Colonel and putting him in the long-boat on tow behind *Lady Luck* was generally considered well-deserved if somewhat extreme. And it was just plain bad luck that the tow rope should snap during the night, according to Charlie Perkins who was on duty when it happened, and he reported it to the Captain when his watch ended several hours later. He also reported having noticed what appeared to be a large collection of floating tree-trunks which drifted by on the far side of the river during the night.

12

Brief Encounter

Lt. Colonel Sir Ferdinand Buckmaster, OBE, awoke from a stupor to find himself in the most unlikely, undignified, and unwarranted situation. Dawn was about to break over a picturesque African skyline. There was a warm glow in the summer sky, tropical birds were twittering and skittering about their business and the placid waters of the Nile were shimmering in the half-light. Unfortunately this idyllic scene was not properly appreciated by the Colonel due to his circumstances. He was sitting on the central thwart of a large dinghy and firmly bound there without so much as a cigar to console him.

Above the natural sounds of bird life and the slip-slap of the water he thought he could hear voices, and after a while, he knew he could hear voices, English voices interspersed with an occasional Scottish brogue. Straining his eyes he could just make out a large collection of tree-trunks and as the dawn broke he could see the out-line of people moving about on them.

Throwing caution and dignity to the winds, he let out one of the bellows for which he was well known, par-ticularly to Chalky White, and then repeated himself for good measure.

On board the *Enterprise*, Lofty Shorthouse reported hearing a distant hippopotamus, and they all fell quiet, remembering only too well the last dramatic encounter with such a beast when Blinder and Augustine had taken leading roles. When the sound was repeated with even greater urgency, they caught sight of the creature moving abreast of them gently downstream, and the Rev. Father called for instant morning prayer.

As the river narrowed and they closed up it became apparent that once again their prayers had been answered, and the hippo was nothing more formidable than an old gentleman in a dinghy. (There are many in Aldershot who would have argued this point.) One young member of the safari party had been in the Sea Scouts and knew the correct procedure.

'Ahoy!' he called.

The Rev. backed him up with a cheery, 'What ho!'

There was a snort from the dinghy followed by:

'What the devil are you idiots waiting for, get me out of here.'

There followed an explanation that without any means of propulsion on either side, any form of closer inter-course between them was in the lap of the gods.

Good neighbourliness seemed to be the order of the day, so while the rafters cooked and ate a hearty break-fast of eggs, beans and brussels sprouts (with eggs only for the Rev.) they kept up a polite conversation.

'Lovely day,' was the standard opener. A snort.

'Nice weather for Wimbledon,' came from Lofty.

'Shouldn't we make the proper introductions?' suggested Augustine, who liked to stick to the social conventions.

'Lt. Colonel Sir Ferdinand Buckmaster, OBE,' came from the long-boat.

'Where are you from?' she enquired.

'Whimby, Wilts.'

'Ever meet the Smithsons down there?'

'Daughter married their son, what. Real nincompoop. Told her so at the wedding.'

'Great friends of mine,' she said. 'Small world.'

Conversation waned.

Then, 'What you doing in these parts then?'

'Came out to look for some idiot parson, don't y'know.'

'Why didn't you bring a friend with you?' asked Pimples. This enraged the Bull, who had in fact been giving a lot of thought to his friend and the comfortable bed she would be lying in at that very moment.

'You should have brought some oars or an engine or something,' said Blinder, and added *sotto voce* to his party, 'Lot of nutty old amateurs think they can roam round the world in piddling little boats.'

In the calm morning air voices carry very clearly, and the Colonel's face reddened even beyond normal. His moustache vibrated with emotion and he seemed about to have a fit.

'Cheeky little whipper-snapper,' he finally blasted out. 'What y'doing on those bloody trees anyway?'

'Going to England,' and Lofty added as a further explanation, 'for Wimbledon.'

'Foolish woman,' said the Colonel. 'It finished a month ago,' and under his breath, 'Can't stand fuddle-headed women.'

As the Colonel's whisper equated to normal conversation, he had at a stroke alienated another six of his new neighbours.

The Christian spirit brought a conciliatory offering from Lord Limpet.

'Looking for something, did you say? Didn't you bring any binoculars?'

A choking sound could be heard from across the water.

'Some crackpot parson – I already told you,' he said. 'Deaf or something?' and added into his moustache, 'No time for skinny bald-headed coots like him.'

They drifted gently on, the sun rose above the trees on a glorious day, and they put the kettle on for elevenses.

The Rev. had been thinking and as they moved further apart –

'Parson, did you say?'

The Colonel grunted.

'Anybody I know d'you suppose?' he called.

'Some old codger named Lincott or Limpole – something like that.'

'Not Limpet by any chance?' shouted His Lordship.

'That's it, Limpet,' yelled the Colonel. 'Came out here to tame the natives, don't y'know. Quite crazy – don't know what gets into people. Know him, do you?'

Now out of earshot, he watched with fascination the figures on the distant raft waving and jumping up and down in some sort of crazy dance.

13

Going About

Up river several miles, the skipper of *Lady Luck* was standing face to face with Miss Gloria Bumpkin. She wished to know if anybody had seen somebody she referred to as Cuddles, as he had promised to bring her a nice cup of tea several hours ago and had failed to do so.

'Colonel Buckmaster has abandoned ship,' he said, and added, 'in a rather unfortunate manner.'

When this was explained to her in greater detail Miss Bumpkin became very distressed.

'Supposing something happens to him,' she said. 'Whatever will I do?' and she went back to her cabin to consider her future. This took half-an-hour or so, if you include time taken to bath and make up properly. She had also made up her mind.

'I think we should go back and look for him,' she said. 'After all, he's paying you.'

This aspect of the matter had until then escaped Rusty McGinty's notice as he had been concentrating his attention on the next set of crates down below.

'Maybe you're right at that,' he said, in spite of a lurking feeling that finding Cuddles might not necessarily lead to a profitable business relationship. Nevertheless, to his eternal credit, he gave orders to Chalky White at the wheel.

'Go about and set course back down the river,' and he went down into the hold to join Charlie Perkins in a glass or two of sherry and a nice cigar.

When they eventually caught up with the Colonel they couldn't help noticing the raft of floating trees on the far side of the river with a group of white people on board. So they asked the Colonel as they put him back in tow and headed up river again, 'Anyone we know, d'you think?'

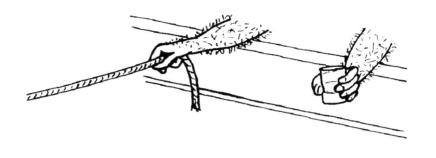

14

5 to 4 On

As the river gun-boat *Lady Luck* chugged its way up the mighty Nile on this glorious summer morning, negotiations were taking place in a none-too-friendly atmosphere. They were between, on the one hand, leaning over the stern rail in what might be called the 'red corner', Captain Rusty McGinty, and on the other hand, in the blue, now purple and rapidly darkening corner, Lt. Col. Sir Ferdinand Buckmaster, OBE, better known to all but one on board as the Bull.

To Miss Gloria Bumpkin, who was also leaning over the rail he was better known as Cuddles, though at this precise moment she couldn't think why.

Negotiations are, as we all know, a trial of strength. On this occasion there was considerable imbalance in their relative positions which heavily favoured the Captain. In his hand he held the tow rope to the ship's dinghy, and at the other end of it, seated and tied firmly to the thwart in a state of apoplectic fury was his adversary.

Nevertheless, the Bull did hold a couple of useful cards in his negotiating hand. One was the awe-inspiring power of his personality and vocal chords, and the other was the fact that he held the purse-strings for the voyage. The stumbling-block seemed to be the Daily Routine Orders issued by the Colonel at 8 a.m. every morning. As noon approached, the tropical sun burned down, and the Captain topped up his glass of gin from the crate at his feet (letting the tow rope slip a little through his hand in the process), it became obvious that the Bull was weakening.

The audience had grown to include Chalky White, batman to the Colonel, Charlie Perkins, the ship's crew at the wheel, and the twelve native porters sitting on their haunches in a little group which was centred on Chalky White. Serious financial commitments were being made in the book Chalky had opened on the outcome of the contest. With the odds changing all the time in the course of the last hour-and-a-half, the porters' pay packets were now fully at risk, mostly in favour of a clear points decision for the Captain within two hours, at odds of 5 to 4 on – easy money on the face of it.

A groan could be heard from the punters when Miss Bumpkin piped up with a compromise proposal.

'Captain,' she said, edging unnecessarily close to him. 'Couldn't you agree to be in charge only when on board, and Cuddles in command when ashore?'

Even the Colonel could see in this a degree of logic and an honourable solution that he quickly seized upon, being further encouraged to do so by the sight of the bottle and the smell of food.

Still smouldering but in no mood to quibble, and with

the agreement of a mellowed McGinty, he was yanked aboard and headed straight for the galley, pausing only to grab a bottle from the Captain's crate. He was far too busy to notice Chalky White in heated argument with his punters on the significance of this freak result.

There followed a period of peace and tranquillity on board, until they ventured ashore for fuel and jungle produce several weeks later.

HENRY

15

The Price of Freedom

From the site on the riverbank where they tied up they could make out in the distance the tops of a few wooden buildings, and on one of them was a flagpole carrying a Union Jack.

The Colonel ordered his bearers ashore, formed them up in fours under his NCO, ex Lance-Corporal White, and set off to march straight through the jungle in a direct line for the village, taking up position ahead of his troops in the time-honoured fashion. It soon became necessary to deviate a little by following paths made by large animals through the thick undergrowth, and this proved to be unfortunate. On reaching a small clearing, they found themselves staring into the tiny eyes of a massive rhinoceros.

It made the mistake of taking on the Colonel in eye-to-eye combat, and anyone in Aldershot could have told the poor beast that there was no chance. To give the rhino its due, it held its ground for all of two minutes (which is more time than it took Chalky White and his troops to disappear over the horizon), before turning round and lumbering off with its little tail between its armoured legs.

On his own now, the Bull pressed on in the general direction of the village, and was making good progress along another animal path until he caught his foot in a loop of creeper. There was a loud twang as the trap was triggered, and the Bull found himself swinging violently in an inverted state, hanging by one leg from a large branch, with his head just three feet above the ground.

The village of Kukukraali had the honour to house the Regional Colonial Administrative Office. In charge of this and his staff was little Mr Leonard Petty, and his staff comprised a sweet careworn little lady by the name of Mrs Amelia Carstairs.

While she was busy helping Mr Petty to administrate, she was in the habit of leaving her six-year-old son Henry in the care of 'Nanny' Bimbu, who was a great believer in 'free range' children. That morning Henry and several of his native friends went off playing hide-and-seek in the bush and drifted further than usual from the village. They came upon a sight that, despite their wide experience of village and jungle life, they thought remarkable.

This large purple-faced gentleman seemed to be hanging upside-down in mid-air making strange signals with his arms and one leg, and bellowing and snorting in a manner they had never seen or heard before. Henry picked up the stray pith helmet and tried it on, and then they all had a turn and finished up fighting with each other for it in a confused mêlée on the ground under the Bull. When they tired of that, Henry got to his feet and

69

said to the suspended body, 'What you doing there, Mister?' while two of his friends were having great fun spinning him around, first one way and then the other.

There was a spluttering from the Bull, followed by, 'Don't just stand there you little freak, go and get your daddy.'

'Daddy went away,' said the boy. 'Never seen him. I like my uncle though,' he added.

'Well get your blasted uncle then,' bellowed the Bull, 'and look quick about it.'

'Can't do that,' said Henry. 'He's busy at work.' Then as an afterthought, 'He ajminstates.'

He tried on the pith helmet again, but it came down to his mouth. He pushed it back and asked, 'This yours? You've got a very big head.'

The Bull had never been very good at small talk, neither was he at his best with small children, even when he was the right way up. He frothed, but he was not finished.

'I'll give you a shilling if you get your uncle straight away,' he said.

'Two shillings,' said Henry, who had his father's genes and was learning fast.

'One-and-six,' offered the Bull, and the deal was done.

So it was that a few hours later we find the Colonel sitting in Mr Petty's chair in Mr Petty's office, addressing Mr Petty and Mrs Carstairs, who were seated together on the visitors' bench. He learned how Mr Carstairs had set up a small sub-office further south, and after a few perfunctory communications via native runners, had seemed to disappear. Rumour had it that there was a woman involved.

One of his reports had mentioned meeting a missionary some ten miles up river, name of Pips or Fopps or something.

'Not the Reverend Featherstone-Phipps was it?' asked the Bull.

'Could have been – probably was,' said Mr Petty.

'I'm looking for him,' said the Colonel. 'Urgently.'

'Why, d'you want to get married or something?' asked Mr Petty, and added 'The drums say he was eaten by the N'Chuyu.'

'Better get back to Blighty then,' said the Colonel. 'Can't sit around here chattering all day.'

16

Bon Voyage

A parley was taking place on board the *Lady Luck*, chaired by the Captain, Rusty McGinty.

The reappearance of Chalky White and his troops in a state of panic had been treated with amusement and Dutch courage in equal quantities by the skipper, and after about a crate of gin had been laid to rest there followed an atmosphere of jittery calm. His assurances that rhinos don't much like swimming seemed to give great comfort to the party.

The subject of the debate was Lt. Col. Sir Ferdinand Buckmaster, OBE.

According to Chalky White's report, when last seen the Colonel was about to be charged by a large number of rhinoceroses. With the help of more medicine, he was able to provide further details concerning the pride of lions and the family of gorillas attacking on their flanks.

Helpful elaboration came from one bearer after another of the brave fight they all put up, and how it was finally decided to create a diversion by racing back to the boat, in order to save their leader.

The decision to be made now was between three options.

One was to go back into the jungle and look for him.

The second was to sit and wait.

The third was to presume the worst and set course for home. This depended on whether they could get by without any more finance from the Colonel, and on this point there was concern, particularly from Miss Bumpkin, as to whether there was any more money to be had anyway.

The Captain carefully explained that it was essential for him to remain with his ship at all times, and proposed Option One. His case for sending out an urgent search party made up in Irish blarney what it lacked in sincerity, but still failed to carry support. There was no seconder.

By a truly British compromise, Options Two and Three were both adopted, subject to an amendment put forward by Chalky White that the waiting time be limited to half-an-hour. One vote was cast against this by Charlie Perkins, who thought that half-an-hour was far too long.

Thanks to the military precision instilled in them by the Colonel, they cast off precisely half-an-hour later. Captain McGinty's sympathetic arm round the waist of the stoical Miss Bumpkin was a gesture in the best traditions of the Royal Navy. On her part, Miss Bumpkin felt it right and proper to recognise the change of circumstances and to demonstrate a spirit of cooperation by resting her head on his shoulder.

Everybody went on deck with glasses of the Colonel's finest sherry to celebrate *bon voyage* for the journey home

on this glorious evening, and sad to say, they all failed
to notice in the distance behind them a familiar rotund
figure ferociously waving his fists at them from the
mooring.

There were difficult times ahead for little Mr Petty,
Mrs Carstairs, the village of Kukukraali, the local tribes,
and the rhinos.

EPILOGUE

In attendance as guests of honour at the wedding of
Lord Bruce Limpet to Miss 'Pimples' Cynthia Pinkerton-
Smythe were Mr 'Blinder' McTavish and his wife
Augustine, together with their good friends Mrs 'Lofty'
Lavinia Sidebottom and her new-found husband Sidney,
better known to everybody as Lofty and Bumsy.

The Lady Buckmaster put in an appearance at the
reception to enquire if there was any news of her husband. The information that he was last seen adrift in a
small boat on the Nile seemed not to disturb her greatly.

The noble lord's latest mother-in-law was pleased to
confirm that at her daughter's new address there were
indeed some thirty bedrooms, fully en suite, with all the
latest plumbing, and thirty staff, which had recently
been augmented by a number of extra servants from the
N'Chuyu tribe of M'Bongabonga in central Africa. She

was particularly attracted to Mr Rutumutu. The model village they had created in the wildlife park of the estate had become a valuable source of income, with its large herd of gnu a very special attraction.

Lord and Lady Limpet lived in bigamous sin and blissful ignorance happily ever after.

'Y're goin' t'need a putter,' said Jock as he checked out the clubs, 'just to help the ball into the wee hole in the green. Y're no finished till that happens.'

With this pearl of wisdom, Jock had identified in a few words the greatest source of self-inflicted misery in the developed world today.

It is not true to say that this book is entirely fictional. A number of the characters might well be recognisable in many golf clubs, and most of the golf swings and bunker shots are taken directly from observations and experiences in my own.

Any claims arising from this confession should be made directly to the author, and addressed to:

The Bunkham Golf Club,
Cawkwell Hall,
Bunkham-on-Ouse.
(Telephone applied for)

Or to his solicitor, Mr Eustace Pratt, unless he is involved in the action.

EUSTACE PRATT

78

GOLF, M'LORD?

Lord Limpet and the Bunkham Bowl

THE REVEREND
LORD BRUCE LIMPET

1

Lord Bruce Limpet of Cawkwell Hall had an idea.

This was unique in itself, and was a revelation to 'Pimples', his beloved wife, on whom had always fallen the responsibility for original thought for both of them. Not that she minded it at all – the division of duties in their idyllic married life had always been clearly recognised, both doing what they were best at quite naturally.

His Lordship's background in 'The Cloth' qualified him perfectly to do the talking and to carry out the social duties admirably, and he was left fully in charge of any major decisions concerning the state of the nation and the world in general, and also the next world. In regard to the management of affairs in this world, when simply concerning Cawkwell Hall, its staff, its maintenance, and any similar parochial matter, such as thinking, these had always been acknowledged as the province of Her Ladyship.

They had been in residence as man and wife for some three years now, having married at the turn of the century soon after their return from an adventurous reunion in the heart of Africa. The Reverend Bruce Featherstone-Phipps had unwittingly become Lord Limpet while heavily engaged in his chosen role of missionary, at a moment in time when he had become assailed with doubt about his chances of success. At that time the N'Chuyu tribe had started to exhibit a number of un-Christian traits, and while he had since achieved a complete understanding with them, this had not appeared likely when he was standing in their ceremonial tribal cooking-pot.

The death of his older brother and his father in quick succession had resulted in his quite unexpected accession to the title and to the responsibilities of a baronial hall with some thirty-odd bedrooms, fully en suite, with all the latest plumbing, and thirty staff, and a very large estate. Also included was his ex-mother-in-law Augustine, who had married his widower father and had become the dowager Lady Limpet. Later still, she became Mrs 'Blinder' McTavish, and they also had taken up residence at the Hall.

Part of the estate had been very profitably set aside as a wildlife park, a rare novelty in those days. A model native village was created in part of the grounds, into which the entire N'Chuyu tribe had been settled, taking charge of a number of duties including managing (and sometimes culling) the large herd of gnu imported from their native land.

This self-sufficient community was benevolently ruled by the tribal chief Tumtumroli, better known to everyone as Fred, with the help of his Witch Doctor, Mr Rutumutu, and their several wives. The native kraal included in its midst a small Mission Hall in which His Lordship held a service once a week involving the distribution of holy bread and a generous ration of holy wine. It was always very well attended. A new large tribal cooking-pot had been provided by the management (Pimples), conditional on its use being restricted to vegetarian dishes only.

It was while His Lordship was paying a visit to the village one sunny day and watched the children whacking each other happily with the femurs of a recently culled gnu the idea came to him.

Golf.

He'd like to take up golf.

2

Blinder McTavish's home town was Perth, and following his betrothal to Lady Augustine they made the long train journey north and across the border to meet her in-laws. To Augustine it was a little too reminiscent of their recent travels through Africa, which had been the culmination of an eventful safari for them both. She remembered too their violent introduction to each other at the hands, or more precisely the nose, of a hippopotamus.

The two-day journey left her sore and weary, and 'home', when they finally reached it, compared more with the Mission Hall than Cawkwell Hall. She was able to have the long soak in a hot bath that she so looked forward to, but only after the large metal tub had been unearthed from an outhouse. It was then ceremoniously placed in front of the log fire in the living room and topped up with many kettles of hot water. Allowing nothing to waste, they each took a turn when she got out before the water could get too cold.

JOCK MᶜTAVISH

No introduction of a bride to her new parents-in-law could possibly be more intimate than that of Lady Augustine, as the four of them huddled in the tiny living room rubbing each other down with rough plaid towels, but the spirit of the welcome was warm enough, and the spirit of the malt was plentiful. With their glasses charged for the second time, Blinder wrapped his towel round his waist and raised his glass to propose a toast.

Before he could do so, however, the door burst open and in bounded two large, mud-caked dogs of a probable labrador-collie parentage, who made their introductions with no formality at all. Their enthusiastic welcome was quite irresistible as they leapt up onto everyone in turn, licking everything in reach, jumped into the bathtub, and then repeated the process.

'Bonny beasties, are they no?' said Jock McTavish as he picked Her Ladyship up off the floor and handed back her towel, which had finished up in the bath.

Meanwhile his wife, little Kirsty McTavish, sat up from where she had been laid out, dodged the flailing wet tails of her pets, and made her presence felt.

'Jock, can ye no stop Ben from snuffling the lady like that, and hold back Nevis fra chewing on Blinder's wooden leg? Where're ye manners mon? Can y'no see a' tha mud on the lady's front parts? Clean her up mon and use y'ain dry towel wi a wee bitty respect fr y'guest.'

Having some time earlier surrendered to this new way of life, Augustine found that she was beginning to enjoy the relaxed intimacy and natural friendliness of her new relatives, as they put on some dry clothes, dried off the dogs and mopped the floor.

Steaming hot cocky-leeky soup and crisp Highland bread went down very well at that stage, and so did the rabbit pie. Then they gathered together round the crackling log fire and got to know each other with clothes on even better, with each bottle from the local distillery that they disposed of.

Jock was a poacher by trade, well known and highly respected as a master craftsman by the local community, especially the butchers and fishmongers. His income was supplemented from two sources. One was Kirsty, the 'little woman' with the magic needle to many of the ladies whose 'own made' dresses, curtains, etc., owed much to her unsung handiwork in the background.

Jock's secondary income arose out of his basic training as a poacher. Roaming the hills and estates as far afield as St Andrews, he had many years back found himself on the famous links, and had watched the activities of the growing band of wealthy golf enthusiasts with close interest. He soon learned that rabbits and birdies had a quite different meaning in that community, and that there were a great deal more of the former than the latter.

He also noticed that the gentlemen seemed to need somebody to carry their bags of implements, and would pay good money for the service. He made himself available, and quickly discovered that a fresh salmon or a couple of plump rabbits in the direction of the club professional placed him at the head of the queue for the best paying club members.

In no time, Jock McTavish was the number one caddie. He added a knowledge of the game to his already clear understanding of human nature, and such a combination of expertise is a rare and valuable resource. His advice on the line to take and the club to use became renowned, and was matched by the good fortune his hirers always seemed to have in finding their ball sitting up sweetly in the rough, and quite miraculously staying out of bunkers. He seemed to have trouble with his nasty cough only when the opposition was on the backswing, and always stopped fidgeting on the putting green when his own man was in play.

As in his basic trade, he became a true professional.

Blinder had in his formative years learned much from his father and had shown great promise in both of his father's specialities. His expert training as a poacher had stood him in good stead when he set up his safari business, and he had always held in reserve his expertise as a caddie. Unfortunately, as his father had been quick to point out at the time, the loss of his left leg to a crocodile on his first safari adventure was not only a black mark against all his careful training, but would make him very unpopular with the greenkeepers if he ventured onto the greens with his wooden one.

However, in the course of their stay, they did make a day trip in Jock's pony-cart to the coast, and he showed the ladies the golf links. Augustine was intrigued by it all, especially the expenditure of the golfing fraternity, so much so that she sent a letter in which she described it all to her step-son-in-law and his wife, the Limpets.

As a result of which, as His Lordship watched the children playing, his idea germinated and developed into a Plan.

SIDNEY SIDEBOTTOM

3

Lord Limpet cracked open his second boiled egg as he shocked his wife with the news.

'Pimples, darling,' he said, 'I've got a plan.'

Lady Limpet remained calm.

'Really, dear,' she replied, as though it was an everyday occurrence.

'You know that letter we had from Augustine the other day.'

'Yes.'

'Well, yesterday I was down at the village watching the children at play and the Almighty suddenly gave me a vision.'

Pimples immediately sat up and took notice. Any plan involving a combination of Augustine and the Almighty had to be something formidable indeed.

'Nothing painful for Augustine I hope,' she said, 'She's much better now that Blinder's around.' A truly Christian sentiment, if a little dishonest about the pain.

MATTHEW
HARDCASTLE

'I want to build a golf course here,' he announced.

There, it was out, and he awaited the reaction.

Pimples considered the pros and cons from her point of view. Space there was plenty of. Expense – there would be plenty of that too, no doubt, but the money was available, thanks to her able management over the last few years and the introduction of the model village, etc.

Of far greater importance was the prospect of giving Lord Bruce some new creative purpose in which to engage the assistance of the Almighty and the rest of the population of the estate, and thereby get him out of the way. Much as she loved him, this aspect of the 'idea' was decisive.

'When can you start?' she asked.

'Tomorrow I should think. Dig a few holes, that kind of thing. Have a game at the weekend if we can find some of those sticks and a ball or two.'

'Shouldn't we wait until Blinder gets back, just in case there's anything we should know about it? Maybe there are some rules or something like that,' said Pimples.

'I'll give them a day or two before I start then. Meanwhile, I'll have a word with Fred so that his men can begin collecting anything useful like large leg bones and horns, and he might set the women to work making some balls.'

He set off, full of a new found enthusiasm, to survey some of his distant acres which till now had rarely been visited. The good Lord, in his infinite wisdom, thought it best to tell him nothing of the problems in store, and you, dear reader, full of foreboding as you are, can do nothing about it either.

Having mapped out in his mind where a golf course might be sited on the estate, the noble lord went back to the Hall and summoned his chauffeur to bring round the

Daimler-Benz, for a trip to the nearby market town of Bunkham-on-Ouse.

'I think we'll just take a look round for some golf sticks, Sidney,' he said. 'We're going to have a golf course.'

'When's that, m'lord?' Sidney enquired.

'Soon as Blinder gets back,' said His Lordship, and they set off for the hardware shop in the High Street.

Sidney Sidebottom was another of the survivors of that notorious African safari. He could in fact be considered supernumerary, as he had been written off, together with his canoe, over a hundred-foot waterfall. His surprise return to England, six months after the main party, had been seen as a mixed blessing by party leader Blinder, who was then obliged to re-adjust all his records and paperwork, including a note of apology to Somerset House, but was still a canoe short.

Blinder found it in his heart to overlook this when Sidney got married to Lavinia 'Lofty' Shorthouse, treating the canoe as his wedding present. Lord Limpet's present was a room for 'Lofty and Bumsy' at Cawkwell Hall, and the job as chauffeur.

Lofty had expected on her return from the safari to continue her studies as a designer. Progress in this direction had unfortunately been restricted as a result of her studies of the mating habits of the crocodile. In the course of those studies, she had lost her right arm, rather carelessly according to Blinder. Since the beast had undoubtedly got the flavour from its earlier encounter with Blinder, his opinion did strike one as a little unfair.

Nevertheless, our noble 'course architect' was to find Lofty's drawing ability to be a great help as the scale of his undertaking began to unfold.

Reminiscing on those exciting memories, His Lordship was brought back to reality as Sidney drew up to the kerb at the premises of Hardcastle and Son, ironmongers, garden equipment suppliers, hardware dealers, builders, decorators, general contractors, and funeral directors. Mr Hardcastle senior was immediately notified by his staff of the arrival of His Lordship, and was out of the shop in time to lead him inside and arrange for a comfortable chair.

'What-ho Matthew, lovely day.'

'It is, my lord, perfect for a spot of fishing. You require a little bait?'

Here was temptation indeed, but the noble lord stood his ground.

'Golf sticks, Matthew, what I need are some golf sticks. What have you got?'

Matthew Hardcastle was perplexed but resourceful. 'Had you any particular type in mind, m'lord?' he asked, this being his standard ploy when playing for time.

'What kinds are there?' enquired His Lordship.

His bluff having been called, Mr Hardcastle resorted to ploy B.

'This is the area in which my son specialises, my lord,' he said, and to his staff, 'Find young Mr Luke for me straight away, if you please. Coffee, my lord?'

'Can I help, Grandfather?' It was the shapely Miss Virginia Hardcastle who was on hand before her father could be found.

'Lord Limpet, we supply a very nice line in brassies, mashies, niblicks and spoons,' she offered, in the most matter-of-fact manner.

This was strange language and surprising news not only to His Lordship but also to old Matthew Hardcastle and the rest of the staff as well.

Virginia was clearly a chip off the oldest block as regards business initiative, provided of course that she could substantiate it. (It was a coincidence that she had noticed in a newspaper article only a day or two ago a reference to the use of these implements in a golf match, and the names had stuck in her mind.)

She went on to explain that they were out of stock at that moment, but if His Lordship would like to place a trial order for half-a-dozen, they would make a delivery as soon as possible, together with any other accessories he might require, such as balls. Lord Limpet was greatly impressed, especially by the winning smile that accompanied the offer, and the initial order was placed.

While there, His Lordship ordered a few extra buckets and spades for the purpose of building the course, wished them all good morning, and set off back to the Hall.

Virginia hurried away to find the newspaper in which there were, luckily, some illustrations of the various golf clubs now in popular use, and before her grandfather could ask too many awkward questions, went down the road to see her friend (and one of her many admirers), Jake, the carpenter and joiner. He saw no problem in making a few sticks like that and was pleased to take the order. Meanwhile, Virginia wrote off to St Andrews for some golf balls.

Grandfather Hardcastle was highly impressed with this example of business initiative from the youngest generation in the family enterprise, even if she was only a woman, and sent a message to the signwriter that very day to add to the text on the shop fascia the legend 'and specialists in golfing impedimenta'.

On arrival back at the Hall, Lord Bruce was pleased to find that the McTavishes had returned from Scotland,

and he joined in the reunion that was taking place on the terrace with his wife and Lofty Sidebottom.

Before long, they were on the subject which would take a lifetime to go away. Golf.

CAPTAIN
MONTAGUE
BUCKMASTER

4

Blinder was enthusiastic about the project, but nervous about Lord Bruce's approach to it. He had an intuition that a little more planning might be advisable, and while His Lordship could not see why, he good-naturedly deferred and suggested that perhaps a small steering committee might be formed. He then went on to decide who would volunteer to be on it.

The outcome was a committee constituted as follows:

Lord Limpet, Chairman.
Blinder McTavish, Technical Adviser.
Augustine McTavish, Treasurer.
Lofty Sidebottom, Secretary.
Fred, Staff Relations.
Mr Egbert Micklethwaite, the head gardener, for diplomatic reasons, on the advice of Lady Limpet.

The first meeting was called at 10 o'clock the following day.

EGBERT
MICKLETHWAITE

JAKE
TRUEMAN

97

'Well, here we are, what,' said the Chairman. 'The idea is to make a golf course.'

'Why?' asked Mr Micklethwaite.

He was in the habit of asking difficult questions, as Mrs Mabel Micklethwaite would be the first to confirm.

There was a brief silence.

'Well, I thought it would be rather fun, don't y'know,' said Lord Bruce. 'Entertain the guests, learn the game myself, keep up with the times, Eggy, what, and maybe form a club for the townspeople, that kind of thing.'

If Mr Micklethwaite was ever to be won over to the scheme, which was very unlikely, the use of 'Eggy' was not going to help very much. He was still adjusting to the arrival of the village of M'Bongabonga, and while his relationship with Fred and Co. was now much improved, there had been some very rough going in the early stages. There was an initial period in which the N'Chuyus had to be dissuaded from foraging roots from his precious flower beds and vandalising his trees, and the cold war that quickly developed was only resolved when Egbert Micklethwaite was introduced to M'Pupu, the tribal tracker.

The common bond that put the seal of brotherhood on this unlikely pairing was M'Pupu's professional talent in tracking and dealing with moles and rabbits, to the great benefit of Egbert's pride and joy, his magnificent lawns. From the moment of that discovery, mutual respect took over in both camps, and Egbert found many other advantages in this new source of assistance, including regular deliveries of gnu manure.

Blinder McTavish made a suggestion.

'Wouldnay y'think, Bruce, tha maybe we sha' draw up a wee plan.'

'Splendid idea,' said His Lordship. 'Could you get it done for us by this afternoon d'you think, Lofty?'

'How many holes will there be?' asked Lofty.

'I thought about five or six,' replied the Chairman.

'There are usually more than that,' said Augustine, 'as many as nineteen according to my first husband, who always blamed difficulties at the nineteenth for his absence from Sunday lunch at home.'

'There are eighteen at St Andrews,' put in Blinder, and that settled it.

Lofty enquired if there was a plan of the estate she could draw on.

'Eustace Pratt might have one, I'll have him bring one over,' and Lord Bruce despatched Sidney Sidebottom off to the solicitor's office straight away.

'A good meeting that,' he said. 'Wake up Fred and let's have some coffee.'

Before they could do either there was a cough from the butler, who had glided into the room.

'Pardon me, m'lord, but there are two gentlemen asking to see you. I would not have troubled you at this time had they not said that it is on the subject of golf. They are from the town, sir,' he added apologetically.

'Better see what they want then,' said His Lordship.

A few moments later Smithers reappeared and made the introductions.

'Lord Limpet, may I present the Deputy Chairman of the Council of Bunkham-on-Ouse, Captain Montague Buckmaster, and the Town Clerk of Bunkham-on-Ouse, Thomas J. Dickie Esquire.'

'Any relation to that old idiot Colonel Sir Ferdinand Buckmaster?' asked the Lady Augustine. 'His wife came to our wedding enquiring about him. He went looking for Lord Limpet in Africa. Probably still is.'

'My father,' said the Captain, 'sometimes wondered where he was. Small world.' Maybe the Colonel, lost in Africa now for about four years, would not have agreed.

'Heard from Ginny Hardcastle that you're building a golf course,' went on the Captain, straight to the point like his father.

'Pleased to meet you,' said His Lordship and shook their hands. 'Have a seat. Two more coffees, Smithers.'

There was a sort of snuffle from Chief Tumtumroli as he recovered slowly from a pleasant nap and murmured *'Zumzum n'gongoli m'nababawali chukchuk mogo n bongobongo,'* which can be freely translated, as you may be aware, as an instruction to bring in wife number three. When he was fully awake, introductions were completed all round. Mr Dickie spoke up.

'The Town Council will be very interested, if you go ahead with a golf course, in whether such an amenity will be available to the public.'

'Thought we might have a sort of members' club, what?' said His Lordship.

'That's the ticket,' said the Captain. 'Who's running the show?'

Lord Limpet bristled slightly.

'It was just a little idea of mine. Got together a small committee to help, don't y'know.'

'You'll need somebody on the committee to represent the Town Members then,' went on the Captain. 'Someone with a bit of authority who could report back to the Council and that sort of thing.' He looked Lord Bruce straight in the eye with all the inherited will-power of the Buckmasters. The rhinos of Africa had been known to wilt under such a gaze from his father, and His Lordship was more in the rabbit class.

'Perhaps you'd like to join us then, and the Town Clerk too. Two heads are better than one, and all that kind of thing.'

Captain Buckmaster was not too sure about that, particularly where Mr Dickie and himself were concerned, but he had achieved his objective, and agreed to make himself available.

'Better have a meeting tomorrow then,' he said. 'We'll get out here at ten o'clock. That alright, my lord?'

He rose as he said it, beckoning Mr Dickie to do the same, bade everybody good day, and headed off back to town.

The committee, apart from Fred, were thoughtful as they sipped their coffee, and rightly so.

THOMAS J.
DICKIE

5

Sidney Sidebottom was shown into the office of Mr
Eustace Pratt, and his request on behalf of Lord Limpet
for a plan of the Cawkwell Estate had a chilly reception.
The deeds would have to be found deep in the archives
of the practice, and the archives were deep in the cellars,
deep in dust.

'What does he want it for?' asked Pratt.

'A golf course,' replied Sidney. 'Today. Wants to play
at the weekend.'

Having witnessed the extraordinary events concerning
the Limpet family over the last four years and been
involved in much of it, Eustace Pratt was not easily
surprised. The very substantial fee income resulting from
administering the African expeditions in search of His
Lordship, followed by the immigration of the N'Chuyu
tribe and a large herd of gnu, had provided great
benefits to the practice and to Mrs Pratt, and he had
learned to be both philosophical and expensive.

Another expedition was unavoidable, this time to the cellars, and an hour later he emerged, covered in a layer of dust, with a large bundle of legal documents which included a plan of the estate.

'I shall have to have a copy made,' he said, 'I can't let this go out of the office. Tell His Lordship I shall deliver it tomorrow morning.'

He went home to take a bath and to muse on how this latest development might once again improve the profits of the practice and the goodwill of Mrs Pratt.

Sidney spent a pleasant hour at the Dog and Duck confirming the current rumours about the town's new golf course.

Lord Bruce was up early the next morning, well before ten o'clock, and went for a stroll in the grounds as he considered his new project. He came upon Blinder doing the same.

'Nice day for a round of golf, what. Pity it's not ready.'

'Just thinking that,' said Blinder. 'Like to be getting on wi' it.'

'Well, you know about these things, Blinder. Why don't you go ahead, so that we can have a game next week. I'm sure Fred can find somebody to give you a hand.'

'What aboot the committee?' asked Blinder.

'They're busy – better use Fred's men,' said His Lordship.

Blinder decided to leave it at that, and was already laying out the course in his mind. He made for the kraal as Lord Bruce returned to the Hall for his kippers and hot buttered toast.

'I put the committee in the library, your lordship,' said Smithers. 'They seem to have made a start.'

'That's good,' came the reply. 'I'll join them after breakfast.' Which he did an hour later.

Eustace Pratt had delivered a hand-drawn copy on paper of the coloured linen map of the Cawkwell Estate. The extensive boundary and the plan of the Hall and the stables in the centre were marked in detail, with the long drive from the gatehouse, the river Ouse winding through, with streams and lakes and woodland areas.

The committee, in the absence of His Lordship and Blinder, made considerable progress under the deputy chairmanship of Captain Buckmaster. The subject of remuneration for service on the committee had been raised by the deputy chairman, and according to the minutes taken by Thomas Dickie, was unanimously agreed, the scale of fees being left to the discretion of the deputy chairman.

It had been agreed that a clubhouse would be required, and Mr Dickie would ask his friend Mr Weatherspoon to submit a design. Messrs Hardcastle would be invited to tender for the contract, and Captain Buckmaster would advise Miss Virginia Hardcastle accordingly.

On a point of order, Mr Tumtumroli had enquired about the coffee, scones and cakes, and this had been communicated to Smithers.

The committee, with the exception of Fred, who went back to sleep, had then gathered round the map and were in the process of instructing Lofty where to mark in the various holes when His Lordship arrived.

'Good morning, my lord,' said the Captain. 'We've made a bit of progress. Hope that's in order.'

'Splendid. Splendid. I've done the same. Sorry I'm a little late, been busy, what. See you've got the map. Leave you to it. Must get on.' It was the sort of morning when one goes fishing, and he did.

They finished sketching in the eighteen holes.

Just as a horse designed by a committee results in a camel, the golf course sketched in by Buckmaster and

Co. could be described at its best as unique. The scale of the map was inevitably a small one, with the result that strictly as shown, the length of the course would have been a minimum of twenty miles, and par in the region of 250.

Little as she knew about golf, Lofty with her art school training sensed there might be something amiss, and suggested that perhaps they should walk the proposed course in case of snags. Augustine, who had traversed Africa with far less detail than that, saw no need, but the Captain felt like a stroll and led the committee off on a tour, without disturbing Fred.

VIRGINIA HARDCASTLE

6

As Lord Bruce had suggested, Blinder made for the N'Chuyu village straight away. In the absence of Fred on his committee duties at the Hall, Mr Rutumutu was in authority, and it was a role he enjoyed exercising.

Blinder's request for a hunting party (as he diplomatically put it) was a welcome break to routine, and a group of tribal warriors was quickly assembled. They were persuaded that assegais would not be necessary on this occasion, but large hunting knives were the order of the day. They leapt about in excitement, many of them hastily decorated in tribal warpaint.

Blinder led them to a point on the edge of the woods from which he decided the first fairway could start. They cut down the long grass in a square patch to represent the tee, and he encouraged them to do a war-dance on it, in the absence of a roller. Then forming them roughly line-abreast he led them along the edge of the wood to the bushes on the brow of the hill, chopping down the long grass and any other plant life, stamping their feet to blood-curdling war-cries as they went, and in the process forming a rudimentary fairway. (Comparable to many club fairways today after the visit of societies.)

Cutting a swathe through the bushes at the top, they danced out brandishing their machetes in feverish excitement.

It was at this point that they encountered the committee (with the exception of Fred), coming the other way, studying their map on their tour of inspection.

The committee took one look at the oncoming warriors and made a unanimous decision. With one accord, and without reference to the deputy chairman, they turned and fled back towards the Hall, with Augustine, who had previous experience at the hands of the N'Chuyu in Africa, showing a very impressive turn of speed.

Blinder's problem was his wooden leg. At the start it had been possible to lead his troops from the front, but as they gradually speeded up their rhythm in response to their natural instincts, he found himself bringing up the rear. When they went 'over the top' he was well behind and quite unaware of the mayhem with the committee. By the time he breasted the hill Augustine and Co. were taking cover behind the wall on the terrace, and the Captain was trying to re-assert his authority and take appropriate military action.

At this critical moment Virginia Hardcastle arrived on her bicycle to see His Lordship, with a set of golf clubs in a canvas golf-bag slung across her back, and the basket on her handlebars full of golf balls. Showing great courage, the worthy Captain dashed out and hurried her, complete with bicycle, behind the 'ramparts'. Having by then seen and heard the N'Chuyu warriors in their frenzied war-dance, Victoria needed no second bidding,

though she felt, quite rightly, that some sort of explanation would not be out of place. Unfortunately, no one present was able to give her one.

The arrival of this reinforcement, with a delivery of weapons in the form of brassies, mashies, niblicks and spoons, and a basket full of golf-ball ammunition was very welcome. Now the Captain could see the way ahead and he rallied his troops.

One of them was becoming particularly agitated. Egbert Micklethwaite had watched with horror as the tribesmen burst through his carefully cultivated privet and laurels in line abreast and then commenced a ritual dance on the lawn and flower beds. He was the first to grab a brassie and, throwing caution to the winds, charged down the steps into the attack. Covering fire was provided by a volley of golf balls from the rest of the committee, while the remaining 'weapons' were issued.

From a first floor window Pimples watched fascinated as the bizarre scene developed. She was in time to see Blinder appear over the hill, apparently driving on the warriors, and Lord Limpet as he wandered into the arena carrying his fishing rod and looking rather pleased with the two fat trout in his net. They were quickly joined in the net by a couple of golf balls, as he entered the battle zone in complete bewilderment.

The commotion was so great that it roused Fred from his nap in the library. He had trouble believing his eyes when he blearily tried to focus them out of the window. He drifted out onto the terrace to join his fellow committee members, but unfortunately for him, it was Virginia who spotted him first. She concluded that they had been surrounded and were being attacked from the rear, and she let fly with some well-directed golf balls, scoring several painful direct hits.

Pimples dashed downstairs and arrived on the scene

just in time to forestall a charge by the Captain, who had by now grabbed a club, though it must be said, not in a true Vardon grip. (The enthusiast might like to know that his club selection for the purpose was a niblick.)

Egbert Micklethwaite had gone berserk, and was to be seen performing a war-dance which compared very favourably with that of the N'Chuyus. Indeed, they were so impressed that before long they retired in confusion, and stood watching the rest of the performance from behind the remains of the privet hedge.

When Blinder entered from stage-left, Egbert turned his wrath on him, as the wooden leg made its mark across his beloved lawns.

Smithers it was who created the calm in which a truce could be declared. Carrying a silver tray loaded with champagne and glasses, he glided to centre stage where His Lordship was sitting on the grass in a daze.

'Should I serve drinks, my lord?' he enquired.

'Certainly,' said His Lordship. 'Didn't know we were expecting guests. Some sort of game is it?'

'Golf, m'lord,' said Smithers.

7

The next day, after all had been explained and most of it forgiven, another meeting of the committee took place. There were apologies for absence from Egbert Micklethwaite, busy repairing the garden, Chief Tumtumroli with a bruised ego, amongst other things, and Thomas J. Dickie, still in a state of shock.

Lord Limpet and Blinder agreed with the others that it might be best if the route for the course was predetermined, and that Blinder's method of producing fairways, although effective, was only feasible if brought under control. A revised plan was drawn up to include most of Blinder's first hole, and he was given permission to proceed strictly in liaison with Fred and Egbert.

Lord Bruce discussed the decision with his wife that evening, and they studied the map together.

'I see the eighth hole crosses the river,' she observed, 'and so does the tenth.'

'So it does. Hadn't noticed. That'll be interesting.'

111

'How will they get across?' she asked.

'With a brassie, I should think.' Bruce had been studying his new clubs.

Long silence.

'What does the square represent?' enquired Pimples after further study.

'Oh, that'll be the clubhouse – good idea, what?'

'Just fine,' she said, 'and so conveniently adjacent to the cess-pit and the piggery.'

'Must mention that to the committee,' said Bruce.

Pimples then appeared to change the subject.

'I wrote to Blinder's parents today. Like to meet them. I asked them down for a holiday.'

'Jolly good.'

'Know about golf, they tell me,' she went on.

'Hum,' came from His Lordship, who was still enjoying the memory of those two fat trout, and humming to himself a rendering of *All things bright and beautiful*.

Ten days later Jock and Kirsty McTavish, Ben and Nevis arrived by train and were collected from the station. Cawkwell Hall was a revelation to them, and they were made very welcome by all the residents with the exception of Egbert Micklethwaite. He had strong reservations in regard to Ben and Nevis vis-à-vis his flower beds and lawns, which were still struggling to recover from the ravages of the N'Chuyu invasion.

At the first opportunity, Pimples took Jock to one side and asked him to take a look at the progress of the golf course, and report back.

Early the next morning Jock and Kirsty took the dogs for a brisk walk to survey the grounds. The size of the estate came as a surprise to them and they were soon lost. Coming upon a path through a small copse, they were happy to follow the beaten track, which led them without warning into the village of M'Bongabonga. The tribal cooking-pot was brewing over a glowing fire, the native women were sweeping the kraal, the men were stirring in their beds, and the children were playing.

To Jock and Kirsty, who had never before been south of the border, this was a severe culture shock.

'Wou'd y'believe tha', Jock,' said Kirsty. 'I a'ways thought the Sassenachs were all white people like oursel'. D'ye think they ken aboot these people up at the hoose?'

Before Jock could reply they had been surrounded by the village children and some of the women, and Mr Rutumutu made an appearance. There was much chatter going on in N'Chuyuese, which when translated boiled down to 'Is that a lady with a beard or a man wearing a skirt?' One or two of the bolder children moved in to investigate in further detail. Ben and Nevis took this as an invitation to play, knocking over the children with a few friendly frolics and then leaping up on the Witch Doctor to give him a thorough licking and thereby undoing his morning application of voodoo cosmetics.

Jock and Kirsty were wary about Mr Rutumutu and the rather sinister-looking cooking-pot. They had read about these things in faraway countries but had thought themselves safe from cannibalism so close to home, despite some of the dreadful rumours about the English.

There followed yet another surprise.

'Would you like some porridge?' asked Mr Rutumutu, giving Ben a clout with the flat of his assegai as he spoke. In the village, he had been the first of the men to pick up the language, and in full tribal regalia found it very profitable to act as guide and host to their visitors.

So began a lasting friendship. They joined the entire tribe in large helpings of their favourite dish, served piping hot straight from the tribal pot, seasoned with salted M'Bongabongan herbs and gnu milk to a flavour

113

superior to anything even Kirsty had ever achieved. The Sassenachs are not so bad after all, she decided.

Jock enquired about the golf course, and was given M'Pupu as a guide.

After his experience of the links at St Andrews this wooded downland course was a complete contrast, but he could see great possibilities for it, especially in the matter of finding and selling back golf balls. It was soon clear to him that an alliance with his companion M'Pupu would be a very profitable one, and M'Pupu could sense a kindred spirit even if he couldn't communicate with him.

Good progress had been made in course construction in the last week or so, and they were half way down the eighth fairway when they came to the river. As they did so they heard the spine-chilling war-chants of the N'Chuyu warriors coming over the hill behind them, and Jock's blood ran cold for the second time that morning as the tribesmen came charging over the top straight for them. Above their heads they appeared to be carrying a very large wooden crate, and behind them Jock noticed with relief the familiar figure of his son.

The warriors continued their run and without pause plunged headlong into the river. Behind them stumbled Blinder, hanging on grimly to a long rope.

'Casual water?' asked Jock.

'Nae free drop,' replied Blinder, and added with a wink, 'Test f'r a goo' caddie.'

'D'ye like the bonny raft-ferry?' he went on, as the men climbed the bank and he made it fast to a post, 'Just a wee charge f'r the crossing, y'understand.'

A son any man would be proud of, thought Jock.

On their return journey to the Hall, Jock and Kirsty came upon His Lordship in the grounds familiarising himself with his new clubs.

'They don't hit the ball very far,' said Lord Bruce, 'and sometimes, not at all.'

Jock had already noticed that, and recognised the swing, but I shall not describe it to you, dear reader, for fear of infection. Jock's friendship with the pro at St Andrews had given him a useful knowledge of the basics, and he asked if he might just have 'a wee go'.

Within an hour, another lifelong golf fanatic was born. His Lordship discovered quite quickly a fact that eludes many struggling golfers to this day – the golf clubs are not always to blame. Copying Jock to the best of his ability, he made contact with the ball on occasions to great effect, giving pleasure also to Ben and Nevis, who were masters at retrieving, if a little severe on the shrubbery.

Egbert looked on with a jaundiced eye.

'Y're going t'need a putter,' said Jock as he checked out the clubs, 'just to help the ball into the wee hole in the green. Y're no finished till that happens.'

With this pearl of wisdom, Jock had identified in a few words the greatest source of self-inflicted misery in the developed world today.

In due course Jock reported back to Pimples, as she had requested.

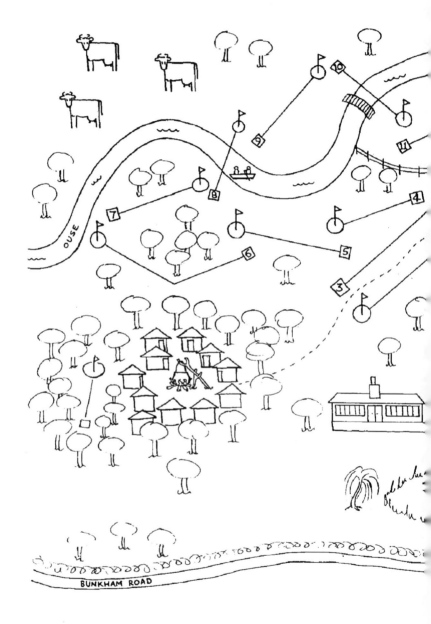

OUSE

BUNKHAM ROAD

116

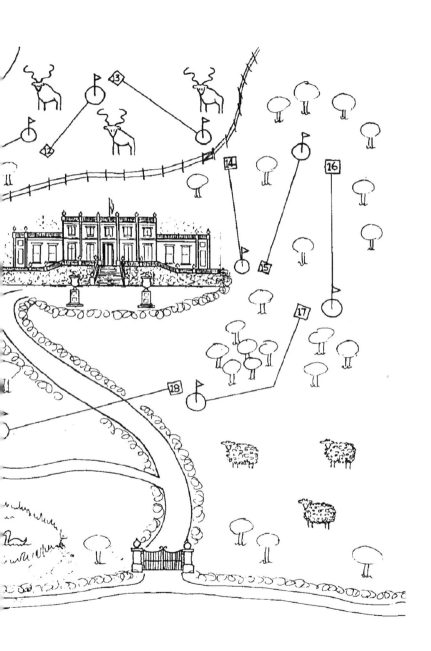

8

The minutes of the next committee meeting record that at the request of Lady Limpet a Mr Jock McTavish was co-opted onto it, and that he made several radical proposals. His suggestion that the proposed clubhouse should be re-sited close to the first tee was regarded as inspired (which in fact it was, by Pimples) and that the eighteenth green should be in the same vicinity instead of five miles away was also accepted.

It was noted that he recommended there should be a club professional to organise caddies, provide clubs and golf balls, and collect fees, and Jock McTavish himself offered to take on this onerous task.

In regard to the course, which was re-routed from the ninth to circumnavigate the Hall, he mentioned that bunkers should be introduced into the design.

'What is a bunker?' asked His Lordship, in blessed innocence.

There are a great many answers to a question like

that, not all printable. Jock tried his best.

''Tis a great hole wi' sand in it. Just t'make the game a bitty harder, y'ken?'

Not surprisingly, Lord Bruce was puzzled.

'A sort of purgatory,' explained Blinder, neatly summarising the view held by countless millions of golfing sinners.

Now in a language the Reverend lord could understand, he asked what misdemeanours would cause a golfer to be put in a bunker and how long he had to stay there.

'Well now,' sighed Jock, 'most players are condemned to a bunker by one o'four very common sins, – the pull, the slice, the top, or the sh.nk.' (Here I must apologise for not daring to print the word in full for fear of repercussions. Jock had no such qualms.) 'Unlike purgatory as ye ken it, Lord Bruce, the sinner is responsible f'r his ain escape, though many seem to spend a lot o'time and energy in the process. The Lord takes strong retribution and can be slow to forgive.'

The noble lord took issue on this point, and a long discussion would have ensued had not Chief Tumtumroli woken with a start and raised his usual point of order concerning the whereabouts of Smithers and the refreshments.

When business was resumed, Captain Buckmaster held forth.

'Bunkham Town Council is very interested in the development of this project,' he boomed, 'and would like some idea of progress and a completion date with a view to planning publicity and an inaugural opening ceremony by the Chairman of the Council.'

As it happened, the Captain was due to take over that office in two months' time.

'What about next Wednesday?' suggested His Lordship.

'More like a year next Wednesday,' murmured Egbert,

who would have preferred a great deal longer, or better still, not at all.

'I think it should be next Easter.' This from Augustine, who was already planning which hat to wear.

'But that's over six months away,' piped up Lofty Sidebottom, who thought, like her author, it was time she said something.

Mr Dickie pointed out that with the clubhouse still to be built, it was probably an optimistic date, but, with the exception of Egbert, they all agreed a Grand Opening on Easter Monday would be highly desirable and should be made the objective of all their plans. Captain Buckmaster was particularly enthusiastic, and he promised to ensure the support of his Council towards unimpeded progress, which he coupled in his mind with the name of Miss Virginia Hardcastle.

The Rev. Bruce had meanwhile lost his concentration and was musing.

'Nowhere in the Ten Commandments do they mention the pull, the slice, the top, or the sh.nk, so why is some form of purgatory involved? Perhaps I should consult with the Bishop on this.'

Jock offered help.

'The Commandments – they were written i'the desert sands, were they no? Tha' woo'd accoont f'the sand bunkers at least, and maybe f'r the green and pleasant land y're aiming t'reach.'

Thomas Dickie threw in a little Lewis Carroll:

> They wept like anything to see
> such quantities of sand:
> 'If this were only cleared away,'
> they said, 'it would be grand!'

None of which was minuted, not in this world at any rate.

MISS FITT

9

On a table of the towns and villages of England rated for excitement, pageantry, entertainment, night-life, or social attractions, Bunkham-on-Ouse would be found close to the bottom, if listed at all. So in the town, news of the progress of the golf course and the Easter deadline for opening (which was common knowledge within ten minutes of the committee decision) was of prime interest to everybody and made banner headlines in the next edition of *The Bunkham and District Crier*.

Virginia Hardcastle ordered a stock of golf clubs, including putters, from Jake Trueman, and as soon as the first few were available (a matter of days for Jake), a complete window was allocated to a display of golfing hardware, with Christmas as well as Easter in mind. As a result of the contract Hardcastle's had received for the building of the clubhouse, copies of Peregrine Weatherspoon's drawings were soon added to the display, together with a large map showing the layout of the course. This immediately became a subject for heated discussion at the Dog and Duck, which suddenly seemed to be full of golf course architects.

The town had by now recovered from the shock waves caused when the N'Chuyu tribal village had been set up a couple of years back. Against all forecasts of disaster, it had proved to be a resounding success, not only for the Hall, but also as a unique attraction for the town. The concern now was whether an invasion of golfing fanatics would compare favourably with the arrival of the N'Chuyu cannibal tribe.

They were to learn of course that in terms of ritual, ceremonials, appetite, thirst, and story-telling ability, there is little to choose, and that while the former may certainly bring more money with them, they are inclined to part with it far less easily.

The subject of the new golf course dominated the next meeting of the Town Council. Mr Lovelace the tailor, whose shop-window display already featured a large range of plaid materials for plus-fours, proposed a special parade of floats down the High Street, featuring golf, for Christmas. His proposal was seconded by Mr Goldbaum the jeweller, silversmith and clockmaker, whose windows were now dressed with a magnificent array of cups and trophies.

Mrs Feathers the couturier and ladies' hat-maker, gave her support on the condition that the forthcoming Easter Parade would receive similar funds and treatment, and the Chairman promised to make himself available for speech-making at both events as he declared the motion carried.

Captain Buckmaster generously indicated that he would be in a position to relieve the present Chairman of that duty on the second occasion. Miss Fitt then raised the subject which had been put back from the last meeting of roof repairs needed at the almshouses, but

MR LOVELACE

SOLLY D.
GOLDBAUM

123

MRS ALICE FEATHERS

unfortunately they had run out of time for the matter to be given due consideration. However, there was just time to take the proposal of Mr Goldbaum that the town should recognise this fine new facility at Cawkwell Hall by offering a trophy for the opening event on the forthcoming Easter Monday, to be known as 'The Bunkham Bowl'. He kindly offered the Council a small discount on the retail price of this prestigious solid silver trophy.

'Thou hast created all things, and for thy pleasure they are and were created' was the Revelation from Thomas Dickie, as he minuted the close of the meeting.

News of the presentation of The Bunkham Bowl by the Town Council reached the ears of Lord Limpet from his wife, who saw the headline in *The Bunkham and District Crier*.

'You'd better find out how to win that, Phippsy,' she said, reverting unconsciously to his old school nickname. It tended to rouse him.

'I'll have a chat with Jock about it,' he replied, and set off right away to find him.

It gave Lord Bruce a welcome opportunity to take another golf lesson and to extend his knowledge of the mysteries of his new craze. Taking his clubs with him, he found Jock exercising Ben and Nevis on the first fairway, and told him about the trophy.

'Well now, it all depends on whither it's t'be medal or matchplay, whither there's t'be handicaps or no, or whither, m'be, it's singles or foursomes or fourball. One round, I presume?' he asked.

So far as His Lordship was concerned it was all or none of these things, and Jock might as well have been speaking N'Chuyuese. However, in less than an hour it became clear to the noble lord that the object of the game was not only to get the ball into each hole in turn, that alone being a major achievement in his view, but to do it

125

with less hits than somebody else, or everybody else, in such an event as The Bunkham Bowl was likely to be.

Having got the hang of that, they moved on to the question of handicaps, a thorny question at any time. To arrive at this, an explanation of the word 'bogey' was necessary, a word that in those days was the equivalent of 'par' in later years. To the Rev. B.F., as he had for many years been affectionately known, the word had only dire connotations for the Sunday school class.

'Bogey f'r the course,' explained Jock, 'is the number o' times a player woo'd ha' hit the ball if a' the bad luck had no' occurred, and if the "if onlys" had. F'r the courses I ken, tha' figure is seventy-two. Anybody who can do tha' regularly is a scratch player.'

(He would have added 'Everybody's itching to do that' if only he had thought of it.)

His pupil struggled hard to absorb this piece of information. He could imagine seventy-two shots for one hole, but that number for the entire course did sound extremely far-fetched.

'Doesn't include air shots or putting I suppose,' he said.

'Afraid so.' Jock nodded his head solemnly.

'Ah, I think I understand now. That's where the handicapping comes in. How do they do it, with a ball and chain on his leg or a blindfold, or something?'

Before answering, Jock pondered this idea for a moment. There may be many readers who would like to do the same.

'I'm afraid it's the other players who get handicapped,' he replied.

This was too much for a simple man of God.

'I'll learn the rules tomorrow. For now Jock, will you please just show me how to hit the ball again.'

Jock found that easier.

NAPOLEON

10

At the next Tribal Council meeting of the N'Chuyus following the announcement of the Grand Easter Golf Challenge for The Bunkham Bowl, the subject was discussed at length. Clearly the honour of the tribe was at stake in the traditional art of projecting a missile with deadly accuracy. Spears and stones were their usual projectiles, but many had been watching with amusement the golf lessons being taken by the Lord of the Manor and felt confident that an entry from the tribe could win them the Bowl, which would make a handsome ceremonial cuspidor.

Mr Rutumutu the Witch Doctor was the obvious candidate, not only because of his acknowledged superiority with the existing spittoon, but also his skill in the art of casting spells over his adversaries. In present-day parlance, a type of strength with the 'verbals' – essential for matchplay but of limited value for a medal round.

Chief Tumtumroli reported that he had received

enquiries from Jock for volunteers to act as caddies on the big day. It was explained that the duties of a caddie involve carrying a bag of sticks, giving advice on which one to use, and collecting money. It occurred to Mr Rutumutu that with a little advance training, his powers and influence could thus be extended very effectively across the field, and plans were laid accordingly.

Where tribal pride and money are at stake, no holds are barred, as any present-day 'sportsman' will confirm.

Although the business of hitting a little ball in a required direction and into a hole would obviously be an easy matter for somebody of the Witch Doctor's capabilities, it was felt that some practice before the big event would be advisable, just to make certain. The team of warriors engaged on preparing the golf course were now so expert at it that it took but half a day to set up a practice ground close to their village, complete with a green. Due notice had been taken of the golf clubs being used by His Lordship, and tribal artisans skilled in the carving of skulls and bones were instructed by Fred to produce a set of clubs suitably tailored to Mr R.'s golf swing, so far as materials available allowed.

Regarding the acquisition of balls, the matter was left in the hands of M'Pupu. His unseen activities in the undergrowth whenever His Lordship was playing in the following week or two resulted in an ample supply, while mystifying Jock and Lord Bruce over the strange depletion of stock. On the other hand, Virginia Hardcastle, the ball supplier, was not unhappy about it.

The N'Chuyus were not the only ones planning for the big event. Sidney Sidebottom and his wife Lofty had been watching the progress of their employer and Lofty had come to the conclusion that, based on what they had seen, it would not be difficult to do better. Lofty even fancied her chances single-handed, but it was decided that, with His Lordship's permission, Sidney would throw his hat in the ring.

From the town, Captain Buckmaster took up the challenge, Mr Lovelace thought he would take up the game with an eye to business, and so did Solly Goldbaum, who had once carried his father's clubs and felt it gave him a distinct advantage.

Virginia Hardcastle established that there would be 'artisan' membership of the golf club before encouraging Jake Trueman to enter, and later set about the more difficult task of trying to interest her father, Mr Luke Hardcastle. Cricket was really his game, but she managed to persuade him to enter the competition by taking him quietly one day to watch Lord Limpet at practice. He booked some lessons with Jock and soon became a very good customer of her new department. In no time he caught the bug so badly his father began to fear for the future of the business.

Good progress was now being made with the course. The tenth fairway included a return crossing of the river, where an existing footbridge avoided additional ferry charges. Blinder's proposal that it should become a toll bridge was not accepted. The next three holes took them through the gnu reserve, a hazard that had so far escaped any references in the golfing rule books of the time. In fact, to this day there seems to be nothing specific in that regard. The tribal gnuherdsmen were instructed to keep their charges off the greens, and with the manure being carefully collected daily and sold to Egbert at a farthing a bucket, it was felt that any other gnu hazard was 'fair game'.

The course now surrounded the Hall, and the eighteenth fairway crossed the drive leading to the Hall. In spite of any advice and guidance given by the committee, the clubhouse was also making excellent progress.

Regular visits by Pimples to the office of the architect and to the building site may have had something to do with this. Her addition of a kitchen and a ladies' toilet were in time to prove a boon on the one hand, and a convenience on the other.

Decisions were made on the siting of bunkers, and pits were dug by the tribeswomen under the guidance of Egbert. They heard that the pits were to be filled with sand, and showing admirable initiative after Egbert had gone, they decided to take what there was of it from the building materials stored for use on the clubhouse building by Hardcastle's men.

It was just unfortunate that the difference between sand and cement was of no concern to these enthusiastic work-ladies. To their delight they found enough of both materials to fill the first half-dozen bunkers, and to make the colours match nicely in all of them, they were careful to mix the two very thoroughly.

There was, inevitably, an overnight shower, resulting in a set of bunkers which would delight all long-handicappers – almost impossible to get into, and a simple putt to get out of.

It is difficult to say who was the least happy about the state of affairs when the result was discovered the next morning. Napoleon, a large gnu bull and leader of the herd, could be heard complaining bitterly when discovered firmly 'set' in the centre of one bunker, and in another the Chief's favourite son together with Mr Rutumutu's young daughter were to be found 'fixed' in a very friendly embrace indeed.

Their explanation that it was an accidental collision while they were on separate rabbit trails was accepted in the tribe as an indication of the talent for camp fire stories inherited from their renowned parents.

It was Napoleon's lucky day, though he may not have

thought so. His plight was first discovered by Jock when exercising his dogs early in the morning, and Jock saw to it that the gnu was dug out rather than 'culled', much to the disappointment of the tribe. The young 'rabbit hunters' were first separated from the cement bunker and then from each other, and with the prospect of interviews with their respective fathers, it was certainly not their lucky day. There is an art in getting out of bunkers which is as much a secret to most players as it was to Napoleon and the young lovers, and they experienced the same sense of annoyance at having put themselves in there in the first place.

Hardcastle's men were not overjoyed about it either. They lent their pick-axes to the tribesmen, who gave them to their women, to deal with the problem. This led to an exhibition of bunker strokes which many of us would recognise, and the accompanying outbursts were not dissimilar even in a strange tongue.

Fortunately, the Reverend was not in earshot at the time.

11

By Christmas, golf mania had taken over in much of Bunkham-on-Ouse and most of the High Street. For those with an eye to entering for The Bunkham Bowl, the large display of 'golfing impedimenta' in Hardcastle's became irresistible, and a visit to Mr Lovelace for the latest in tartan suiting essential. When properly equipped and attired, often with the help of huge hints to Santa Claus, a booking for lessons with Jock was the normal procedure, and he was soon fully booked for all the hours of daylight. Even Blinder's limited knowledge of the game was eagerly sought, and paid for.

The steering committee continued its regular meetings, but they were no longer directly relevant to anything of a practical nature that was going on, so the building remained on schedule. Lord Bruce as the Chairman tended to contribute to the meetings a record of his most recent practice game, shot by shot, together with comments on the latest advances in club design and manufacture now available from Jake Trueman via Hardcastle's.

'What were you saying about handicaps, Jock?' he asked at one particularly lengthy session.

'Every golfer has t' have one,' came the reply, 'unless it's all off scratch.'

'Postponement due to weather, I suppose. That kind of thing?' said Lord Bruce, which led to a debate prompted by the Captain on the ceremonial arrangements to be made in the event of rain.

'Y're going t'need a handicapping committee,' said Jock, 'woo'd ye like me to take it on?'

That ideal situation of power without responsibility appealed to him, and as he was the only one present who had the slightest idea what he was talking about, that was agreed.

Next, Augustine asked a question which had been 'planted' by Pimples – 'Will ladies be allowed on the course?'

The Chairman hesitated, so Captain Buckmaster gave the answer.

'That won't be necessary. Arrangements have been made for Fred's people to do all the caddying.'

Thus the matter was settled for several generations to come.

Lord Bruce was brooding again. 'Tell me, Jock,' he said, 'how do people remember how many shots they have taken?'

'In my experience, not very well,' replied Jock, 'but I'll be selling a wee card and a pencil tha' might help a little.'

'He that increaseth knowledge increaseth sorrow,' quoted the Town Clerk as the meeting broke up.

As a result of the regular publicity given to the new course by *The Bunkham and District Crier*, a number of applications for entry in the opening day competition for The Bunkham Bowl were received from outside the town. It became necessary to decide if the event was to be open to all. The decision was complicated by the fact that young Smithson of Whimby, Wilts., was the son of old friends of Lady Augustine and was also Captain Buckmaster's brother-in-law, and Lord Humphrey Dinglefoot, another applicant, was a distant relative of the Limpets and not the sort to take no for an answer.

Lord Bruce consulted Jock, who consulted Pimples, and a decision was reached.

The competition would be open. It would be a four-somes matchplay knockout, and entries would be limited to sixteen people, in eight pairs. Easter Monday could then feature a semi-final round in the morning, followed by a grand final in the afternoon.

This format would necessitate a preliminary quarter-final round beforehand. As His Reverence would not hear of it being played on the Sabbath, it was scheduled for Easter Saturday, leaving a day clear for the players to offer up such prayers as may be thought appropriate to the occasion.

The good Lord was certainly going to have great difficulty in fulfilling more than two of them.

The announcement of the programme for the competition led to long arguments at the Dog and Duck about what it all meant. Jock had to be called in, and with the help of several drams was persuaded to explain it. First, the competitors would have to form partnerships. In each match, the partners would play alternate shots against their opponents, and the winning pair would go forward to the next round.

Partner selection was clearly of vital importance, and intense lobbying with a touch of intrigue was inevitable. So little was known by anybody except Jock and Blinder about the form of the local contestants, and even less about the outsiders, that judgements had to be made on the basis of appearances backed up by rumour, of which there was plenty.

Entries were accepted from the Lord Humphrey Dinglefoot with his son, the Hon. Dominic Dinglefoot, from the Smithson brothers of Whimby, Wilts., and from a Major Potts and Mr Ernest Hunter of the Strangeways Golf and Sporting Club somewhere in East Anglia.

The two remaining spaces were quickly filled, one by Mr Isaac Cohen, from Hatton Garden, a friend of Mr Goldbaum, and by Mr Lovelace's young nephew, Archibald Smart.

As Lord Limpet spent so much time and money in Hardcastle's, his invitation to Mr Luke to partner him was an offer he could not avoid or refuse. Latest reports on the noble lord's progress were hardly encouraging, and the response of Mr Luke could fairly be described as 'luke warm'.

Captain Buckmaster, having checked the list, found himself with the choice of Sidney Sidebottom, Mr Rutumutu, or Jake Trueman. On the basis that he had seen Sidney Sidebottom and that he didn't know or like the sound of the Witch Doctor, he made straight for Jake Trueman who looked pretty powerful and was quite easy going.

News of the format for the contest reached Mr Rutumutu from Jock and came as a nasty shock, especially when he discovered that his partner would be Sidney Sidebottom. With the help of a unique assortment of clubs made from willow, bones and gnu horn, he had developed a very effective game. His swing was more personal than classical, and his practice sessions on the tribal practice hole had become regular entertainment for the entire tribe. They would line the fairway and the green, cheering or jeering as the performance deserved, until he had achieved a very creditable level of skill. His putting with the complete hind leg of a young gnu was particularly impressive.

There was one advantage in having Sidney as a partner. He had not developed any bad habits. The disadvantage was that he had never had an opportunity to do so. Not only had he never played golf, but he had never played anything, apart from truant from games at school.

An emergency meeting of the Tribal Council was called to consider the problem, and the only possible solution seemed to be that Sidney would have to be intensively trained. His duties as chauffeur were likely to be far too restrictive, so plans were laid to overcome that obstacle for as long or as often as necessary.

This decision accounted for several mysterious incidents involving the Daimler-Benz, which became so unreliable that mechanics had to be brought out from the town, and it was later towed away to their garage for overhaul and to await new parts. This difficulty did not bother His Lordship much, as he was generally busy practising on the golf course, and it left his chauffeur to do the same, though not at all publicly.

Sidney's surprise at the problems with the motor car was as nothing to the shock he received when he was led away from the faulty vehicle by Chief Fred Tumtumroli to the N'Chuyu village and introduced to his golf partner, the Witch Doctor. He was promptly measured for a set of 'Rutumutu' clubs, and after being sworn to secrecy with the most terrifying threats of cannibalism if he broke faith, he was shown the tribal practice ground and given a demonstration by Mr R.

A period of intense and unremitting training lay ahead, and while the slightly adventurous spirit which had once led him into the African jungle on safari was still just alive, he couldn't help wishing that he had found any other partner, even His Lordship, or else that the ground would open up here and now and swallow him.

However, when a few hours later he discussed the affair with his wife Lofty, they decided it was not all bad.

'Would you rather be playing with Mr Rutumutu or against him?' asked Lofty, and Sidney could see the force of this argument, though the third alternative of not playing at all, which he favoured, was not mentioned.

Sidney's clubs were quickly made and he was soon put to work on the practice ground under the instruction of the Witch Doctor. This he had been prepared for, but not for the tribal initiation ceremony that followed. It seems the proud N'Chuyu tribe could not allow themselves to be represented by anybody who had not received the full ceremonial treatment.

In a state of shock, he was stripped off, painted in a variety of colours in various places and then invited to experience the tribal brew with each of the elders in turn. Then having reached a more relaxed, indeed, a carefree mood, he took centre stage in the compound in a wild dance with the maidens of the tribe all similarly unattired.

All would have been well had not a large party of visitors arrived on the scene at the height of proceedings, led by his wife Lofty and the Deputy Chairman of the Council of Bunkham-on-Ouse, Captain Montague Buckmaster, JP.

Sidney had a lot of explaining to do at home later that day. How lucky for him, and what a pity for us, that cameras were not standard tourist equipment at that time.

12

When Blinder opened his 'book' on the result of The Bunkham Bowl, he found the utmost difficulty in setting the initial odds. He consulted his father on the subject of handicaps.

'From wha' I can see so far,' said Jock, 'the handicapping limit o' twenty-four needs to be doubled before they qualify. The ootsiders are a problem, but they a' claim to be twenty-four handicappers onywey so I think we'll dispense wi' handicaps for this event and make it a' scratch. If necessary, when we see the standard o' play, maybe we'll think o' individual handicaps in some other form.' This was accompanied by a flicker of an eyelid which Blinder well understood, and it enabled him to set out his book with greater confidence.

His opening offers, which he posted below stairs at the Hall and in the public bar at the Dog and Duck, created a lot of interest but not many takers, due not only to lack of information on the form of the players, but also lack of news of the draw for the first round. Blinder made this known to Jock, who raised the question of the draw at the next committee meeting. At the suggestion of Captain Buckmaster it was decided that the draw should take place under his chairmanship at the Town Hall, and so it was.

The Town Hall was packed for the occasion, and all the local entries were present with the exception of Messrs Rutumutu and Sidebottom, who were busy practising.

Captain Buckmaster made an introductory speech, mostly on the subject of the new golf club and who was likely to be the most suitable first Captain, and he might well have spent half an hour on it had not Solly Goldbaum marched onto the stage with The Bunkham Bowl and, to a round of applause, invited Lady Cynthia (Pimples) Limpet to draw the first slip from it.

She did so, and the Town Clerk recorded the names.

The Smithson brothers.

In a now tense silence, she drew their opponents.

Major Potts and partner.

Next came

Lord Humphrey Dinglefoot and partner, versus

Lord Limpet and partner.

A noble contest indeed. Betting prospects were warming up.

Captain Buckmaster and partner were next out.

In a hushed hall Pimples drew another slip.

Mr Leslie Lovelace and partner.

This left the final pairing of

Solly D. Goldbaum and partner, versus

Mr Rutumutu and Sidney Sidebottom.

The Chairman rose to round off the proceedings with thanks to Her Ladyship and to ... by which time the hall was empty, and first orders in a growing crush were being placed at the Dog and Duck.

There was a clamour to put money on 'Lord Dingle' and partner at even money against 'Lord Limp', which was felt to be like finding money in the street, and those who knew Sidney Sidebottom thought the same way about backing 'Solly D' against him at evens.

Too little was known about the other runners to attract much business, although Virginia Hardcastle had a flutter on the Buck–Trueman partnership at eleven to ten.

There were now just four weeks to go to Easter, and the subject of the contest was paramount throughout the town, Cawkwell Hall and the village of M'Bongabonga.

The course was laid out and was receiving the finishing touches of Egbert and his staff. The clubhouse was sufficiently advanced to cope with the opening, and the committee had arrived at a decision on the colours for decoration – leave it to Pimples. Spring was in the air, practice rounds were being played at every opportunity, Jock and Blinder were fully booked for lessons, and spies were out everywhere.

Danger lurked in the corridors of the Town Hall and Cawkwell Hall, where putting practice was rife. Secretaries learned to step warily at all times when certain Council Members were in the building, and most of the staff at Cawkwell Hall did the same, with the unfortunate exception of Smithers.

The disaster would not have been so bad had he not been carrying a large breakfast tray loaded with porridge and soft-boiled eggs on the occasion when His Lordship's putt went astray. It was as a result of this and the subsequent incident involving Lady Augustine and the staircase that Pimples found it necessary to declare all areas above the ground floor 'out of bounds'.

In defence of His Lordship it must be said that his putting was not at fault in the second unfortunate mishap. He had played half-a-dozen perfectly good shots

SMITHERS

to the top of the stairs, prior to practising chipping down them, and he could not have been expected to know that while he was changing his club, Her Ladyship would give up waiting for Smithers to bring her breakfast in bed, and go downstairs for it. Or try to.

By a coincidence that might be considered lucky for Augustine but less so for a certain Miss Peabody, a party of tourists were visiting Cawkwell Hall at that time and had been given special permission to view the magnificent Adam staircase. Miss Peabody was their guide, and the visit inside the Hall had promised to bring a little nearer the ambition she had always cherished to meet a member of the aristocracy, and to even have the chance to introduce such a personage to her party.

Her ambition was on this occasion quite suddenly and unexpectedly fulfilled, as they climbed the stairs.

The Lady Augustine arrived at waist height and approximately twenty miles per hour, gathering speed. Their introduction was, inevitably, very informal, as Miss Peabody and the entire party were skittled down the Adam staircase with insufficient time to really appreciate it. In the circumstances there were surprisingly few serious injuries, and many of the party were able to complete the tour unassisted.

For Miss Peabody, the incident had its compensations, as this close connection with the upper classes permanently raised her social standing at her local Women's Institute, entitling her to take the chair.

So far as Her Ladyship was concerned, she decided that in future she would wait for Smithers.

Lord Bruce waited patiently for the 'course' to be cleared before chipping the remaining three balls down the stairs.

In the N'Chuyu village they had no staircase problems, but were not without other reminders of the imminent match and the presence of their star competitor. The children made miniature golf clubs and spent much of their time trying to imitate their hero, the Witch Doctor. Chipping and putting practice took place all over the compound, and it was an unusual day if breakfast porridge was served without several helpings of golf balls. Indeed, it indicated that more practice was needed, as the tribal pot was used as a regular target by Mr R., and even Sidney Sidebottom on his daily visits had been known to 'hole out' in it from time to time.

Great interest was aroused when it was reported that some of the visiting entries had arrived at Jock's office, and that they had received permission to play practice rounds to familiarise themselves with the course. The odds shortened sharply when Major Potts and Ernest Hunter were seen to play, and any punters who had managed to get on at five to four realised how lucky they had been. Blinder closed that page of his book immediately.

Lord Humphrey's arrival caused great consternation for all those with money riding on him to beat Lord Limpet. It had been assumed that anybody could do that.

The noble lord weighed in at a good twenty stones, and was only a pound or two above that of his son. Blinder issued urgent instructions for the footbridge at the tenth hole to be strengthened, and a new large raft to be built for the river crossing at the eighth.

Nothing had been seen of the Smithson brothers.

ANGEL

13

Mrs Feathers, the couturier and hat-maker, reminded the Town Council of its promise to promote an Easter Parade, and it was arranged that the event would take place after church on Easter Sunday. The river walk and park was the obvious venue, with the nearby carriage-way for the use of motor and horse-drawn floats and for those on horseback.

The theme for the floats was to be 'Golf', and the first prize, funded by the Council, to be six free golf lessons from Jock McTavish.

Mrs Feathers kindly offered to donate a small cup for the finest hat on parade, and also generously offered her time and expertise as judge of the contest. Not surprisingly, she was very busy in the remaining few weeks, and made good use of Kirsty McTavish's services at a sewing machine at the Hall.

Lord Limpet intended to hold an Easter Sunday service at the Mission, so he and Her Ladyship had no plans to attend the parade. When his chauffeur Sidney asked, on behalf of Chief Tumtumroli, if he might be allowed to use the Daimler-Benz for this special occasion, permission was given and the hope expressed by His Lordship that the car would be more reliable than of late. Fred and his Witch Doctor were confident that it would be.

Another request made to Sidney by his golf partner was the attendance of his wife Lofty at a special tribal meeting. It is a tribute to her support and loyalty to her dear Bumsy that, with vivid memories of her last visit still fresh in her mind, she agreed to go. She was flattered to discover that it was her design expertise that was required.

The ladies of the tribe had heard about the hat contest.

The week leading up to the Bank Holiday was one of special excitement for the town. Bunting and flags appeared the length of the High Street, in the park, and on the bridge over the river. The spring weather looked set fair and the gardens were ablaze with colour. Publicity in *The Bunkham and District Crier* had created widespread interest in the 'float' and 'hat' competitions, and secret developments were afoot throughout the town and in the surrounding villages.

Whether they were completely ready for the parade or not, most of the local population downed tools and were to be found at the golf course on the Saturday morning, lining the route to the clubhouse and in a crush around the first tee and all over the fairway. A ceremonial war-dance by the tribal warriors was found to be a very effective solution to this problem, but it did create another when some of the more excitable young N'Chuyus complete with assegais continued the chase as far as the river and a number of innocent citizens had an early season swim.

145

A draw was made for the order of play, and the first on the tee was Smithson Major. With his brother, he had materialised at the last moment, and they were of special interest to Blinder and the punters as a pair of very dark horses. They looked athletic, studious and positively dangerous by comparison to most of the field, and they shortened their odds even further by declining the carefully trained and selected caddies that Jock and Mr Rutumutu put at their disposal. They were equipped with an impressive selection of golf clubs, and with casual confidence, Smithson Major drove his ball two hundred yards down the centre of the first fairway.

Jock then announced his opponent, next on the tee.

Major Clarence Potts.

The Major had brought with him his own caddie, and the flatness of his nose and the thickness of his ears was evidence of his regular appearances in the regimental fist-fighting ring. 'Angel', as he was called, glared round at all the spectators as the Major prepared to take his drive.

To the horror of the Smithsons, it flew past their ball by some thirty yards. Sociable conversation seemed to be in very short supply as the four players set off up the fairway.

Much as I know every golfing reader and golfer's wife would like to be given a shot-by-shot report on this and every match, I fear that time and space are too limited. However, full information is available from *The Bunkham and District Crier*, if provided with a large stamped addressed envelope.

Such a report would also include more background detail on the cause of the altercation on the seventh green, and the fighting that broke out on the ferry at the eighth. Luckily, the tribal ferryman was an excellent diver and successfully recovered Smithson Minor's clubs

146

ISAAC COHEN

SMITHSON MAJOR   SMITHSON MINOR

LORD HUMPHREY DINGLEFOOT   HON. DOMINIC DINGLEFOOT

LUKE HARDCASTLE

MAJOR POTTS   ERNEST HUNTER

ARCHIBALD SMART

147

after the Major's caddie had taken matters into his own hands. Unfortunately it was not possible to save Smithson Major's deerstalker, which drifted away as he swam ashore. From this point it appears that the game deteriorated somewhat, particularly the Smithsons' game, and it was all over by the fourteenth.

The Smithson brothers returned that day to Whimby, Wilts., and reportedly took up croquet.

14

The first to tee-off in the second match was Mr Leslie Lovelace. Little was known of, or expected from, the tailor, except that he had been missing from his shop for long periods of every day, and that he had selected as a partner a very capable and aggressive-looking young man, a distant relative, who talked a good game of golf at the Dog and Duck.

To the surprise of everyone including Mr Lovelace, his drive travelled in a straight line along the fairway and although staying in contact with the ground throughout, it cleared the tee by a good fifty yards.

Jock then announced his opponent, next on the tee.

'Captain Montague Buckmaster, Chairman of the Bunkham-on-Ouse Town Council.'

The Captain was a credit to the House of Lovelace in his immaculate plus-fours and peaked cap, though some might question the suitability of white spats for the occasion. He tee'd up and carefully selected his highly polished brassie, had several smooth practice swings, and then addressed the ball. It had nothing to fear from his first two attempts, but good contact was made with his third shot, which sliced off to the right and was traced to the front lawn of the Hall.

Archibald Smart promptly drew to the attention of Jock that two rules of golf had already been broken. One, that the second (attempted) shot should have been taken by the Captain's partner, Jake Trueman, and two, he had thereby been guilty of a practice shot on the course during the match.

'Ha' ye no hear'd o' a mulligan?' was the sharp reply.

Not surprisingly, nobody had, as this was probably the first time the term was used for a free shot on the first tee, and that may well be the origin of it. (If not, the author claims a literary mulligan.)

Thereafter, the contest was played to Jock's rules.

There was a race to the ball on the front lawn between Egbert Micklethwaite and Jake Trueman which was narrowly won by Egbert. Before he could be stopped, he picked up the ball from his precious lawn and threw it back onto the fairway, where it finished forty yards ahead of the opposition. Jock's ruling of a 'free drop' was received with no more than a black look from Archibald, followed later by another when Jake played his shot to within a foot of the pin, while Archibald's finished in a bunker.

Leslie Lovelace refused to risk his personally tailored sporting suit by playing in a bunker, so the first hole was conceded to the Buck–Trueman partnership. This was to be the pattern of the round, with a frustrated Archibald and the unblemished tailor being obliged to concede the match when Jake Trueman drove the green at the three hundred yard sixteenth and Leslie Lovelace was faced with, and refused, his umpteenth bunker.

15

Solly Goldbaum and his partner accepted the free caddies offered by their opponents without hesitation, which proved to be unwise. His first clue to this was being offered his putter on the first tee, but he presumed that an African tribesman could not be expected to be expert at the game, and he selected his brassie. Perhaps his caddie was right – he might have done better than thirty yards with it at that.

Mr Rutumutu took his well-tried gnu femur, which had been intricately carved and shaped to his swing, and with a tribal war-cry and uproarious response from his native supporters, he wound himself up like a clock spring and released a drive that James Braid would have been proud of, finishing not far short of the green. There were whoops of joy from all the N'Chuyus present, and from Blinder, who now felt more comfortable about all the money riding on Solly Goldbaum.

However, Solly's partner Isaac Cohen was no pushover,

especially as his was some of the cash involved, and he placed his shot onto the green. Sidney Sidebottom only needed to make a short chip after his partner's fantastic drive, but in a highly nervous state he snatched at it with his spoon and stubbed the ball across the green and into the rough on the other side. Had it not been for the acrobatic work of his caddie's feet in 'setting it up', the return shot might have been very difficult. As it was, the Witch Doctor was able to lay his chip dead by the hole.

While this was in progress, Isaac Cohen's ball seemed to have drifted somehow to a nasty dip at the edge of the green, where his caddie must have inadvertently trodden on it. Solly did his best with it, using the brassie handed to him by his caddie, and they did well to make a six, though they lost the hole to their opponents' five.

After losing the first six holes in similar fashion, Solly and Isaac began to get a little suspicious, and started to watch the activities of the caddies carefully. Mr Rutumutu was not a Witch Doctor for nothing, he sensed the changing atmosphere, and gave the appropriate signals.

Solly and Isaac were pleased to find themselves winning the next four holes, and felt badly about those obviously unfounded suspicions. Consequently their luck suddenly seemed to change and they lost the match at the fifteenth. They shook hands amidst the war-dance of the massed tribal fan-club, making sure to smile all round, just to be on the safe side.

The noble Lords Limpet and Dinglefoot were the last team leaders to start in the quarter finals, and Lord Humphrey tee'd up. To be more precise, he had the ball placed by his caddie, as that operation was a difficult manoeuvre for a man of his, or his son's, build. Once it was placed, he was just able to see it.

For full details of this round I would again refer you to *The Bunkham and District Crier*, or alternatively in this case, to the record in His Lordship's diary, although the two accounts may not exactly tally. Doubtless His Lordship did have a lot of bad luck as his record shows, but other versions suggest that the Dinglefoots (or feet?) had a lot more of it, and even go so far as to imply that, strictly amongst themselves, the caddies may have had more to do with it than the Almighty.

All versions are agreed that the number of strokes taken overall would qualify as an all-time record, and that it was only the long hours of daylight and the clear skies that made a result possible that night. The match was decided on the last green, where Luke Hardcastle holed out for a ten. The Hon. Dominic had a tap-in for the half, but sadly his caddie dropped his bag of clubs just as he took his putter back out of his line of sight, he hit his foot in mistake for the ball, and the game was lost.

It was left to Jock to congratulate all the caddies on their mastery of the technical details of their new trade.

FIFI

MARMADUKE

16

Some animals, like some people, seem to attract trouble and bad luck. Napoleon, the proud leader of the gnu herd, was such an animal. Having only just recovered his self-esteem and dignity in the herd after that embarrassing bunker incident, his luck deserted him again on Easter Saturday evening, during the very last round of the day.

The strange disappearance of Luke Hardcastle's drive in a massive hook over the trees at the tenth hole was already common knowledge wherever the story of the round was told. What they were unaware of was the involvement of the unfortunate Napoleon who, having received the shot as a direct hit between the eyes, collapsed in a daze on the bank of the river and tumbled in. Struggling in the tide, he collided with the large raft at the eighth, scrambled onto it, and fainted.

He awoke the next morning still groggy and a bit peckish, and he chewed at the nearest thing available, which happened to be the sisal mooring line. The raft floated gently out into the tidal stream.

His arrival at the town centre coincided with the climax of the parade and celebrations. The raft bumped into the small landing stage, and letting out a roar of pent-up frustration and hunger, he staggered ashore and tried to take in the noisy festive scene that greeted his eyes.

The parade of horse-drawn floats, beautifully decorated and depicting golfing scenes, dresses and equipment was approaching down the High Street. The street was lined with cheering crowds which included many from Cawkwell Hall. Jock and Kirsty with Ben and Nevis were again studying the strange traditions of the Sassenachs and enjoying a respite from their duties at the Hall.

On the lawns by the river, dozens of ladies were beginning to parade their ingenious hat creations, with Mrs Feathers taking up a judging position on a raised dais in the centre.

At that moment a loud honking from the horn of the Daimler-Benz announced its approach from the opposite direction, and all eyes turned to the extraordinary display it contained. A dozen nubile N'Chuyu ladies were standing on the seats and the running boards wearing the most spectacular and colourful hats and very little else, apart from small and fairly inadequate grass skirts. Winning entries, without doubt.

The ladies of the town looked shocked, Mrs Feathers looked 'daggers', and the men just looked.

Eye-witness reports vary widely on the exact sequence of events thereafter. According to the *Crier*, the trouble started when the parade horses shied as a result of the persistent blasts on the horn from Sidney Sidebottom. Others have the view that it was Ben and Nevis breaking loose in the excitement (and while Jock's eyes were elsewhere) that caused the horses to bolt. Most are agreed that the problem might have been controllable had not Napoleon become bored with inactivity and decided it was time to exercise his authority.

He put his head down and, with a great bellow of warning, charged across the lawns, scattering the screaming ladies and collecting on his horns a selection of their precious Easter bonnets. Thus adorned he proceeded to attack the already confused horses, and might have caused even greater mayhem if his horns had not been so effectively muffled, and if Ben and Nevis had not decided to join in on the side of the horses.

As Napoleon backed off and turned away, he noticed the grass skirts and remembered how hungry he was. This novel and very attractive cereal breakfast led to the *Crier*'s most famous headline:

THE MAD HATTER'S BREAKFAST
GNU CHEWS N'CHUYUS

Fortunately, the beast calmed down after eating half-a-dozen skirts and several hats, and, still bewildered, allowed himself to be quietly led back to his pastures by the gnu herdsmen, who saved him from further embarrassment in the herd by removing the remains of the hats.

By lunchtime, Sidney had extricated the Daimler-Benz and returned to the village of M'Bongabonga with his full complement of ladies. They had a lot of explaining to do to the tribal elders, who were quick to notice the absence of their hats.

By the evening, some degree of order was being restored in the High Street of Bunkham-on-Ouse, and most of the population settled down for the night in anticipation of an exciting Easter Monday at Cawkwell Hall. Presentation of the Council's 'Best Float' prize was

157

postponed indefinitely, although the general view at the Dog and Duck was that it should have gone to Napoleon.

Mrs Feathers' Cup, which was found flattened by the wheels of the Daimler-Benz, was returned to Solly Goldbaum with a sharp note concerning its quality.

The Town Clerk called for an Emergency Meeting of the Town Council.

The meeting might have lasted no more than a few hours, but for the problems resulting from so many broken shop-front windows. Mollifying the owners and clearing up the mess was an operation which could be left to the Highways Department (Will Tidy and his son), but it was the effect on the Council Chamber that caused the most trouble.

All the broken glass scattered down the High Street caused Miss Fitt to be very concerned about her cat's paws, so she thought it best to bring Marmaduke with her to the meeting. This might have been a satisfactory solution had not Mrs Feathers felt the same way about Fifi, her poodle.

Open warfare did not break out immediately, although some spitting and growling on their exchange of greetings was ominous. It was when Mrs Feathers stood up to speak on the deplorable behaviour of Mr McTavish's dogs that Fifi fell off her lap and was free to investigate Marmaduke.

Most of the action in the encounter took place on the top of the polished walnut table, ranging from one end to the other and providing an interesting contrast in styles, as the dog lunged and the cat parried, the papers flew, and the Chairman seethed.

When he could stand it no longer he climbed onto the table to separate them, and the three-cornered contest that ensued was the most colourful episode ever recorded in the annals of the Bunkham Town Council.

After extra time, the clear winner was Marmaduke, with little more than a torn ear. Fifi, with a bloody nose and both eyes closed, was a defiant loser, and the Captain had to retire wounded. With his right hand bandaged and a patch over his left eye, it was a strangely subdued Chairman who concluded the meeting as dawn was breaking.

The Town Clerk's minutes closed on a quotation from The Bard.

'When the hurly-burly's done,
When the battle's lost and won.'

Miss Fitt and Mrs Feathers left separately.

17

Easter Monday dawned bright and clear and promising. With the semi-finals and finals to be played in one day, an early start was necessary. The first pairing was Lord Limpet and Luke Hardcastle versus Captain Buckmaster and Jake Trueman.

Before a very small crowd of early risers, Lord Bruce took the tee, and viewed with sinful pride his magnificent drive soaring down the middle of the fairway.

It is customary for most golfers at such a moment to make some kind of excuse before taking their turn on the tee. Bad cold, bad leg, haven't played for weeks – that kind of thing. In the Captain's case this procedure was unnecessary, as he had to be helped onto the tee by his partner, and almost propped up to take his shot.

It was clear that the Chairman of the Bunkham Town Council had had a busy night. Everyone presumed that his eye patch and bandaged hand could be attributed to some heroic involvement with the dozen horse-drawn floats running amok in the High Street, and were duly impressed. He made no comment, thereby manfully shielding Marmaduke and Fifi from the blame.

Having been pointed in the right direction, he took a swing at one of the balls he could see, and it is to his credit that he made contact with it sufficiently to get it off the tee, almost as far as the divot. Jake Trueman hit a powerful recovery shot, and continued to do so throughout the game, with a cheerful smile of resignation in face of the inevitable result.

He conceded the match on the twelfth green, where the Captain fell asleep in a bunker and was carried back to the clubhouse by Jake and four caddies. There, His Reverend Lordship gave him a blessing and Mr Dickie gave him several double brandies. The Captain gradually perked up, and it is debatable which of the two treatments did the trick.

The second semi-final matched Mr Rutumutu and Sidney Sidebottom against Major Potts and Ernest Hunter, and promised a close game. The Potts–Hunter combination had shown itself to be a serious threat, and the Witch Doctor had received detailed reports. Naturally he set about casting some of his most powerful spells in their direction, and at the same time left nothing to chance by planning the strategy of his game, and theirs, in a thoroughly practical manner.

He arrived on the tee in full tribal warpaint and regalia, with his and Sidney's caddies similarly attired, together with a full supporting cast. Sidney had resisted their attempts to give him the same tribal treatment, under very firm instructions from Lofty. Among the crowd were a careful selection of the most shapely of the young ladies whose attributes had been so effectively displayed in Bunkham the day before. New grass skirts had quickly been run up for the occasion and the remaining few hats were also on show as further embellishment to their other attractions.

The Witch Doctor tee'd up his ball on an old knuckle bone, and winding himself up in a tight coil, he then released the sort of lethal attack on the ball usually reserved for enemy warriors. To the chanting of his supporters it rocketed down the fairway, and he performed a triumphant little dance on the tee of the kind usually displayed in the present day by footballers.

The Major took his turn in a contrasting silence that was almost deafening. As he set up his ball, a few movements in the crowd facing him made him look up, and he noticed that the supporting N'Chuyu warriors had acted in the most gentlemanly fashion by moving back to allow the shorter young maidens to get a better view of his shot. They smiled and waggled their hips a little in a friendly, encouraging manner.

His tee shots were always extremely reliable, but on this occasion he must have taken his eye off the ball for some reason, and for the first time in their long partnership around the country, Ernest Hunter found himself playing the second shot from his partner's tee. No mulligans in this match.

Taking out his brassie, he took up his stance opposite the 'chorus line' and with commendable will-power, kept his head down long enough to make an adequate shot. One of the shapeliest girls was seen to give him a special little cheer and a wink, which brought a blush to his cheeks, and a dreamy expression to his eyes, as he fumbled putting his club back in the bag.

In this fashion, it was unnecessary for Sidney to play more than a supporter's role for his team to be six up by the time they reached the river at the eighth. The crowd could not very well follow the players across the water, and were left to pick up the game at the tenth green. Major Potts took Angel, his caddie, to one side and suggested that he might stay on that side also, and try to do something about the N'Chuyu crowd problem.

Sidney's tee shot on the eighth predictably entered the river Ouse, and in general, things took a turn for the better for the Potts–Hunter team in the absence of the crowd. They won the ninth with a birdie two, and Sidney found the water again at the tenth. Now there was only three in it, and their spirits rose.

After crossing the footbridge to the tenth green, Major Potts had carried his clubs long enough, and looked round for his caddie. Angel seemed to be missing, so the Major prepared to tee off from the eleventh without him.

He couldn't help noticing as he took his stance that the 'chorus line' was still prominent, but the one he had regarded as the leading lady was no longer in evidence. In the course of his swing, he gave further thought to the significance of this, with the inevitable result that, once again, it was necessary for his partner to play from the same tee.

When the match was over on the thirteenth green, the celebrations of the N'Chuyu supporters could be heard from the clubhouse, and Sidney and Mr R. were carried shoulder high back to the village. There they were to be rested and prepared for the afternoon final.

To Sidney's surprise, they found another visitor already there, being suitably entertained by Primrose, the 'leading lady' of the village. Angel was never the same man again, and never wanted to be.

Major Potts failed to solve the mystery of Angel's disappearance, and had to find another caddie. Ernest Hunter left, still wearing that dreamy, far-away look.

18

Chief Fred Tumtumroli and Mr Rutumutu and all their wives had dutifully attended the Easter Sunday service in the Mission Hall, given by their Reverend landlord, not only to offer up prayers and sing hymns, which they did with enthusiasm, but also to receive their ration of the holy wine in the course of the service.

They had become firm believers in the mystical power of the bread and wine, especially the wine, to the extent that they even took into the tribal safekeeping any spare crates of it that the Reverend Father might happen to leave lying around. In this way they created for themselves an emergency stock of their own for use at any time they felt the need to reinforce their faith in the Almighty, or simply to celebrate his existence.

Mr Rutumutu was without doubt a first-class Witch Doctor. He was, nevertheless, also only human, when all was said and done. He and his Chief felt that the outstanding success of their tribal campaign that morning was the sort of occasion when such a celebration was justified, and the wine flowed freely.

It followed that when the time came to commence the final round against His Lordship and Luke Hardcastle, Mr Rutumutu was a little the worse for wear. Even so, he was in a very happy frame of mind and full of confidence, and while the situation bothered Sidney somewhat, he felt that a slight handicap of that kind was unlikely to matter much, in view of the quality of their opposition.

On arrival at the first tee, it appeared that the entire population of Bunkham and district was present. Captain Buckmaster had by now sufficiently recovered to see it as his duty as Chairman of the Council to mark this auspicious occasion by making a speech, and was about to do so when Virginia Hardcastle, at the suggestion of Jock, overwhelmed him with a bewitching smile and an invitation to 'get away from it all'.

Instead, Solly Goldbaum was on hand to exhibit The Bunkham Bowl, and Jock spun a coin for first to play. Mr Rutumutu won the honour and with a wide grin and a sweeping bow, he took his stance. Or tried to.

On wobbly legs he managed to tee the ball up on his favourite knuckle bone and then remembered the need for a golf club. His trusty gnu femur was handed to him by a bemused caddie, and he went into his routine winding-up procedure. His swing, when it came, had all its usual power, but his mind had wandered to the days of jungle warfare and he aimed his club like a throwing spear. It sailed fully forty yards before plunging deep into the fairway.

Jock generously declared a mulligan, but the second try was no better, and Sidney had to take over. Aided by the caddies, they put up a token fight, but reached the river seven holes down.

165

The pride of the N'Chuyus was now at stake, and risking dire revenge later, they heaved the Witch Doctor into the water and let him struggle across to the far bank. The cure was complete and immediate. Dripping wet, he set about the tribesmen, the caddies, Sidney, and finally, the game.

His Lordship and Luke, who had been coasting to an apparent early victory at nine or ten shots per hole, found to their surprise that by the seventeenth hole they were all square, with just the eighteenth to play. Sidney and Luke had the responsibility of the drives, and with everything now at stake, both did well to get across the road and leave their partners a shot to the green.

A large crowd was packed around it, as the contestants approached and prepared to chip on. Suddenly there was a commotion in the centre of it, and the cause was soon to become very apparent indeed.

Lady 'Pimples' Limpet, in a state of high excitement, had collapsed and was carried out of the crowd into the clear air of the green. The reason for her quiet reticence in the last few months then became obvious as she was made comfortable in the centre of the green and immediately commenced the final process of presenting His Lordship with a son and heir.

A tribal midwife was on hand who, together with the customary attendance of the Witch Doctor, helped Pimples to bring forth a bonny lad in no time at all. On arrival in the world he let out a noble cry. He was joined by his exultant father in a duet of praise to the Almighty, who was himself already familiar with the way sons tend to appear unexpectedly at Easter.

There will of course be arguments in golfing circles as to whether such an event should be allowed to interfere with play, but in this case it was generally agreed that The Bunkham Bowl would make a perfect christening present. In due course the name of 'The Honourable Pascal Bruce Limpet' was engraved on it as its first inner.

Smithers was equal to the occasion. The entire staff of Cawkwell Hall soon appeared carrying trays loaded with champagne for everybody. The two small winners' replicas were presented to Mr Rutumutu and Sidney Sidebottom. As a cuspidor, the small tribal cup was a challenging target that only the Witch Doctor could confidently use.

Sidney's cup was proudly mounted on the radiator of the Daimler-Benz, where he could admire and polish it every day.

Blinder's 'book' was declared void.

Mr Thomas J. Dickie was heard to quote from the *Rubaiyat*...

The Ball no question makes of Ayes and Noes,
But Here and There as strikes the Player goes;
And He that tossed you down into the Field,
He knows about it all – He knows – He knows!

LATE EXTRA...

On the Tuesday after Easter a special edition of *The Bunkham and District Crier* carried the headline

EASTER EGG WITH HEIR
LAID IN THE BUNKHAM BOWL

At the request of Lady Augustine, the Sports Editor was invited to resign, and a second edition favoured

BUNKHAM BOWL WON WITH A STYMIE

GOLF, M'LADY?

Lady Limpet Tells All

NATHANIEL GAWTHORPE

'Tell me, Mr Gawthorpe' said Lady Limpet with the hint of a twinkle in her eye, 'what would be your views on the introduction of lady golfers on the course?'

MRS JEMIMA GAWTHORPE

1

The Bunkham and District Crier was established in the year 1855 with the issue of a handwritten leaflet by Mr Joshua Gawthorpe on the need for a new larger bridge over the river Ouse at the town centre. He expressed the view that whilst the existing footbridge was still negotiable with care, the losses of children and old people through the rotting planks was beginning to affect the morale of the remaining inhabitants. He withheld any serious criticism after watching his dear wife Jemima disappear into the river, but became very angry when Spot, his beloved collie, went the same way.

There was also some incentive to take action with the prospect of additional passing trade for his general store.

Now, as the newspaper prepared to celebrate its fiftieth anniversary, history has shown that his judgement had been entirely justified in regard to the effect of the new bridge on the store, which he had by then unwisely sold, and now it flourished under the control of the Hardcastle family. Correct too in the writing of the leaflet and thus developing into journalism, thereby creating the publishing empire of the *Crier* of today, with a circulation of at least one thousand, if the fifty circulated free to advertisers are included.

A very special 'Celebration Edition' was called for and the editorial committee (Nathaniel Gawthorpe and his staff, Miss Mabel Fitt) had given many hours of consideration to what might make suitable copy. Obviously a review of the highlights in the progress of the town in that period would be its basis, but first some evidence of progress had to be identified, and that was not immediately apparent. It would be true to record that the gas street lights in the High Street, installed five years before, were now working quite well for most of the time, and that some improvements in the sewage disposal facilities had taken place within that period, but they could not visualise a headline or an editorial that might turn this information into exciting reading.

Views were of course freely available on this subject as on any other at the Dog and Duck, and advice could be obtained in unlimited quantity for as long as ample lubrication was forthcoming. Most were of the opinion that few of the issues of *The Bunkham and District Crier* were in the least memorable and had only been worth the one penny cost to those whose births or weddings had been recorded, and perhaps to those who hoped to benefit from the sad news of the dear departed.

All were agreed that the most surprising and worrying news that had ever appeared in its pages had been some five years ago when up at Cawkwell Hall on the outskirts of the town, the Reverend Bruce Featherstone-Phipps, the second son of Lord Limpet of the Hall, had returned from his missionary work in Africa to take over the title as a result of his father's long overdue demise

172

and his elder brother's early, but not surprising, end in the vast wine cellars. The well-preserved condition of his body when finally found was regarded by connoisseurs as a credit to the noble lord's palette.

It was not the return of the new Lord Limpet that was so memorable, nor his very popular wedding to Miss Cynthia Pinkerton-Smythe (better known to everybody by her nickname 'Pimples'), but their decision to create in the spacious grounds of Cawkwell Hall a native village to accommodate the entire N'Chuyu tribe of (hopefully) erstwhile cannibals from central Africa, in whose cooking-pot they had for a short but worrying period been their guests.

The experiment had been confidently forecast by all at the Dog and Duck and their wives at home as a certain disaster, a view held also by Mr Eustace Pratt, the Limpet family solicitor, Smithers, the butler, and Egbert Micklethwaite, the head gardener. Instead, the so-called 'model village' became a highly successful attraction to visitors and so also to the town, whilst its inhabitants added greatly to the effective management of the property. That was only the beginning, and when His Lordship, guided not only by heavenly inspiration but also by Pimples as well, created a golf course on his estate with the help of the tribe and took up the game himself, the town took on a new life and the *Crier* was gifted with events and stories on which it could not fail to produce saleable material.

Clearly the half-century of the *Crier* would have to focus on the events at Cawkwell Hall, especially golf. It was no secret from anyone that to go to the fountain-head of management and knowledge at the Hall was to consult Lady 'Pimples' Limpet. An appointment was arranged and Nathaniel himself attended on Her Ladyship for the first interview.

173

On his arrival at the Hall promptly at 10 o'clock on a bright and clear February morning, Mr Nathaniel Gawthorpe was ushered into the library by Smithers to await Lady Limpet who, according to Smithers, was busy with 'young Master Pascal', this being confirmed by the cries from upstairs of a lively two-year-old baby. A few minutes later the lady appeared, petite, buxom, flushed and attractive, and offered him a chair with a welcoming smile.

'How can I help you?' she asked, perhaps being responsible for initiating that overworked cliché even before a telephone had been installed.

Nathaniel explained how anxious he was to give the fiftieth year of *The Bunkham and District Crier* the sort of celebration issue it deserved, and Pimples was kind enough not to express her hope that it would be a lot better than that. Cawkwell Hall being the major centre of attraction to the area, and more recently bringing a great deal of trade to the town, he felt the Hall should be strongly featured and that Lady Limpet might be the one to help in providing some interesting stories.

Pimples' eye for business was as bright as ever.

'Could we not combine the past with the future, d'you think? Some sort of event to bring this eminent moment in history into focus? That way you might well have copy for many issues leading up to it as well as a central point from which to look back.'

'Just what I was thinking, Ma'am,' lied the journalist. 'Perhaps Your Ladyship would be kind enough to make some proposals along those lines in the next week or so, and at the same time give consideration to some articles on the outstanding memories you have since taking over the Hall. I'm sure His Lordship could be a great help on the subject too.'

They both knew there was not much truth in that, but the attempt at diplomacy made it acceptable.

'Tell me, Mr Gawthorpe,' said Pimples with a hint of a twinkle in her eye, 'what would be your view on the introduction of lady golfers on the course?'

A tricky one for Nathaniel. He knew very well the views of that very influential gentleman, the Chairman of the Council, Captain Montague Buckmaster, and of most of the leading members of the Council and the Golf Club, and their support and advertising was essential to the survival of the *Crier*.

'I can't afford to have any, Your Ladyship,' he replied, that being as close to the truth as he had ever been.

'Good,' came her response, 'that means I can expect your support should that matter arise in connection with our plans for a "celebration event" at the Hall. Thank you so much for calling – I'll be delighted to collaborate with you and I'll be in touch as soon as I've developed some ideas.'

Clearly they were already developing, and it was an apprehensive Mr Gawthorpe who Smithers saw to the door and wished a good day.

Pimples remained in the library deep in thought, then sat down to set down some of them on her writing pad.

'Opportunity knocks,' she decided.

THE
CAPTAIN

HIS
LORDSHIP

2

Out on the course Lord Bruce Limpet was engaged in his usual mid-week round of golf with the Chairman of the Council. It was not so much a pleasure as a duty, from both their points of view. His Lordship liked to feel he was keeping in touch with the town, and Captain Buckmaster knew very well how important the course was to the town and so sacrificed himself to this good cause.

Naturally, what started as a 'friendly' fixture in the early days had tended to develop into something rather more competitive. There had been improvements in both their games over the months since the highly memorable opening of the course two years ago, that event having been indelibly commemorated by an incomplete final round, due to interference when young master Pascal was born to Lady Limpet on the eighteenth green.

Under the tutelage of the club 'professional' Jock McTavish they could now get round the course in not much over one hundred, air shots excluded, and the matches had become fiercely fought affairs. For the first seven holes the conversation was limited to the usual polite enquiries of the family and concern about the weather, and they were level as they prepared to tee off on the eighth. (In case there are still any readers who are unfamiliar with the course at Cawkwell, this is the first of two holes crossing the river Ouse and reachable with a well-struck mashie-niblick and then by the raft moored nearby.)

'Strange thing,' observed His Lordship as the Captain tee'd up, 'my dear wife actually enquired at breakfast this morning whether she might actually walk round with me sometime and perhaps even try a shot or two. Have you ever heard of such a thing?'

The Captain blanched and his moustache twitched. With a swish and a loud 'plop' his drive looped gently into the Ouse. His opponent's expressions of sympathy were rewarded with a glare. Lord Bruce tee'd up.

'Read about it somewhere once,' came the reply, 'women actually allowed on the course to play the game. Thank God there's no danger of that kind of non-sense here. They'd never get across the river for a start. I trust you told her not to be so damned silly.'

It was with the thought of ever doing so that Lord Bruce addressed his ball and watched it skitter along the ground and take to the water.

'Pity,' said the Captain, cheering up noticeably, 'funny thing though – Alice Feathers said something of the sort at the Council meeting just the other night. Quite a coinci-dence, what? Told her to shut up and stick to the agenda of course, but I saw her muttering to that idiot Lovelace later on. Hope he didn't fall for any ideas of that kind.'

He obviously brooded on it as he despatched another ball into the river.

His Lordship tut-tutted, and then with true Christian charity considered for a moment whether he should offer the Captain a half and move on. Such is the power of the game, however, that even the Reverend Father could not bring himself to make such a sacrifice. Instead he sent up a short, rather selfish, prayer to his Maker and the response was a shot to the green that settled twelve inches from the pin. They took to the raft in very contrasting moods – the Reverend lord sinfully proud of his best shot for weeks, the Captain deeply troubled not only by the prospect of going one down, but suffering a sense of foreboding he couldn't quite put his finger on.

Needless to say, His Lordship went on to enjoy a clear-cut victory which he enthusiastically described in ball-by-ball detail to his devoted, ever patient wife over lunch as she fed and chatted to their gurgling offspring at the same time. She was by now one of those rare angelic spouses who had mastered the art of appearing to be interested and contriving to make encouraging noises in the right places. In this case, there were also ulterior motives.

'I expect you're wondering what to get for my birthday, darling,' she said, 'now that I've got a full set of handbags. It's only three weeks away.'

His Lordship thought it best not to mention the rather smart patent leather bag he had purchased in Mrs Feathers' shop only yesterday. Pimples had of course already decided the same thing.

'Did you have anything special in mind, dear?' he asked.

'Well, perhaps something different in the bag line would make a nice change,' she said. With visions of a possible swap, her husband brightened.

'A golf bag,' said Pimples, with one of her most innocently seductive smiles, 'Jock says I'll need one to put my new clubs in. You invited me to go round with you. Remember?'

His Lordship swallowed hard. A major crisis in the affairs of Bunkham-on-Ouse and Cawkwell Hall was clearly on the horizon.

3

The general store in the High Street of Bunkham-on-Ouse was these days under the management of three generations of the Hardcastle family. Old Matthew Hardcastle rarely failed to be on duty to keep a watchful eye on the staff and particularly on the attention given to important customers. His son, 'young' Mr Luke, was in charge of the day-to-day management, though it had become a matter of concern to old Matthew in the course of the last year or so that 'day-to-day' had become more like 'week-to-week' ever since Luke had been bitten by the golf bug.

Nevertheless, the 'golf bug' had its compensations. Thanks to the initiative of his attractive granddaughter Virginia, a very significant addition to the turnover of the business had resulted from her creation of a department described on the shop fascia as 'specialists in golfing impedimenta'. Their range of brassies, mashies, niblicks, spoons and putters was not only unique but enjoyed a monopoly of the local business thanks to the skill and the production capacity of Jake Trueman, the local carpenter. At the instigation of his heart-throb Virginia he had added this range of products to his regular supply of coffins to their funeral department, and had developed a complementary working relationship with Andy Small, the blacksmith, in the design and production of the heads.

Virginia had been watching the development of the game since the opening of the Cawkwell course with growing interest, and had discovered over afternoon tea at the High Street Café that Lady 'Pimples' Limpet had similar aspirations, and to her surprise, so did Alice Feathers. When an order for a small lady's set of clubs came through, via her agent the course professional Jock McTavish, she felt encouraged to suggest to Jake that he might produce an extra similar set for herself.

'You might like to take me for a walk round the course one day,' she suggested, knowing that would settle it. She knew better than to mention the matter to her father.

Mrs Alice Feathers' interest in the game had rather different origins, and arose out of her habit of taking her French poodle Fifi for a daily walk in the vicinity of the course. It was in the undergrowth beside the sixth fairway that she came across dear Mr Lovelace searching for a ball. At the same moment Fifi appeared with a ball in her mouth, tail wagging madly, and dashed off in the direction of the green, dropping it neatly in the hole and thereby providing Mr Lovelace with the first (and probably the only) birdie of his life. Quite uncharacteristically he snatched up Alice Feathers and gave her the hug and kiss he had secretly longed to do since their first meeting on the Council. Alice's resistance was minimal, indeed it appeared to his opponent Solly Goldbaum, who was impatiently watching the proceedings from the fairway, that she might even be clinging on, having thrown her handbag to the ground.

Alice decided there and then that she liked this game of golf and fancied more of it. Solly Goldbaum, who went on to lose the game by one hole, had a different view.

Jock McTavish meanwhile was finding this insidious interest from the ladies both profitable and embarrassing. So far the orders for clubs he had received, and the lessons he had been asked to give, had all been dealt with in secret, but clearly this could not go on. He decided to take Augustine into his confidence, and explained the situation to her.

'It'll need to be mentioned at the committee meeting on Friday,' she said. 'We all know what the Captain's views are on that kind of thing. Even if there are only four ladies wanting to play, he'll still explode.'

'Three,' said Jock.

'Four,' replied Augustine, 'I fancy a game myself.'

There's only one thing for it, thought Jock, we'll have to consult Pimples.

Jock had spent many years as a caddie at the home of golf, St Andrews, before he and his wife had been invited down from Perth to take up residence at the Hall. His consultation with Pimples was therefore a formidable partnership in which Pimples was able to formulate her plans with the benefit of much useful background and helpful connections. Her first move became evident at the next club committee meeting.

JASPER
CLAWHAMMER

4

The picturesque market town of Little Winkleton lies on the river Ouse in unspoilt rolling countryside about five miles east of Bunkham-on-Ouse, as the crow flies. Very few crows actually made that journey in the first decade of the twentieth century, and a return trip was even rarer. In fact it could only happen in the dead of night or at Jasper Clawhammer's meal times. Only then did he fail to patrol his seventy-five acres which lay on the outskirts of the town in the direct flight path, shotgun at the ready, daring anything to move across or fly over his patch.

The property known as Woebetide Farm comprised undulating meadowland broken by small copses and wooded areas, and had been the natural inheritance of eldest son Jasper at the turn of the century, earning him a regular small income by letting the grazing rights from time to time. He generously allowed his sister Rosie to remain as housekeeper, but their older sister had escaped by befriending the local baker as passionately as custom and opportunity allowed, and becoming Mrs William Arthright in time for the birth of their son to be credited as decently premature.

It was over breakfast on a fresh and bracing early spring morning in the year 1905 that history was made in the Clawhammer household. He had as usual made a plea to his long-suffering sister to take over the shotgun patrol so that he could enjoy his meal in comfort, but this time instead of the standard shake of the head she went into the attack.

'Time you knowed my mind on tha', Jasper Clawhammer,' she said, snatching away the greasy remains of his eggs and bacon, 'time you thought of something better to do wi' yer time an' all yer money. Time you got out sometimes, met a few people, an' got me out o' here f'r a break now an' then.'

She so rarely spoke up that Jasper was momentarily tongue-tied. Rosie made the most of it.

'Hear say they built a golf course over on the Cawkwell place... Why don' e try somethin' like that? Here you are, bald as a coot, nearly fifty an' looking more like sixty, wi' precious few friends an' nothing better to do than shoot everything in sight. You could shave off that horrible beard, clean up a bit, and take us over there one day t'see what it's all about – an' leave that bluddy gun behind f'r once.'

Jasper got up from the kitchen table, picked up his twelve-bore, and went off on patrol without a word.

But the point had been well made and had touched a raw spot. Patrolling the fields had given him plenty of time to ruminate over many years, and his aggressive temperament and general hatred of everything that moved, including the human race, had left him a very lonely man.

184

The following day straight after breakfast he got out the pony-cart, gave his sister five minutes to get in, and set out for Cawkwell Hall. There they joined a group of visiting Americans, toured the 'model village' of the N'Chuyu tribe with them, and in the process became an additional source of interest to the group with their 'traditional country dress' and their 'quaint old ethnic brogue'. Such a lucky bonus for the visitors – they couldn't wait to tell the 'folks back home'.

Somehow Rosie contrived to prevent Jasper from expressing his thoughts on the visitors, which would have brought their lovely visit to 'dear little old England' to a very unpleasant conclusion, and led him off to watch the activity on the golf course.

Lord Limpet's weekly golf lesson from Jock was in progress and today was concentrated on finding a cure for a nasty slice that had crept into His Lordship's game. Proof of this came with his very first practice shot. It sailed off across the fairway and arrived on the lengthening forehead of Jasper Clawhammer at maximum speed, laying him flat on his back. Rosie showed admirable self-control, picking up the ball and throwing it back with surprising power and accuracy and then walking over to where the noble lord and his mentor were busy discussing possible changes to his stance and grip.

Introductions were made and Rosie apologised for being unable to properly introduce her brother due to his temporary indisposition, and went on to enquire about the golf club and the game. In the course of the conversation, in which Lord Bruce described in detail all the horrors of the slice and the shank, Rosie mentioned how her brother had become familiar with it at first hand, and on receiving the news Jock thought that perhaps they should take a look at him. By the time they got there Jasper was sitting up, shaking his head, and reaching for his gun which, fortunately, did not on this rare occasion exist.

'If that's your way of keeping people off your property it's a damn good one,' he said. 'Prefer a twelve-bore m'self but I might try it for a change.'

A sizeable lump had now appeared on Jasper's head and Lord Bruce's Christian spirit came to the fore, to the extent of sacrificing his golf lesson and inviting the Clawhammers back to the Hall, calling Smithers to offer hospitality, and introducing them to his wife, Pimples.

'My brother has just discovered the game of golf and would very much like to learn to play,' volunteered Rosie, and was inspired to add, '...I think it has gone to his head. Would it be possible for us to join the club?'

In such innocent, unpredictable ways are the turning points in the development of a golf club reached and its history made.

5

When, about three years ago, Lord Limpet had been inspired by his Maker through the medium of his ex-mother-in-law Augustine and her second husband 'Blinder' McTavish to create the golf course, a small committee had been formed to help the Almighty and Pimples give His Lordship further guidance. Although the basic work had now been done and membership from the town had built up to nearly a hundred over a period of two years, that committee, with one or two changes, continued in charge under the nominal chairmanship of the noble lord, whose deputy, Captain Montague Buckmaster, JP, gave very generously of his time, and even more, of his authority.

'Blinder' remained as 'Technical Adviser', relying heavily on advice from his father, Jock.

His wife Augustine, Treasurer.

187

Thomas J. Dickie (the Town Clerk of Bunkham Council), Secretary.

'Fred' Tumtumroli, the N'Chuyu Chief, Staff Relations.

Egbert Micklethwaite (head gardener at the Hall), the Green Committee.

Luke Hardcastle, because he once partnered Lord Bruce.

The meeting that Friday followed the customary pattern, His Lordship describing in some detail his round with the Captain, the Captain complaining that the deplorable state of the greens had cost him the match, the Green Committee threatening to resign, Augustine calming him down with compliments on the rhododendrons, and Mr Dickie throwing in his regular supply of quotations.

It was when they reached the item headed 'Applications for Membership' that the proceedings took an unusual turn and we would do best, perhaps, to refer to the minutes taken by Mr Dickie.

The following applications have been received.
Mr Jasper Clawhammer and Miss Rosie Clawhammer.
(Proposed by Lord Limpet.)
Lady Cynthia Limpet.
(Proposed by Lord Limpet.)
Mrs Augustine McTavish.
(Proposed by Mr B. McTavish.)
Miss Virginia Hardcastle.
(Proposed by Mr J. Trueman.)
Mrs Alice Feathers.
(Proposed by Mr N. Lovelace.)

Mr Jasper Clawhammer was unanimously accepted as a member.

At this point Captain Buckmaster took over the Chair as Lord Limpet remembered an urgent appointment. He welcomed the idea of membership for these eminent ladies, acknowledging that there were many useful jobs they could do in and around the clubhouse while golfing was in progress, and they might in particular choose to assist Mr Micklethwaite with his suggestion (inspired by Her Ladyship) to create a small putting green near to the clubhouse (something Jock had seen in his time at St Andrews). When completed, they might even try an occasional putt on it, when not in use by golfers.

Mr Hardcastle thought that allowing ladies on the putting green, unless to weed it, might be going a little too far, and was very concerned that should the idea spread, the household duties of many ladies could suffer, particularly Sunday lunch. The Chairman thanked him for drawing attention to this important point. He felt that the question of allowing ladies to putt, in the event of creating a putting green, should be a special item on the next agenda. The applications for membership were therefore put in abeyance, and the meeting moved on to the next item.

'Delays have dangerous ends,' was the quotation from the Bard that Mr Dickie scribbled in the margin.

When His Lordship received his copy of the minutes a few days later, Pimples asked if she might study them.

'That must have been the day you came back with those three beautiful trout, darling,' she murmured.

'Probably was,' he replied. 'Sorry to miss the last bit of the meeting, but what a good job I did. Been after those beauties for weeks now.'

His wife smiled indulgently.

'They were so tasty. Why don't you try for a few more today? I'm expecting a visit from Mr Gawthorpe and you don't want to get trapped by him, do you, dear?'

A wonderful, thoughtful, considerate wife, thought His Lordship as he wandered off to find his fishing tackle.

Pimples' meeting with Mr Gawthorpe lasted roughly an hour, in which time he took copious notes and four cups of coffee. The result, or at least part of it, was to be seen in a leading article in the next edition of *The Bunkham and District Crier* under a headline

BOLD PLANS FOR BUNKHAM

Congratulations are due to the management of the Bunkham Golf Club on their imaginative proposals to follow the lead given by St Andrews.

The plan to create a new separate putting green in the vicinity of the clubhouse will be warmly welcomed by all members, and will be of special interest to the ladies, who can look forward to taking part in putting competitions.

We hear that in appreciation of this far-sighted development an anonymous donor has offered a valuable trophy to be played for at Easter while that major event, The Bunkham Bowl, is in progress, to be known as 'The Pascal Putter'.

It was a very thoughtful Lord Limpet who read this article for a second and third time.

The effect on Captain Buckmaster was a severely bruised ego, followed by a sort of mental recoil in readiness for a counter-attack. That earlier sense of foreboding was taking recognisable shape and the thin end of a dangerous wedge was clearly in sight.

So was a leak in the minutes.

BERT JENKINS

ROSIE
CLAWHAMMER

6

Over at Woebetide Farm extraordinary changes in the lifestyle of the Clawhammers were taking place. Old Bert Jenkins, their ancient paid hand, had to be told at least three times to create a golfing fairway across the meadow closest to the house, and found the order for a lawn at the end of it even more difficult to understand. Putting a hole in the middle of it with a flag in it was finally too much, and was a job that had to be given to the lady of the house.

Then came a visit to Hardcastle and Son in Bunkham, where Virginia not only succeeded in selling Jasper a full set of their finest clubs and a gross of balls, but also noticed the keen interest being displayed by Rosie Clawhammer. She quietly showed her the set of clubs recently completed for herself and a deal was done. The subsequent dramatic fall in turnover on twelve-bore cartridge sales was to be well compensated for in the golf ball department.

The arrival of Jasper's clubs sounded the death knell of his twelve-bore. Rosie had yet to learn about an eighteen-hole bore and she set about enjoying her new lease of life. So did most of the wildlife in the area as they discovered a new freedom restricted only by a regular spray of golf balls and the swish of a spoon if they lowered their guard too unwisely. For the first time ever Rosie heard and enjoyed bird-song, and so did the birds.

Unfortunately nothing is perfect. Jasper Clawhammer was blessed with very few good qualities and patience was not one of them. Neither could he be described as even-tempered. As a result, in the early days the fairway was made to suffer for his 'learning curve' (a very shallow one), as was the green, his clubs, his sister and Bert Jenkins, but he thrashed on and by sheer will-power and cussedness he began to develop a swing which produced some acceptable results, but owed nothing to elegance.

His approach to the problem was a natural development from his attitude to creatures over or on his land. He eyed the ball with all the malevolence of a hungry tiger to its prey, and pounced in much the same way. First he stalked the ball, then he crouched over it waggling his club menacingly; once the decision to attack had been made, his grip tightened and he swung the club in a figure of eight several times in the manner of a discus thrower, then hurled himself at the ball in a fit of pent-up fury, finishing with a sort of two-footed pirouette.

Repeated failure to disturb the ball resulted in a greater concentration of ferocity, and only when it was finally despatched did he calm down sufficiently to snort, and then start over again. But there was one quality he had in abundance and that was persistence, to which could be added brute strength.

192

Slowly he improved.

Meanwhile Rosie took advantage of Jasper's pre-occupation to take time off for 'shopping' in Bunkham, and by arrangement with Jock she included a set of lessons with her new clubs. These she kept in Jock's store, well out of sight of her brother. Rosie was a quick learner, deceptively powerful and very steady, and Jock soon realised that she could become a force to be reckoned with against the men, never mind the women.

At home she listened attentively to Jasper's report on his day's work, calmed his temper with a large roast supper, and displayed as much sympathy as she could muster – such a rare quality in normal golfing circles.

Jasper entered his name for The Bunkham Bowl. The event had begun two years before as a knockout foursome competition, but with growing membership and ever larger entry lists the format had been changed to an individual medal round, and Jasper needed to get an official handicap. Jock McTavish was the recognised arbiter in such matters so Jasper made arrangements to play a round with him at the first opportunity.

It was here that Jasper's inexperience of human nature quickly became apparent. Not only did he fail to 'oil the wheels' by producing the obligatory bottle of Jock's homeland brew before subjecting himself to the handicap check, but also failed to raise a smile at Jock's opening remark on the first tee.

'Ha' ye decided to use a golf club now instead o' ye head to propel the ball the noo?'

Nevertheless Jock bore in mind the income he enjoyed from Jasper's sister. He watched with horror the home-made swing that Jasper had so painstakingly perfected, and withstood the barrage of blasphemy released by Jasper over the eighteen holes, awarded him the maximum handicap of eighteen, and headed at full throttle for the bar.

Jasper went into the clubhouse, studied the notice-board, and entered his handicap beside his name on the list for The Bunkham Bowl, now only a fortnight away. Another notice attracted his attention, headed 'The Pascal Putter'.

Members will have noticed the recent press announcement of a proposed putting competition to be held on Easter Monday, and also the excellent progress being made in the preparation of the putting green by Her Ladyship's head gardener.

In the event that the Club Committee should decide to proceed with this novel development, a list is attached inviting the names of lady entrants who would wish to take part in the competition.

Signed Augustine McTavish
Treasurer

Jasper rode back to Woebetide Farm feeling rather pleased with himself and announced with pride to Rosie his entry into his first golf competition, complete with an official handicap. He mentioned too the strange idea he had seen on the club noticeboard of a putting competition to be held at the same time involving ladies.

'Dunno what the world's comin' to,' he said as he settled down to his evening roast, 'next thing you know even people like you'll be havin' a go!'

He failed to notice the smile that crept over Rosie's face and stayed there right through the washing up.

A meeting of the Bunkham Golf Club Committee took

place a few days later and when Lord Limpet returned from it he was delighted at the unusual degree of interest shown by his wife in the proceedings.

'Told old Buckers a thing or two about his chipping on the fourteenth. No follow through, what? Dreadful putting stroke too – no idea. Then he became a fearful bore on the subject of my spoon shots, and kept reminding me of my four putts on the twelfth... Pretty poor meeting, really.'

'Nothing else to report, dear?' she enquired.

'Well, Luke Hardcastle tells me Jake has come up with a rather special new driver – could add twenty yards for me. Must get down there in the morning and take a look at it. It'd be a big help on the eighteenth – always have trouble there.'

Patience, Pimples told herself, patience.

'Anything on club business at all?'

'Nothing much dear... Augustine asked for extra staff for the Bank Holiday weekend. Eggie seemed to think the weather might turn nasty before long, but you know what a misery he can be. Gets some sort of pleasure out of bad forecasts – can't think why.'

Pimples began to wonder, just for a weak moment, what made her love this maddening creature, and what was stopping her from throttling him this very minute.

She counted to ten. 'No new members I suppose?'

'No. But about five ladies came in. That was all.'

'How nice,' said Pimples, 'I've been accepted.'

'And you're going to be allowed on the putting green on Bank Holidays and Thursday afternoons between two and five o'clock... That was old Buckers' proposal... pretty good eh?'

Her Ladyship's response was to ring for Smithers and order a large pink gin.

'Anything for you, dear?' she asked.

195

Pimples' next meeting with Nathaniel Gawthorpe took place the following day. He was already aware of the decision of the club committee, having been informed by the Vice Chairman himself of the new extensive facilities and privileges being extended to lady members resulting from his personal proposals.

'In regard to your fiftieth anniversary celebration, my ideas are not yet finalised,' said Pimples, 'but I would like to suggest that our plans should aim at making August Bank Holiday the date for some suitable festivities, and to offer facilities here at Cawkwell Hall for the occasion. Would that be helpful?'

'Excellent, ma'am,' he enthused. He paused as Smithers appeared with a tray of tea and biscuits.

'There is another development you might like to bear in mind, ma'am. As you know, *The Bunkham and District Crier* has a wide readership even beyond the boundaries of Bunkham itself, and I have been contacted on the subject of this great anniversary year by the Chairman of the Council of Little Winkleton with a view to involving the town in some suitable activity, in the hope of putting Little Winkleton's holiday and entertainment attractions on the map.'

Her Ladyship was aware that these consisted of a church (one wall of Norman origin), three boarding houses, a park with three swings (two operational), a cricket pitch, four pubs with accommodation, and eight without.

'I know William Arthright well enough,' she said. 'I think his bread is so much nicer than anything in this town. I'd like to talk to him next time I go over there. Tell him I'll look in at his bakery.'

With that she wished the journalist a good day and hurried off to another secret golf lesson with Jock while her husband was in town studying the addition to

Hardcastle's 'golfing impedimenta' – Jake's new improved driver.

'Jock,' she said, 'you told me once that when ladies play golf they do so from special tees placed nearer to the green. Is that right?'

'Saw them mesel',' replied Jock, 'but they'll no be seen on this wee course if the Captain and his crew hae anything to say in the matter.' Studying the expression on Pimples' face, he decided he would not like to put money on it either way.

'Anyway, it would be simple to mark out ladies' tee positions anywhere up the fairway if such an eventuality ever came to pass,' he added.

With so many ladies now taking lessons from himself and from his son Blinder, he knew well which side his bread was buttered on, and had long ago decided to occupy that uncomfortable and undignified position known as sitting on the fence.

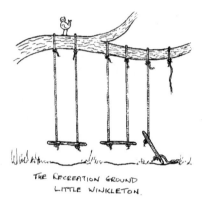

THE RECREATION GROUND
LITTLE WINKLETON.

7

Willy Arthright, the Chairman of Little Winkleton Council, was a happily married man, and often felt sorry for his sister-in-law Rosie living such a lonely existence with that misery Jasper out at Woebetide Farm. They saw very little of each other, so the news he received from Lady Limpet when she paid a call on him came as a great surprise. Indeed, several surprises.

'Jasper without his gun? 1 don't believe it. Jasper playing golf? Impossible! Somebody playing with him? Out of the question!'

'That's not all,' went on Pimples, 'but this has to be very strictly confidential – just between you and me.'

A very difficult commitment for Willy to make, this. His bakery was the town's acknowledged centre for local information and the early morning starting point for almost every worthwhile rumour in the district. But in family matters maybe he could stretch a point, and by now he simply had to know.

'Rosie plays golf too, and very well. You should see her! At present only with the professional, taking lessons, but she's got the bug alright.'

All this was too much for Willy. They had retired to his local for this little chat and he ordered a double brandy with cider chaser, along with Pimples' pink gin. He stoked up his pipe.

'Did you say, ma'am, that Jasper has put in a practice fairway?'

'That's right. And a putting green. Spends all his time at it these days. Surprising you haven't heard.'

It certainly was, but now he had absorbed this astonishing piece of news he began to see some possibilities.

'Maybe it's time I had a chat with Rosie,' he said.

A smug expression was in evidence on Pimples' cheerful face as she bade Willy Arthright *au revoir*.

The very next day Willy Arthright paid a visit to Woebetide Farm, making a long overdue call on his sister-in-law the excuse. Her absence, due apparently to a shopping trip into Bunkham, suited him perfectly well as an opportunity to try to talk with Jasper – never an easy thing to do. Willy strolled out into the meadow in the direction of a steady stream of invective, and watched from what he thought was a safe position as Jasper went through his routine golf swing procedure. A cry of 'Fore' meant nothing to Willy, especially as it was only one word out of many, but he got the hang of it as a golf ball whistled past his ear a moment later.

'What the 'ell are you doin' there,' yelled Jasper, 'distractin' me in the middle of a perfect swing. Serve you right if I got yer fair an' square – wish I 'ad!'

'Agnes asked me to look in on Rosie,' said Willy.

'Always shoppin' these days, she is. Dunno what for but it suits me alright. Getting this golf business sorted out is a lot of 'ard work. Costs a lot on balls too, it do.'

'Maybe I can help in that,' offered Willy, seeing a golden opportunity to attract Jasper's attention. He'd brought with him a couple of bottles of beer (he was not Chairman of the Council for nothing), and the combined effects on Jasper were sufficient to persuade him to put down his club and listen.

'One fairway and a green are surely not enough to provide really good practice, are they? Better surely if you had, say, nine holes.'

Before Jasper could interrupt on the subject of cost, he went on, 'I could arrange help to do the work if you would be willing to look after it and let other people use it at a moderate charge.'

Jasper brooded.

'You see, Jasper, Little Winkleton needs one or two attractions as well as the swings at the recreation ground. Questions are always being asked at the bakery, and even in the Council. And maybe you might find a little extra income useful.'

'Let ye' know,' said Jasper, picking up his clubs and returning to his full-time occupation.

During his day's work he began to realise the limitations of his present training ground, and to imagine the challenge a small course would provide. The need to communicate with other members of the human race was an obvious drawback, but golf itself necessitated the same supreme sacrifice so he might as well get used to it, and there would be some very positive advantages. A greater challenge should enable him to improve his golf to the point when he could give a thrashing to any opposition, and also the income would always be welcome.

Furthermore, Willy Arthright and the Council would be in his debt, and he'd find a way of turning that to his advantage.

Next morning he went into Willy's bakery and said 'Yes', and went home to his breakfast. When he told Rosie about it he expected some sort of mild objection to such a radical development on their land. Instead, to his surprise, she seemed quite enthusiastic and actually asked if she could be of any help in creating the nine-hole course, and he was surprised too at how much she seemed to know about what would be needed.

Naturally he told her to be quiet and get on with her business, and he would get on with his. He made it a rule always to be considerate and fair-minded in matters of that kind.

THE LATE
ARTHUR FEATHERS

8

Since the sad demise of Mr Arthur Feathers some ten years before, life for Alice Feathers had been interesting without being very exciting. It had been a tragic moment in her life when the shocking news reached her of his misfortune, and to this day she could not imagine how he had contrived to drown himself in a brewer's vat. His profession, so far as his social status was concerned, was a civil servant, and Alice had always been at pains to avoid going into any further detail wherever possible.

Tax collector never had quite the same ring.

Perhaps he had been a shade over-zealous in his work, particularly in his dealings with the local brewery, which gave every appearance of flourishing success despite its evident lack of taxable profits or duty in its accounts. Had he not been teetotal, he might have been able to reach a better understanding with the management. As it was, the police put the accident down to something to do with 'weights and measures', beer being a subject on which Ned Drinkwater, the local constable, was so well versed. His investigations at the brewery took up a great deal of his time before a satisfactory verdict could be reached, and the brewery generously took no action against the estate in regard to the spoiled vat of beer, as it was only half full at the time.

For Alice Feathers there had been some practical consolation in the substantial life insurance she felt it wise to carry in recognition of the hazards of his profession. This enabled her in her widowhood to set up her couturier and hat-making business in the High Street of Bunkham, to raise her daughter Florence, and to enter into the management of the town's affairs as a councillor. But there was still something missing in her life, and the little incident with Leslie Lovelace had drawn her attention to the problem, and also to a possible solution. She set about learning to play golf with assiduous care, almost in the class of Jasper Clawhammer.

This was made easier for her now that her daughter, just seventeen, was off her hands. There were in fact many pairs of hands in the town willing to take her on, especially at the Dog and Duck, where 'Flossie' Feathers, its latest barmaid, had become a star attraction. She had quickly become a very useful mine of information emanating from no less a source than the backstairs of Cawkwell Hall itself. It happened that her best friend from her school days, Doris Goodbody, was Her Ladyship's chambermaid, and was well able to pass on much of the gossip, suitably embellished, should there be a 'slow news day'.

It took Pimples very little time to work out what was going on when a few unimportant domestic issues became public knowledge, and she was quick to realise what a valuable conduit this leak could be if carefully used. She fed in several trial tit-bits just as a check and found it worked quicker than the post. Thus, news of golf course developments at Little Winkleton was served with the first pint at the Dog and Duck on the day after Jasper's momentous decision.

Other strange rumours were afoot, emanating from the poaching and hiking fraternity, claiming to have seen ladies carrying bags of golf clubs on the course, and not only that – actually handling the clubs and attempting to strike golf balls with them. All those familiar with Captain Buckmaster, which included every local person of voting age (and also women), knew perfectly well that such was not possible, and moved on to more likely and more interesting subjects such as Flossie, and some-times her mother, who had noticeably blossomed in recent weeks.

There was also betting on The Bunkham Bowl to con-sider. The trouble this year was the open nature of the event, resulting in a serious reduction in scope for local knowledge, leading to flagging interest. It was Sidney Sidebottom, Lord Limpet's chauffeur, who suggested that the ladies' putting competition might offer more scope, and Blinder, who could always be relied upon to make a book on anything that moved, announced such a book was open with just seven days to go before the event. News of it circulated quickly back through the system to Doris at the Hall, who then acted as runner and agent for the heavy betting from 'below stairs'.

The favourite seemed to be Lady Limpet herself, although rumour had it that an unknown 'dark horse' had signed on under the name of Miss Clawhammer, who showed definite signs of form. With two days to go it was not unusual for staff at Cawkwell Hall to see heads bobbing about in the bushes close to the putting green when any ladies were spotted sneaking in to prac-tise, and on one occasion there was the unmistakable reflected sheen of Smithers' pate in evidence. This was confirmed when he placed sixpence with Doris on Augustine – on the nose.

His Lordship's mid-week round with the Captain this week was, in effect, a warm-up practice for the imminent Bunkham Bowl, and was unhappily punctuated by disturbing tit-bits of news and rumour. According to the Captain, interest in the event appeared to be waning in favour of the ladies' putting competition, judging by gossip in the Town Hall, and Lord Bruce added the intelligence that he had reason to believe that the rules concerning the ladies' use of the putting green were being regularly flouted.

All this was bad enough, but His Lordship had even worse news to report, and thought it wise to save it for the eighth tee in the usual way.

Captain Buckmaster tee'd up.

'Couldn't believe my eyes a couple of days ago,' he said, 'saw what looked like Alice Feathers out there with Jock on the practice ground... with a set of clubs...'

The Captain addressed the ball.

'...playing!' said Lord Bruce.

There was a plop.

His Lordship tee'd up.

'Strange, that,' commented the Captain. 'You'd never guess who Luke Hardcastle thought he saw doing the same thing only yesterday...'

Lord Bruce took his stance.

'...your wife!'

There was a swish.

Followed by another swish.

Followed by a plop.

It was a game they both chose to forget, as they set off for home from the eighteenth green with a lot on their minds.

FLOSSIE
FEATHERS

9

It was customary at Bunkham-on-Ouse to celebrate the Easter Festival in style, decorating the High Street with bunting and floral displays, and enjoying a traditional carnival, fêtes and parties, starting on Easter Saturday. In recent years Easter Monday had tended to become a day out at Cawkwell Hall for a great many citizens, where family parties were made welcome and much interest centred on the golfing event of the year, The Bunkham Bowl, and on the first cricket match of the season with Little Winkleton.

Visitors greatly enjoyed the festive atmosphere, and at Cawkwell Hall were specially intrigued by the N'Chuyu village in the grounds, where the native villagers had adapted their cannibalistic instincts to a more acceptable form of entertainment and enterprise. Under the benevolent leadership of Chief 'Fred' Tumtumroli and Witch Doctor Rutumutu they had developed a businesslike acumen for keeping their visitors alive, healthy and charitable. Mr Rutumutu had displayed a natural golfing talent when the game was first introduced at Cawkwell Hall, and now found more satisfaction and profit in giving exhibitions of his skill on the 'practice' ground in the kraal, and occasional lessons to anyone bold and muscular enough to adopt his unique swing.

This year there were, unfortunately, some clouds on the horizon. Literally. Maundy Thursday saw the start of the drizzle which by Good Friday had become a downpour. Bedraggled shopkeepers, gardeners and visitors alike packed into the Dog and Duck, whose landlord spent much of his time expressing his sorrow and sympathy whilst making copious transfers from his till to his safe and from his safe to the bank. With no apparent likelihood of improvement in sight, the events in the town were cancelled or abandoned one by one in favour of indoor pursuits, and speculation was rife about the programme scheduled for Easter Monday at Cawkwell Hall.

This had also been exercising Pimples' mind, and on Friday she decided to do something about it. She paid an urgent call on Matthew Hardcastle, and by Saturday afternoon a large marquee had appeared at the Golf Club, and was erected over the putting green. News of this was fed through the Doris–Flossie system and became common knowledge in the town by the time the churchgoers set out in the pouring rain for the first Sunday service. This included a prayer for the blessing of some sunshine, which the Almighty must have thought fit, at such a busy time, to put into the pending tray.

Easter Bank Holiday Monday dawned ominously red. Threateningly heavy black clouds were moving in and there was an occasional lightning flash and the rumble of distant thunder. Nevertheless, the hardy souls of Bunkham, having little alternative by way of entertain-

207

ment and many having a serious financial interest in the result of the putting competition and the cricket match, set out for Cawkwell Hall complete with families, picnic baskets, raincoats, umbrellas and groundsheets. Twenty-four entries for The Bunkham Bowl tee'd off in fours under the direction of Jock, who then took time off to give some exercise to his dogs, Ben and Nevis.

The rains came. And came. And came.

Inside the marquee the ladies' putting competition for The Pascal Putter got under way with Blinder in charge, his wooden leg suitably muffled against damage to the green. The start had to be delayed for at least half-an-hour as spectators fought their way in, some to watch, plus many to take cover. These soon included the cricket teams and their supporters, and any stalwarts who had troubled to watch the golf. Later still a growing number of the bedraggled golfers themselves started to show up.

When the five lady competitors finally started the match space had become very cramped indeed, so that each hole had to be cleared before it could be played, with all the others fully occupied by spectators, golfers, cricketers and children of all ages trampling with complete disrespect on Egbert Micklethwaite's sacred turf. Betting was rife on every hole, and sometimes on each shot, the crowd pressed forward cheering on their favourites, and there were multiple running commentaries for those at the back.

After five holes had been fought out it became clear that Pimples, Virginia Hardcastle and Augustine were destined to be the 'also rans', and the finish would be a close call between Rosie Clawhammer and Alice Feathers. By the twelfth they were out on their own and still level, the other three having retired from what had become more like a rugger scrum moving en masse from hole to hole.

Out on the course Jock and his dogs took cover under a tree where a view of the final hole was possible. One by one he watched the competitors trudging and slushing their way in from all parts of the course and heading for a rub down, a change of clothes and the blessed relief promised by the club bar. Their soggy score cards had long ago been allowed to disintegrate and wash away.

Jock was about to do the same when through the driving rain up the eighteenth fairway he made out a sorry-looking figure stumping after his golf ball and stopping at regular intervals to swipe and splash it a few more yards. He counted fifteen shots himself before the ball arrived on the green, which could better be described as a pond, and a further six before it disappeared in the hole.

The figure then crouched over a pappy piece of card with his pencil, then tucked it inside his raincoat and trudged towards the clubhouse.

Full of admiration for such devotion to the game, Jock went over to make him welcome, letting Ben and Nevis off the lead as he offered to help with the clubs.

Sad to say, Jasper Clawhammer's temper and language were at their worst, taking no account of the religious significance of the occasion, so unfortunately an exact quotation is unpublishable. The gist of it, apart from the references to the weather, was an expression of his opinion of his playing partners, and with a measure of diplomacy that was missing from Jasper, they shall remain unnamed. Evidently they fell by the wayside one by one in face of the teeming rain, though to his credit he did make some allowance for the one who slipped into the river, because he lost his clubs.

His chief concern was whether his card, marked by himself and unwitnessed, would be acceptable in the

210

competition. Jock took a quick look at what remained of it, noted a return of 322 shots, and gave it his blessing. There being no others, Jasper Clawhammer was the clear winner.

As they splashed their way back Jock looked around for Ben and Nevis but they had obviously gone on ahead. Evidence of this was close at hand. Skipping through the water-logged ground had put them in a playful mood, and the guy-ropes and tent pegs of the marquee offered a tempting target. Worrying and tugging the pegs in the soggy ground was rewarding fun and they ripped them out with growing enthusiasm. Jock and Jasper were in time to see the result with no hope of preventing it.

Inside the marquee tension was at its climax as Rosie Clawhammer faced up to a three-foot putt to win the match. Luckily she had quite a short backswing, and was just able to go through with the stroke before the first layer of canvas descended on the crowd, who in turn descended on the hole as the ball was set in motion. There followed much creaking and groaning of straining guy ropes accompanied by muffled screams and shouts as the whole edifice gently collapsed onto a sizeable percentage of the population of Bunkham-on-Ouse.

10

It was about the same time as 'The Great Cover-up at Cawkwell' (to quote the headline in the *Crier*) that the good Lord must have found time to make reference to his pending tray, and to kindly accede to the prayers of the Sunday congregation of Bunkham-on-Ouse. Belatedly, perhaps, in the view of his devotees, but from his point of view what are twenty-four hours in the scale of the millennium?

The dark rain clouds gradually gave way to lighter skies and then to watery sunshine, giving promise of a cheerful sunny evening, and it revealed a chaotic scene on the putting green of Cawkwell Hall. A cacophony of muffled sounds was issuing from under the heaving canvas of the collapsed marquee, heads and bodies were bobbing about, and from time to time dishevelled figures would burst forth from the edges. Jock, Jasper and those golfers still at the bar of the club rallied round once they had downed their drinks and began the task of rolling back the edges, which was a welcome help to those nearest the edge, but resulted in a heavyweight trap surrounding the last of the struggling figures in the middle.

When the canvas was finally lifted and dragged off by many hands, several strange sights were brought to light. By some extraordinary coincidence Mr Lovelace seemed to have fallen heavily onto Alice Feathers and found himself unable to move, not only due to the weight of the canvas but perhaps also because her arms seemed to have become locked around him. A similar fate had evidently befallen Rosie Clawhammer and the Captain, though in her case there was some evidence of a struggle going on as the curtain went up, so to speak. There was no such evidence on the part of Flossie and Blinder and he had to spend several days convincing Augustine that it was because the poor girl was so frightened that his protective cover had been necessary.

A number of bodies were found to be prone across the eighteenth hole, refusing to be moved unless witnessed by Blinder. When this took place he was invited to examine the hole, in which he found Rosie's golf ball. It was no surprise to Blinder to find that three of the gentlemen concerned happened to have their money on that very competitor, at three to one, and were heard to complain bitterly in the Dog and Duck that evening about the unpleasant rumours circulating as to the exact route taken by the ball before being found in the hole.

When Rosie discovered that Jasper had won The Bunkham Bowl as a result of his pig-headed obstinacy, she felt fully justified in accepting 'the rub of the green' and being the first winner of The Pascal Putter in the same adverse conditions.

Presentation of both trophies was made on the steps of the Hall by Lady 'Pimples' Limpet, whose little speech congratulating their two visitors from Little Winkleton included a mention of the new golf course now under construction there. With such an accomplished lady putter on the premises, they would presumably welcome lady golfers there, and she went so far as to suggest that there might be several ladies she knew of who would like to have the experience.

Jasper was embarrassed and tongue-tied but very proud of his success in his first golfing competition. Rosie's putting ability had come as quite a shock, and suspicions began to creep into his mind about the frequency of her shopping expeditions recently – and what further surprises might be in store. But he had to concede that in spite of being a woman she was after all a Clawhammer, so he stammered his thanks on behalf of both of them, and by making no comment on Pimples' suggestion left it open for Nathaniel Gawthorpe to draw the conclusion in the *Crier* that it had been accepted. At the same time he headlined June 1st as the opening date for the new nine-hole course, 'available to golfers and also ladies'.

The die had been cast.

Letting no grass grow under her feet Pimples paid a call at Willy Arthright's bakery the very next day, and then made arrangements for another session with Nathaniel Gawthorpe at the Hall. The following week the compositor for the *Crier* set up a headline in his heaviest eight-point type above the editorial.

50 YEARS OF CRYING

THE TROPHY

It is with great pride that the management of The Bunkham and District Crier *this year records its semi-century of devoted service to the community of Bunkham-on-Ouse and far beyond.*

To celebrate this outstanding publishing achievement a special edition will be issued in August featuring all the changes and developments that have led up to the sophisticated modern town and society of today.

The new golf course now being completed at Little Winkleton will add yet another attractive facility to the area, and is a fine example of the progressive initiative so abundant in the community. The Crier intends to use this as a focal point for the celebration of its fiftieth birthday by offering as a challenge between the two towns and their respective golf clubs a Commemorative Trophy to be played for on August Bank Holiday Monday, nine holes at each venue.

The trophy will be known as 'The Bunkham-on-Ouse and Little Winkleton Crier Memorial Cup'.

Nathaniel Gawthorpe was not best known for his snappy prose or titles, but in this case he had made it easy for a wit at the Dog and Duck to pronounce its inevitable pseudonym –

'The Bunkup'.

11

Unusually, there was in the atmosphere over the breakfast table at Cawkwell Hall a slightly distant, slightly chilly air, and it was oozing from His Lordship. Lord Bruce was puzzled.

'Anything bothering you, darling?' enquired his beloved wife.

Lord Bruce cleared his throat, then came out with it.

'Something old Bucky said on the eighth the other day. Been thinking about it ... and all that ladies' putting stuff that was going on... Then there was that birthday present business of yours, a golf bag. Makes me wonder a bit, what?'

'It was such a lovely, thoughtful present, dear, and Jock supplied some beautiful clubs. You did say I could come round with you sometime, didn't you, sweetheart?' She buttered him another slice of toast.

His Lordship flushed and floundered, taking a spoonful of marmalade and applying it to his boiled egg.

'It's so difficult,' he said, 'setting such a bad example. Love to take you round, but where would it all stop?'

Where indeed! thought Pimples.

'...trouble enough brewing now, after that idiot Gawthorpe's proposal in the *Crier* this week. Can't imagine where he got a crazy idea like that.'

Deep in his righteous indignation and shaking a little at the prospect of the next committee meeting, Lord Bruce took a mouthful of his egg and went on to apply a liberal spoonful of salt to his coffee. He was following a dreadful train of thought.

'Where can they possibly find a team capable of giving us a game with only a month or two to go to the Bank Holiday? No chance for any proper practice if they let the ladies on the course. Thank the Lord we shan't have that problem here.'

'Don't worry, darling,' comforted his ever-loving wife, 'I quite understand.' Lord Bruce realised once again what a treasure she was. 'You won't mind I suppose, if I use the Daimler-Benz on Wednesdays when you play your round with the Captain. I thought I might go over to Little Winkleton sometimes and have a chat with Rosie Clawhammer. She leads such a lonely life stuck out there with her brother and we seem to have quite a lot in common to talk about. Might take some friends with me to cheer her up and there's not enough room in my little trap.'

His Lordship nodded. Dear woman. So thoughtful and considerate. Christian to the core.

Strange to say, the atmosphere at the breakfast table at Woebetide Farm closely matched that at the Hall. The jubilation they had both experienced as a result of their triumphs at Bunkham was followed by some serious reflection, particularly on the part of Jasper. He tried hard to remember how it had come about that he had

217

made his new course available to lady golfers, and what, if anything, he could do about it.

Perhaps it was when he started putting marmalade on his eggs and then a large spoonful of salt in his coffee that Rosie sensed the problem facing her brother.

'What a clever idea it was for you to open our new course to ladies, Jasper,' she said. 'That should soon make f'r a very profitable membership. Don' know where they would have come from otherwise, around here...'

Silence from Jasper, as usual, but a more thoughtful, congenial silence than was normal.

'...got talking to Lady Limpet while we were over there. She comes over to the bakery quite often and said she might just look in wi' some friends when the course is open. That would raise the tone and get plenty of people interested, that would. Even Agnes might come out here if the word was to get around.'

And it most certainly did, with the first loaf of bread.

The golf course, as it developed under the enthusiastic supervision of Willy Arthright and his helpers, egged on rather than assisted by Bert Jenkins, made use of the hilly wooded terrain and several ponds to create a challenging nine holes. As a course architect Willy Arthright had the distinct advantage of never having played the game, and so was not restricted by the slightest sympathy for the player. Jasper was too busy practising to take much interest, and Rosie's opinions were of no concern to anybody.

There were no bunkers, but there was no lack of hazards. As well as the streams, ponds, bracken and undergrowth, there were liberal contributions from cattle and sheep enjoying their new-found freedom. Holes and hillocks made by the badgers, foxes and rabbits peppered the fairways, and the greens could fairly be described as 'challenging'.

The phrase 'if you can play here you can play anywhere' might well have originated at the Little Winkleton golf course.

They built a small timber clubroom close to the farmhouse, and it was considered ready to open before May was out. To put the course on the map, Willie Arthright insisted that there should be a proper opening ceremony, and that, if possible, publicity should be enhanced by the invitation of a suitable local celebrity. Lord Limpet was the obvious choice and he agreed to attend, make a little speech, and drive off the first ball.

Opinions varied in different sections of the community on the wisdom of this decision.

The last Saturday afternoon in May was innocently cloudless, disarmingly beautiful and innocuously warm, giving not the slightest hint of potential doom or disaster. There were in attendance all the local dignitaries, councillors, shopkeepers and the press (Nathaniel Gawthorpe), and attracted by the spring sunshine, a sizeable crowd of Little Winkletonians ranging from curious mothers and ladies' maids giving their brood an outing, through youngsters of all ages, to some well-lubricated regulars from the local hostelries where 'time' had not long before been called.

The function started with several welcoming sherries at the new clubhouse bar for the dignitaries, where the welcome was a little too generous for His Lordship, but not for ladies, with whose absence went any degree of control over the intake. Willy then led them all outside towards the first tee and there he introduced his noble guest of honour to a slightly restless gathering and invited him to say a few words before officially opening the course. With his background as a missionary in darkest Africa, His Lordship's style fell naturally into the category of a sermon.

His opening – 'Dearly beloved brethren' – was ominous. 'We are gathered together here today to shelebrate...'

'You've done that already, guvner,' came from a peaked cap at the back.

'Got any to spare?' from a battered trilby.

'...to shelebrate the completion of thish fine new shporting fashility for the...'

'Councillors,' offered a brown bowler.

'...good people of Little Winkleton...'

'And the councillors,' shouted Brown Bowler.

'...And for thish magnifishent golf course in this bright and beautiful setting we must offer our thanks to The Almighty...'

'Assisted by Bert Jenkins and me' – from a black beret.

'And me' – from Battered Trilby.

'...And to Mr Jashper Shcrewdriver...' – there was a hurried aside from Willie Arthright – '...shorry... Clamhopper, who so kindly made the whole shcheme possible...'

'Shot 'is bleedin' bolt, he did, miserable ol' b...' from Battered Trilby.

'....for the golfers and alsho...' lowering his tone, 'for ladies, I believe...'

'Never believe them!' came heartfelt from Peaked Cap.

A well-built lady behind Peaked Cap obviously took exception, showing her feelings by landing a very effective blow on the centre of the cap with the handle of her parasol.

'That's enough from you, 'Enry bloomin' Appleyard.'

At this point Peaked Cap made the mistake of reacting in a most ungentlemanly manner by stepping back onto what he thought was the lady's foot. It was that of her husband who, although agreeing in principle with

220

Peaked Cap's sentiments, instantly responded with a kick in the shin.

The scuffle that followed was in no way sexist. Everybody joined in, including Jasper Clawhammer, who had been waiting to get back at Battered Trilby for his earlier contribution. He was doing pretty well against Battered Trilby, the hat soon disappearing under foot and shortly followed by Battered Trilby himself, but then found himself outnumbered by a variety of Caps and Hats, and was very pleased to find Rosie by his side using her trusty putter to good effect once again.

Lord Limpet surveyed his 'audience' and felt a little disappointed that their behaviour compared so badly with his N'Chuyu congregation at the Mission. He then recalled their earlier treatment of him in the tribal cooking-pot, took heart, and blessed their high spirits. He was rewarded first with a flying mince pie, then with a lull in the fighting, and was about to continue his speech when, in the absence of her husband in the middle of the fray, Agnes Arthright stepped forward and suggested that His Lordship might like to open the course by driving the first ball.

This was promptly tee'd up for him by his chauffeur, Sidney Sidebottom, who handed him his driver.

The subsequent report on the event in *The Bunkham and District Crier*, written with consummate tact by its editor, stated that Lord Limpet performed the ceremony before a large audience of well-wishers, and despatched the ball with a creditable drive of some two hundred yards.

What it failed to mention, presumably due to lack of space, were the fifteen previous attempts, nor was it recorded that the final drive took place long after the audience had made clear what it was 'wishing' by rapidly disappearing in the direction of the nearest first aid and refreshment tents.

221

ERNEST GOODBODY

12

The agenda for the June meeting of the Bunkham-on-Ouse Town Council was devoted almost entirely to planning for the town festivities on August Bank Holiday weekend. In attendance under the chairmanship of Captain Montague Buckmaster were the Town Clerk, Mr Dickie, and a dozen Councillors including Mrs Alice Feathers, Miss Mabel Fitt, Mr Solly Goldbaum and Mr Leslie Lovelace.

The occasion this year would have two special ingredients – the celebration of the fiftieth year of the *Crier*, and also the involvement with Little Winkleton resulting from Nathaniel Gawthorpe's offer of 'The Bunkup'. For this reason the Chairman had taken the unusual step of inviting the Chairman of Little Winkleton Town Council to attend, but it was with great regret that he was unable to do so due to being 'indisposed'.

Willy Arthright did not think it fitting to dwell on the nature of his injuries or to broadcast all the details of his

222

part in the opening ceremony at Woebetide Golf Course and the courageous support he had given to Jasper Clawhammer and Rosie. His black eye was clearing up nicely and he expected to be rid of his crutches well before the big event.

It was with some misgivings that he did the only thing possible by sending his Town Clerk, Mr Ernest Goodbody, to represent him. It was the correct thing to do, though not necessarily the most advisable.

There was no harm in Mr Goodbody, none at all. Everything he did was for the best. That was why he had held the job for over twenty years now despite some limitations to his faculties which, in his eightieth year, were still not as obvious to him as to his fellow Councillors. He might have agreed that his vision had become a little hazy through his bottle glasses, and that his hearing was not quite what it used to be, but only if he heard the question, and that was unlikely.

He was delivered to the Town Hall in good time for the six o'clock meeting by his Council chauffeur, and met at the door by Captain Buckmaster himself, who led him to the Council Chamber and invited him to take a seat at the table. Unfortunately Solly Goldbaum was in the process of seating himself into the one Ernest Goodbody selected, and Solly Goldbaum, who had had a bad day, continued to do so. In the absence of his chair he finished up on the floor, and after rolling under the large walnut table, he crawled out in not the best of tempers, only to meet head to head with the visitor as he peered down to see what had happened. The clash of heads sent Mr Goodbody's spectacles flying, but did at least serve the purpose of silencing Solly Goldbaum before he was able to express his views on the matter. He was out cold.

Mr Dickie's minutes show that the meeting proper

223

started thirty minutes late, and record Mr Goldbaum's apology for absence due to 'unforeseen circumstances'. A hearty welcome was proposed for their distinguished visitor and passed almost unanimously. He also scribbled in the margin 'Better late than never', but later in the meeting changed his mind and crossed it out.

The next ten minutes were spent by the Council members crawling around the floor in search of their visitor's spectacles, until he was found to be sitting on them. The Chairman then called the meeting to order and after a brief reference to the town events scheduled for the Saturday, he proceeded to set out the programme as he saw it for the golf competition on the August Bank Holiday Monday.

'I suggest there should be a team of six from each club, to play in singles, match-play. Twelve players, six matches. Would that be agreeable, Mr Goodbody?'

'Don't worry, Mr Chairman,' said Ernest, 'I've got a boxful somewhere, Swan Vestas. Last me all day when I'm fishing. Go ahead, light up. Think I'll do the same.'

Whereupon he produced from one of his voluminous pockets an ancient charred pipe that was later described by Mr Dickie as a cremated faggot. He added to its blackened contents a fingerful of tobacco from a wodge he filtered from the other pocket and proceeded to light up, puffing clouds of acrid smoke in all directions.

Captain Buckmaster, a confirmed non-smoker, recognised his obligations as a host and choked without comment.

'May I ask, Mr Chairman,' broke in Mrs Feathers, 'if we plan any other events for the entertainment of our townsfolk while the golfers are playing at the away course for half a day? Once before we had a fashion parade, for instance.' Mrs Feathers happened to be the couturier in the High Street.

'Wasn't that the one ruined by an escaped gnu?' Miss Fitt rather enjoyed reminding her. 'Why not have an event more suited to the special occasion, something to round off the weekend. What about a firework display, for example?'

'That sounds interesting,' said the Chairman. 'Any other ideas?'

Mr Goodbody said he had one. He sucked hard on his pipe, which had gone out, and went through the lighting-up procedure again, spraying the used matches into what appeared to him to be a large ashtray behind him.

'May I make a suggestion? Sometimes we have a fireworks display on special occasions at Little Winkleton. Why not do that to celebrate this special occasion?'

He became aware of a stony silence and a glare from Miss Fitt. 'If the cost worries you, my Council will contribute, and I've got plenty of matches – that should save money.'

'Thank you,' came from the Chair. 'Talking of matches, shall we go to Little Winkleton in the morning and Bunkham in the afternoon?'

'I'm afraid they won't be ready for you all yet,' said Ernest. 'Shouldn't we wait until August? Far better to plan ahead a little, don't you think?'

There was no immediate response, so Ernest carried on.

'On that occasion, it was the view of our Council that we should play a golf match, half of it at each of the two golf courses.'

No comment.

'Nine holes in the morning and nine in the afternoon.'

'At alternate venues?' enquired Mr Dickie, with singular patience and courtesy.

'We didn't discuss the food,' replied Ernest, 'I'll enquire if they have any special menus in mind. Our

225

Chairman usually takes care of the catering side, you know. Have you tried his hot cross buns? A bit late for that now, I suppose, but next year...'

It was uncharacteristic of Mr Dickie to interrupt, but he did so on this occasion. It had become apparent to him that not all the smoke and fumes which now thickened the room were from Mr Goodbody's pipe, and he drew the attention of the Chairman to the waste bin behind that gentleman's chair. As he did so, the waste papers burst into flames. They all jumped up in alarm, and Mr Goodbody pushed back his chair, knocking over the bin onto the Persian carpet and under the plush velvet curtains...

Mr Dickie's minutes, re-written from memory, record that the meeting was presumed closed when the Town Hall was evacuated and as the Town Hall clock sounded nine o'clock. In a postscript he was able to confirm the time when the clock was rescued three days later from the smouldering ashes of the Bunkham-on-Ouse Town Hall.

Ned Drinkwater was called in from the Dog and Duck to take statements from all concerned, and the fire brigade (Bill Cheeseman and his son Fred) arrived shortly after to take over dousing the flames.

Mr Goodbody's report to the next meeting of the Little Winkleton Town Council took three-quarters of an hour. From it Willy Arthright and his fellow Councillors learned that there had been a close meeting of minds (which is not the way Solly Goldbaum would have described it) and one of the Council had been taken ill. Mr Goodbody's proposal for a golf match had been accepted and he had succeeded in postponing the date until August Bank Holiday Monday. His suggestion of a fireworks display to open the event had also been accepted, on the condition that Little Winkleton provided the matches. Catering had been discussed, and enquiries had been made about the supply of hot cross buns.

He reported too that the Bunkham Council meeting had ended in a more spectacular fashion than any he had attended at Little Winkleton. He expressed his surprise to them as he had done to Captain Buckmaster, that it had been thought necessary to light a fire in the Council Chamber in the middle of June and had advised that in future they should stick to a paraffin stove of the type used at Little Winkleton, and only in the winter months.

He told the meeting of his courteous, indeed, hearty reception and recommended that in appreciation of it and of their kind acceptance of his proposals and guidance, they should send a present to Captain Buckmaster, who evidently smoked Players cigarettes so heavily that he ran out of matches.

A presentation pack of Players Medium Cut was duly sent to him, care of the temporary Council Offices, together with a gross of Swan Vesta matches, with greetings from the Little Winkleton Council.

13

On the first Wednesday in June, Lord Bruce's Daimler-Benz arrived at Woebetide Golf Club, Little Winkleton, chauffeured as always by Sidney Sidebottom, with four lady passengers and four sets of ladies' golf clubs. With Lady Limpet and Lady Augustine were Alice Feathers and Virginia Hardcastle, and they were made welcome by Rosie Clawhammer and signed in as members.

They were surprised to discover that they were the first playing members to join the new club. The presence of Jasper Clawhammer may have had something to do with a lack of enthusiasm in the community, and the signboard at the entrance to the new golf club, the work of Jasper Clawhammer himself, did little to help.

WOEBETIDE GOLF CLUB

By kind permission of Woebetide Farm, golfing on the 9 hole course is permitted to members only.

Membership of Woebetide Golf Club is limited to applicants familiar with the course and subject to the approval of the proprietor.

JASPER CLAWHAMMER

P.S. The following should not attempt to apply –

(The list of names scribbled below bore witness to so many long-standing feuds that only Willy Arthright and Ernest Goodbody seemed likely to qualify, should they ever lose their passion for fishing.)

Where ladies were concerned, Jasper was a very shy man, and it was only thanks to his curiosity about their playing ability and that momentous meeting with Pimples at the Bunkham prize-giving that he could be persuaded by her to join them. Playing in two sets of three, Jasper was able to introduce Pimples and Alice Feathers to the course, while Rosie did the same for Augustine and Virginia.

Jasper presumed it would be necessary to give an exhibition of each shot in the game, and took the first drive with this in mind. He gave the ball his usual series of threatening waggles before winding himself up in the customary way and letting fly with his most powerful swipe. Although the ball was never seen again, they were all duly impressed with its elevation over the trees and the probable distance it travelled, and they made their admiration very plain.

As a result his morale was raised sufficiently to withstand the shock of their shorter but far more accurate expertise, which continued to surprise and impress him as they neatly negotiated the many hazards of the course. Pimples' and Alice's expertise also extended to the skilful massaging of Jasper's ego, so that by the end of the round he found himself in a somewhat dazed and

229

unusually pleasant mood, particularly when in close proximity to Alice Feathers.

When the following threesome came down the last fairway he watched in something of a trance as Rosie sank a ten-foot putt for a birdie, and announced a round of eighty for the eighteen holes.

Whilst he was in this extraordinary state the ladies found it easy to persuade him to say nothing of his experience that day to anyone at Bunkham – a promise he found easy to make, since the only repeatable thing he had been heard to say there during his six months of membership was 'Fore!'

The significance of these golfing revelations was not lost on Sidney Sidebottom, who had parked the Daimler-Benz and then stretched his legs round the course, and under cover of the undergrowth followed the play. Since his involvement in the first contest for The Bunkham Bowl as successful partner to Mr Rutumutu, Sidney had played very little – he found the pressure of competition to be an unnecessary strain and preferred the role of spectator and critic. And sometimes, punter.

His knowledge of the game and of the capability of most members of Bunkham Golf Club told him that he was onto a good thing. He heard the promise of confidentiality given by Jasper, and there was certainly no chance of a leakage from him until Blinder had opened his book on The Bunkup at the Dog and Duck in the usual way and Sidney had been able to take advantage of probable long odds to make a substantial investment.

He was humming happily as he drove the party home, and so were they.

14

The mid-June meeting of the Bunkham Golf Club was also devoted to matters concerning August Bank Holiday and the Bunkham-on-Ouse and Little Winkleton Crier Memorial Cup, with Lord Bruce Limpet in the Chair.

He opened the meeting with a detailed description of the new 'spoon' now being made for him by Jake Trueman and the hope that it would be available to demonstrate to the Captain at their next meeting. This was followed by an expression of regret at the sad loss of the Town Hall, and a word of advice to the Council Chairman, Captain Buckmaster, against encouraging smoking in the future. He went on to remark on the kind expression of sympathy and the thoughtful gift from their neighbouring town he had read about in the *Crier*.

He called on the Captain who, at that moment, seemed to be suffering some sort of choking fit, to announce the team for the memorial match.

The Captain, red-faced and exhibiting an attitude more of malicious intent than sporting competition, read out the six names. (Team selection had followed the principles familiar to most golf clubs.)

Luke Hardcastle (generous discounts in his store).
Jake Trueman (golf clubs made to measure).
Leslie Lovelace (golfing attire, ditto).
Solly Goldbaum (discount on trophies).
Lord Limpet (unavoidably).
Himself.

'Rumour has it,' he went on, 'that membership of the Little Winkleton club is very limited, probably due to their misguided policy of allowing lady members. I just hope they can raise a team.'

The same question had occurred to Nathaniel Gawthorpe, who foresaw the dreadful possibility of the focal point of fame and celebration for himself and the *Crier* falling flat. He raised the issue at his next meeting with Her Ladyship. Her reply was both comforting and flattering.

'May I call you Nathaniel?' she asked, and receiving a blushing nod, 'Nathaniel, it is thanks to your far-sighted promotion of ladies' golf at Little Winkleton that the competition will be a very special one with far-reaching consequences and wide circulation. I suggest you might care to express your concern in the next edition that it would not do for the great town of Bunkham to be beaten by Little Winkleton – without reference please to what I have just said. Do we understand one another, Nathaniel?'

Her winning smile sealed it, and the resultant editorial also had some bearing on the level of betting at the Dog and Duck. In that matter, Sidney Sidebottom was suffering severe disappointment at being offered by Blinder no better than even money, not being aware that his secret knowledge of the ladies' golfing prowess was matched by Blinder's confidential information from Jock, their coach. Still, even money on a dead cert is not too bad thought Sidney as he put on two weeks' wages, £1 18s. 6d.

He was very pleased that 'his team', four of them anyway, continued their regular Wednesday practice visits to Woebetide Golf Club in the Daimler-Benz, and not surprised when, at the height of the July heat wave, Pimples called upon Smithers to provide them with a picnic hamper, beautifully stocked, for them to enjoy on their way back from the morning round. The road between the towns ran for much of the way beside the Ouse, and they pulled off the road where, in a copse of small trees and undergrowth, there was a perfect clearing down to the water's edge.

As they were laying out the tablecloth on the grass and the little rugs to sit on so thoughtfully provided by Smithers, Sidney suddenly remembered His Lordship's request that he should collect the new spoon from Hardcastle's store. With Her Ladyship's permission he made off in great haste, promising to return within the hour.

After the heat of the golf course, the ladies found there was still little relief from the midday sun. The seclusion of their picnic site gave them the confidence to follow Augustine's lead and begin stripping some clothes off, and they were even tempted to seriously consider a dip in the river. Their minds were quickly made up for them by the ants on whose home they had unfortunately settled and by the close attention of an unfriendly swarm of wasps. Off came their remaining garments and into the cool water they went. Oh, the joy of the delightful river Ouse.

These were also the precise sentiments of Ernest

Goodbody as he parked his bicycle nearby and settled down for a bit of quiet fishing in his favourite spot, just beyond the bushes shielding the ladies' clothes. Their cries when he made a few practice casts were wasted on Ernest, who was now concentrating on packing his pipe and lighting up. The procedure always took half-a-dozen goes, the matches being tossed away in disgust with each failure.

The ladies' clothes had been neatly stacked together on a branch above ant level, and anybody familiar with Murphy's Law will know what inevitably followed. The lingerie seemed to ignite much easier than the pipe, though Ernest was quite unaware of it until the fire spread in the undergrowth around him. Taking advantage of this diversion, the distraught ladies scrambled up the bank and snatched up the tablecloth and rugs before the fire could get to them. Thus attired, choosing to cover whichever portion of their anatomy they felt most vulnerable, they attempted to break in on Ernest to explain their predicament. But Ernest had his own problem.

The light breeze had driven the fire through the long grass towards him, and as he backed away he slipped on the edge of the river bank and fell in.

One of the many things that Ernest was incapable of was swimming, which was soon obvious to the ladies. In their present mood the ungallant question in all their minds was whether to save him or not. It was lucky for Ernest that, in Pimples' case, common humanity prevailed and she plunged back in to the rescue.

It was at this moment that Sidney returned. Faced with the trio of ladies wearing nothing but tiny rugs and Her Ladyship swimming naked with Ernest Goodbody, his first concern was quite naturally the danger of his team catching cold and handicapping themselves for the big match, costing him £1 18s. 6d. He then realised that

Her Ladyship was engaged in a struggle with Ernest, and thinking the obvious worst, did not hesitate to plunge in to her rescue and push her 'attacker' further out into the river, where he promptly sank.

Once again Mr Goodbody's fate was in the balance, and if subject to majority vote, it would have been sealed. But after brief discussion, Pimples and Sidney, who first needed to dispense with the restriction of his clothes, jumped back in, dredged him up, and dragged him ashore. He gurgled a few times, readjusted his glasses, then went off in search of his pipe.

Jasper's return to Little Winkleton after a golf lesson with Jock was timed to perfection from his point of view, and possibly that of Ernest. It was the sight of the Daimler-Benz and the sound of familiar voices that caused him to draw up his buggy and try to take in a sight he would never forget. Especially Alice Feathers, whose rug was certainly the smallest and was not very accurately positioned. This was love at first full-frontal, but he had some misgivings concerning the conduct of the two gentlemen with the other three ladies, whom he did not immediately recognise until he raised his gaze.

Ernest then gratefully thanked the five kind gentlemen who had been so helpful, and went off to Little Winkleton with Jasper. Having first loaded his bicycle and fishing rod on the back of the buggy, he then tried desperately to light the sodden tobacco in his soaking pipe. Luckily for Jasper (and for Ernest), the matches that landed on Jasper's golf bag were just too wet to do any damage.

Sidney Sidebottom's drive back to Cawkwell Hall took him through the centre of Bunkham. His parade of the four semi-naked ladies would have compared favourably with that of Lady Godiva, if the reports emanating from the Dog and Duck are to be believed. Fortunately for Sidney and the ladies concerned, Pimples' connection with Nathaniel Gawthorpe ensured that the *Crier* concentrated its story on the courageous rescue of a drowning man by Sidney Sidebottom, who happened to be passing at the time.

However, the Dog and Duck version was soon common knowledge at the Hall via the Flossie–Doris network, giving Sidney Sidebottom a very hard time with his wife Lofty.

At the Limpets' breakfast table, Smithers noticed a distinct chill in the air so far as His Lordship was concerned.

15

The heat wave continued through July and into August, to the great joy of the citizens of Bunkham-on-Ouse and Little Winkleton. The annual Fair on the common at Little Winkleton did record business and so did the circus in the grounds of Cawkwell Hall – a new innovation this year, instigated by Pimples.

Nathaniel Gawthorpe ensured that the *Crier* gave due prominence to his promotion of the golf match between the two towns, and succeeded in creating much curiosity about the team selection at Little Winkleton, which remained unannounced. He carefully played on the natural rivalry of the two communities so that when the Bank Holiday dawned two charabanc-loads of Bunkhamites set out early for the opening nine holes to be played at Little Winkleton, and a further small flotilla of river craft did the same, complete with picnic hampers and all the paraphernalia of a family day out.

A festive atmosphere pervaded Little Winkleton;

flowers, banners and bunting were everywhere, even including the entrance to Woebetide Golf Club. The team of six from Bunkham arrived in a convoy of motor cars and buggies, led by the Daimler-Benz carrying Lord and Lady Limpet and the Lady Augustine with her husband Blinder. Next was Captain Buckmaster, who had with him Luke Hardcastle, his daughter Virginia and Jake Trueman. Jock McTavish and Kirsty followed in their buggy accompanied by Alice Feathers and Leslie Lovelace. Solly Goldbaum and his wife brought up the rear in his Armstrong-Siddeley coupé.

They were welcomed by the Chairman of the Council, Willy Arthright, and by his Town Clerk. The handshake given by the Captain to his opposite number could not have been described as cordial, except by comparison to his frosty acknowledgement of Ernest Goodbody. His father's recent confrontation with a rhinoceros in darkest Africa would have been considered more genial.

The atmosphere did not improve when he was handed the Little Winkleton team sheet and found there was only one man in the team of six, and not one of his favourites at that. He was drawn to play against Rosie Clawhammer, who was by this time ready on the first tee in her golfing attire, taking a few practice swings. He swallowed his pride, and still in a black temper, prepared to play. Rosie was so accustomed to her brother's moods that she found the Captain comparatively good-humoured, and as this became apparent, even to him, the atmosphere gradually improved even as he lost the first five holes. He had to concede that she played remarkably good golf, despite her sex, and to his further surprise she looked quite attractive doing it.

Prompted by a pre-match briefing from Pimples that it would be counter-productive to embarrass their opponents, she relaxed her game at the sixth hole, and by conceding several lengthy putts managed to end up only two up over a very changed Captain Buckmaster.

Luke Hardcastle and Alice Feathers were next and, with some difficulty on the part of Alice, a similar result was achieved. They were followed by His Lordship versus... his wife.

Lord Bruce was nothing if not a gentleman.

'Don't worry, my dear,' he was heard to say, 'I'll get you round somehow.' The result, calling upon all the reserves of Pimples' good nature, was all square.

Solly Goldbaum found himself with Augustine, who was immediately eyed very suspiciously by Mrs Goldbaum, who thought it advisable to follow them round. This did nothing to help his game, and as it was not in Augustine's nature to give anything away whatever the circumstances, and especially in the tiresome presence of Mrs G., they turned dormy nine.

Jake Trueman was happy enough. Having been responsible for making everybody's clubs, the team sheet came as less of a surprise to him, and the prospect of the company of Virginia was a dream come true. At the end of an enjoyable round he was delighted to be one down.

Now Jasper Clawhammer versus Leslie Lovelace – that was very different, and the difference was Alice Feathers. The Bunkup had a very different meaning for them, and there was an edge to this match of almost gladiatorial proportions. The only things given away in this match were black looks – not an unusual condition for Jasper but quite abnormal for the gentle Mr Lovelace, and in a state of frenzy at the thought of Jasper's interest in the lady, he did well to finish all square.

The very chastened team from Bunkham sat down to lunch alfresco in a strange variety of moods. The Captain was so mellow in the presence of his playing partner that even the sight of Ernest sitting opposite and lighting his pipe could not seriously upset him. Luke Hardcastle was eyeing his daughter with a mixture of shock and pride, while Solly Goldbaum was shepherded by his wife to the opposite end of the table from Augustine. This freed her to perform a useful service in smoothing the path of Pimples with her somewhat deflated husband.

Jake and Virginia watched with amusement the manoeuvrings across the table between Jasper and Leslie Lovelace in their efforts to avoid each other but not Alice Feathers. Finally sitting on either side of her, they began a conversational battle which Jasper won hands down in Alice's eyes by not saying a word.

Pimples' plan was clearly well on course. Ladies' golf at Bunkham would be achieved only by demonstrating that they could 'play the game' in every respect, and not actually beating the men was surely an advisable game plan at this stage. How to accomplish the perfect result was now exercising her mind, but she need not have worried. The outcome was in even more capable hands than hers – the hands of Eros, Goodbody and the Almighty.

16

Pimples' chambermaid Doris Goodbody and her grandfather had very few opportunities to meet, so Ernest's visit to Bunkham golf course at Cawkwell Hall with the team gave them a rare chance to do so. They went to the circus together.

There were a number of family traits that had noticeably carried through the two generations that separated them, such as a generous friendly nature and a twinkle in the eye. There was also a similar though less pronounced tendency to be accident prone. A combination of the two was, nevertheless, ominous.

The disaster, when it duly arrived, started simply enough and owed something to that admirable family trait, generosity. Edward the performing elephant was going happily through his routine with his trainer on his back, circling the ring with forefeet up on the rim, tickling people with his trunk and accepting buns and sweets. Doris attracted him with a piece of her home-made cream cake, and he must have lost his concentration for a moment as he swept away in his trunk Ernest's pipe, which was well packed and fully alight. Letting out a piercing screech, Edward went completely berserk, careering through the side of the Big Top, trumpeting at full power and knocking over everything in his path, including the caged tunnel leading from the lion's quarters to the ringside.

Harold was an aging lion, but he knew how to put on a good enough performance to make him the showpiece of the circus. He still had several good teeth left, and could produce a fearsome look, which he liked to combine with a few hearty roars. Plenty of applause followed by plenty to eat and then to bed – that was the routine he enjoyed. Any variations to it, such as being invaded by an elephant, he found tiresome, even if it was only old Edward. Shaken out of his dreams, he wandered out into the grounds, yawning as he went. This was easily misunderstood by the holidaymakers and had the effect of evacuating the entire area in a flash. Meanwhile Edward was making a beeline for the river to cool his trunk, trailing large sections of the Big Top behind him.

All the golf matches were fully in progress and delicately poised. The ladies were struggling to bring about the result recommended by Pimples, but not finding it easy to lose holes convincingly. The intervention of Edward was at first seen as a sort of mixed blessing in the eyes of the embarrassed Bunkham losers and also in the eyes of the ladies. However, as Edward charged across the course, he was followed not only by bits of the tent but also by a panic-stricken crowd. This mystified the golfers until Harold came into view, by this time putting on one of his best performances.

Even the most enthusiastic and dedicated golfer might be forgiven for losing his concentration in a situation of this kind, and it is certainly not conducive to a relaxed swing or an accurate putt to be faced with either a trumpeting elephant or a roving lion, let alone both. This point was clearly made by Augustine, who had a twelve-inch putt to win her match but dropped her putter and joined the throng sprinting headlong for the river.

Not far behind her was Nathaniel Gawthorpe, who had been waiting with pencil poised to record the first result in the contest for his memorial trophy and the special edition of the *Crier* being held over awaiting this headline news. Augustine could produce an impressive turn of speed when really necessary, and it is to Nathaniel's credit that when he reached the river and plunged in, it was a dead heat.

In no time the river contained what appeared to be most of the population of Bunkham and Little Winkleton, many of whom needed to be rescued by the small armada of pleasure boats. On several of these were stored the fireworks, in readiness for the evening display, and it was thanks to Willy Arthright, who was in charge of them, that they were put to more immediate use.

Neither Edward nor Harold had any previous experience of rockets or fire-crackers, and faced with a volley from Willy, they decide to seek the safety of their familiar surroundings and head for home. Edward had in any case cooled off and drunk his fill, and Harold was getting tired – so much so that he found himself a comfortable spot in the sun on the eighteenth green and fell asleep. He was led back to the circus later in the evening by Egbert Micklethwaite, who strongly disapproved of animals on his precious greens.

Various acts of heroism were meanwhile taking place in the waters of the river Ouse. Nathaniel Gawthorpe was saved as he sank for the third time by the ever vigilant Pimples, although the report dealing with this incident in the *Crier* contrived to get it the wrong way round. Alice

Feathers was conveniently close to Jasper when she found herself in difficulty, and to his great joy had to be carried out in his arms. A strong bond was thereby established, loosened a little perhaps by the encouraging wink she gave to Leslie Lovelace in the process.

It transpired that another non-swimmer who had been swept into the water with the crowd was none other than Captain Buckmaster. His rescue by Rosie put the final touch to a liaison that had been blossoming throughout the day. Not only was it to lead to the altar, but also to a fresh assessment of lady golf members in the Bunkham Golf Club and a highly satisfactory conclusion to Lady 'Pimples' Limpet's campaign.

The main headline in the 'celebration' edition of the *Crier* ran as follows:

CATASTROPHE AT CAWKWELL

Bank Holiday bedlam gave way to widespread acts of heroism in face of jungle monsters on the loose...

Followed by editorial of a colourful nature in which the rescue work of the paper's 'representative' was given coverage suitably dramatic for this memorable occasion.

Page 2 carried the headline:

COMPETITION FOR THE BUNKHAM AND LITTLE WINKLETON CRIER MEMORIAL CUP POSTPONED

Agreement has been reached between the two towns to replay the matches in full in the Christmas holiday period when it is understood that all participants and council members will again be available to give their support with the exception of the Town Clerk of Little Winkleton. He will be away with his granddaughter visiting family

*in America, the fare and all expenses having been gener-
ously donated by Captain Buckmaster, and a booking
made for the maiden voyage of the SS Titanic.*

Three other items caught the eye in this bumper edition
of the *Crier*:

Announcements of the engagement of Mr Jasper
Clawhammer to Mrs Alice Feathers, and of Captain
Montague Buckmaster to Miss Rosie Clawhammer.

An invitation to lady golfers to apply for full membership to the Bunkham Golf Club, Cawkwell Hall. And
thirdly, under 'Lost and Found':

*A reward is offered by the Town Clerk of Little Winkleton
to anyone finding a large slightly scorched briar pipe lost
recently in the grounds of Cawkwell Hall.*

There followed a very strong rumour going the rounds
at the Dog and Duck that when it was found by M'Pupu,
the N'Chuyu tracker, he had been rewarded by a better
offer from an unidentified source in the temporary head-
quarters of the Bunkham Town Council, and that it was
never seen again. The only clue was a quotation from
the Bard attached to the minutes of the Council meeting
that month by Thomas J. Dickie.

O, how full of briers is this working-day world!

MORE BULL

Colonel Buckmaster heads for home

The further adventures of Lt. Colonel Sir Ferdinand Buckmaster, OBE (retired), pick up from the denouement of the first of this series, and is in response to complaints from all those readers who have had sleepless nights worrying about him.

Lady Buckmaster was not one of them.

LEONARD + AMELIA

1

Kukukraali

Lt. Col. Sir Ferdinand Buckmaster, OBE (retired), better known as the Bull, stood on the bank of the Nile, approximately in the centre of Africa by his judgement, shaking his fist in the direction of the river gun-boat *Lady Luck* as she disappeared round a distant bend in the river. At no stage in his long army career had he ever found himself at the top of the popularity chart, but in his experience military discipline had always made good any difficulties of this kind. Until today.

Revenge would be sweet and merciless if ever their paths should cross again, but this was such an unlikely event...

He turned his mind to his immediate problem and realised that a second visit to the administrative village of Kukukraali would be necessary. In the distance above the trees he could still see in the evening light the Union

Jack hanging limply on a flagpole over the office of Mr Leonard Petty, whose acquaintance he had made on his visit earlier in the day. As he looked, the flag was being lowered for the night, and he set out to follow the track he had found the first time, but taking care on this occasion not to step into any lion traps again. His one-legged suspension earlier in the day was an embarrassment he would prefer to forget.

He remembered too that he still owed the little boy Henry one-and-sixpence for arranging his release.

It was getting dark by the time he reached the outskirts of the village, but he could follow the sound of activity and could make out a few lights.

Suddenly he became aware of a rustling sound in the undergrowth and as he stopped and prepared to meet any attack with his customary dominant eye contact, he found himself being dragged to the ground in a tangle of rope netting.

'*M'bingong chuchu tingmumu chungchung jumbo bongabonga,*' somebody cried.

The Bull, who was by no means pleased with this reception, would have been even more upset had he understood this outcry, and for those readers equally unfamiliar with the dialect, I give a rough translation.

'Hold tight, I think we've got a baby elephant!'

The roars that followed led his captors to change their minds, and they moved back for fear of the claws of a lion or the horn of a rhino.

The citizens of Kukukraali had good reason to fear night attacks from the many dangerous denizens who inhabited their suburbs. Indeed, there were many comparisons to be made with city life as we know it today, but the Kukukraalians were generally inclined to be rather less conciliatory or forgiving than it is today considered to be proper, and were not disposed to try to reason with or re-train those they managed to catch, whatever their human rights might be. Consequently it was extremely lucky for the Colonel, though he never acknowledged it, that his captors had omitted to bring their knives or spears with them. Had they not been so tardy, this would certainly have been one of the shortest short stories ever told.

Instead they bundled him up and dragged him unceremoniously into the centre of the village, where there was enough light from the fires to identify the 'kill'.

'I know what that is,' shouted a young voice, 'it's that funny man who keeps coming here and doing silly things... If he promises any money to let him free, don't trust him. Get it first... and my one-and-sixpence too!'

The Bull had by this time almost reached the final stages of apoplexy.

'When I get out of this thing I'll break every bone in all your blasted bodies!' was his least offensive outburst, from which it can be deduced why his early career in the diplomatic service was of a very short duration.

His captors were so disappointed with their catch that they simply retired to their huts in disgust, leaving the Colonel to bellow to his heart's content. This brought little Mr Leonard Petty, the local colonial administrator and representative of HM Government, onto the scene.

'Hallo again,' he said, 'did you forget something?'

'Yes, he did,' said a small voice, and by now we all know what was bothering Henry.

Mr Petty examined the bundle and went off to find a pair of scissors. Meanwhile the Bull remembered his sheath knife, and working his arms free he slashed his way out of the net. When Mr Petty returned with the scissors he also brought with him his assistant, Amelia Carstairs, who brought with her a cup of tea.

'Milk and sugar?' she enquired.

253

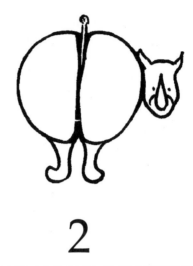

2

White Rhino

It had been a long day for the Bull, and not one he would wish to commit to memory. He ate the meal of boiled zebra tripe and corn cobs because there was no alternative, drank the remainder of the 'visitors'' sherry, and fell into a deep sleep on the visitors' camp bed. In his dreams he found himself back on board the river gun-boat *Lady Luck* and was sorry to wake up suddenly just as he was in the process of wringing the neck of Captain Rusty McGinty. He tried hard to get back to sleep again just to finish off the job, but there was Amelia Carstairs beaming down at him, saying, 'Was it one lump or two?'

For Mr Petty this promised to be a busy day. He had received notice that a hunting party of Americans was expected to pass through Kukukraali, and his instructions were to treat them with diplomatic civility but minimum

IVOR PYLE   DONNA PYLE

hospitality. His capacity for hospitality being already severely limited, this subtlety of treatment was in his view going to be very difficult to achieve effectively. The Bull had already concluded, and made clear, that the treatment he had received was in much the same category.

His customary bombastic personality, when exercised on the meek and mild Mr Petty, had the inevitable result that, by ten o'clock, he had taken over Mr Petty's office, so that when the party arrived at about eleven, they were led into the administrator's office, where the Bull was sitting at the desk and Mr Petty and Mrs Carstairs were sitting on the visitors' bench receiving instructions.

From HM Government's point of view, the result was as required, if not strictly in accordance with protocol.

The party was led in by a large rotund ruddy-faced man in a multicoloured shirt, chewing the remains of a cigar, and he was followed closely by a loud falsetto voice emanating from a small well-upholstered lady of indeterminate age.

'Ivor, this is so sweet – we really must get a cute little hut like this built down by the lake at home. I can just see Mary Lou and all the darling little ones down there in the box-wood furniture and all...'

Behind them, in unfortunate contrast, came a quietly attractive young lady with large blue eyes, a seductive smile and an hour-glass figure, followed by a tall dark-tanned man. His bushy eyebrows shielding slitted eyes, his aquiline nose and heavy growth of beard, needed only the standard colonial pith helmet to identify him as an Englishman.

'Ivor Pyle,' announced their leader.

'Bad luck,' replied the Bull, 'haven't got any more chairs anyway. Who is everybody?'

'I'm Donna Pyle,' piped up his wife, 'and this is our

MILLICENT
MARTINI

PERCY
UNDERWOOD

257

niece, Miss Millicent Martini, and our hunting guide, Percy Underwood.'

'Nice of you to call in – pity you didn't wipe your feet though... suppose no one bothers in America.'

This was not quite the reception Mr Petty had in mind, and he rose to say something more diplomatic.

'Sit down, Petty,' ordered the Colonel, and he did.

'Where are you heading for, Pyle?' he asked. 'And how soon?'

'We're following the trail of the white rhino,' said Percy Underwood. 'Mr Pyle would like to get a shot at one.'

'We thought the mounted head would look so nice over the mantelpiece in the trophy room back home, and maybe a tiger-skin rug to go with it.' As she said it, Donna Pyle was looking round the room and caught sight of Amelia Carstairs. 'You know what it is, dinner parties, conversation pieces, can't do without them, can we!'

In fact, Mrs Carstairs was thinking how happy she would be to do without them for the rest of her life – not only the rhinos, but everybody in the room, with the exception of Leonard Petty. She went on to imagine their heads mounted on the walls of this office, and what a wonderful conversation piece that would make, especially the Bull. She would have been much relieved in any case had she known what was now going on in the mind of that particular 'trophy'.

'Don't see too many tigers around here,' commented the Bull, 'better try another continent perhaps – saw plenty of 'em in India... Seen a rhino though,' he added.

A stratagem had gradually dawned on the Colonel, whose objective was to move on in any direction from Kukukraali.

'What you need is some military experience to

out-manoeuvre such a quarry in a situation like this. I'd better come with you and take over.'

'We wouldn't like to put you to all that trouble,' said Percy Underwood, shuddering at this very unwelcome turn of events. 'If we can just bed down somewhere for the night, we'll be on our way by daybreak.'

'Or before,' added Pyle hastily.

'I think it would be rather nice to have a change of company for a day or two,' twittered Donna, whose husband could happily have killed her there and then.

'I'll start packing a few things for you right away,' offered Amelia Carstairs, and Mr Petty said he would be glad to lend her a hand.

Outside the office, the Bull was pleased to discover that the party included half-a-dozen pack mules and a dozen or so native porters and servants. They seemed to be well equipped with stores, water containers, rifles and ammunition, and the Colonel sensed a turn for the better in the foreseeable future. As it happened, he was the only one of the entire hunting company who felt that way about things, but Mr Petty, Amelia Carstairs, her son Henry and the entire population of Kukukraali were completely in sympathy with his mood.

Amelia went so far as to cook them all another potful of zebra tripe and corn cobs, and Mr Petty suggested a toast of 'bon voyage' should be drunk with the remains of their small stock of native hooch.

Ivor Pyle provided a bottle of bourbon whiskey to help 'conserve such precious stocks', as he diplomatically put it, and they were able to properly celebrate or drown their sorrows, as the mood took them.

The discovery of this additional attraction in the Americans' stores was for the Colonel something to celebrate in itself, and he opened a second bottle.

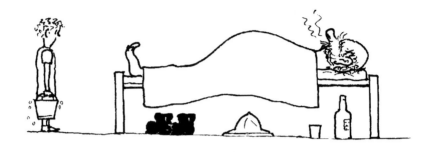

3

Bull-Dozed

Before first light the party set off quietly in a southerly direction, very considerately trying not to disturb the Colonel who, with the aid of the second bottle of bourbon, was enjoying deep slumber. If it had not been for the vigilance of young Henry, he might even have been left behind. Henry woke early, still thinking about a certain outstanding account, and decided to go into the Bull's bedroom and deal with the problem on a direct debit basis.

This he did, and clutching his one-and-sixpence, was going back to his own room when he saw the party preparing to leave. He thereupon did the Bull a favour which was never fully appreciated, by fetching a bucket of water and pouring it over the Bull's head.

Wisely, he then ran for it.

The Bull roared – perhaps bellowed describes it better

– leapt up, and dashed out of the door in pursuit of Henry, almost colliding with the tail end of the hunting party as they slunk quietly into the jungle.

The Bull was no good at taking a hint, especially an unwelcome one. In his most commanding manner he called the party to a halt whilst he put on his trousers and boots, and then strode to the head of the 'column' and gave the order to quick march.

Mr Petty and Mrs Carstairs were not at all put out by their guests' failure of common courtesy and protocol. Heaving a sigh of relief, they wished the party a long and distant journey with plenty of rhinos. On hearing young Henry's story, they of course chastised him for taking the money, then gave him a bonus and a large breakfast.

Before his journey to Africa in search of Lord Limpet, the Colonel had taken the trouble to study a map of the continent, and it might be helpful if at this point I reprint the copy from *The Pot Thickens*, with some additional detail.

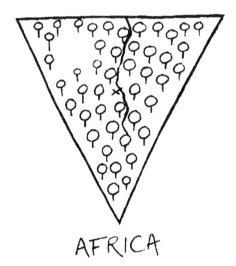

AFRICA

He had equipped himself at the start (out of the grant provided by the solicitor handling the Limpet estate) with a river gunboat for use on the Nile, and three camels for use in the deserts. To the relief of the camels he made no use of them at all, and as for the *Lady Luck* – well, he could think of more appropriate names.

The continent being entirely surrounded by water, he now evolved a plan to try to reach it by heading in what he vaguely imagined to be a south-easterly direction where the triangle got thinner. As it happened, this was the direction in which the hunting party intended to go anyway, hoping in the process to get on the trail of the white rhino and any other unfortunate beast whose head might, in the judgement of the Pyles, make a good impression on the visitors in the trophy room back home. Just like Amelia Carstairs, it crossed the mind of Donna Pyle that the head of Sir Ferdinand Buckmaster could well qualify for a prime position, and there were times in the course of the next month or two when, so far as Ivor Pyle was concerned, it was a damned close run thing.

Percy Underwood was a hunter by nature as well as by profession. Wild animals were his professional prey but in the course of his forty-odd years he had also had two other targets, namely, women and money. Drink might also be mentioned, but it was not so much a target as an essential commodity at all times. His success rate in the second objective had been largely satisfactory, apart from the occasional encounter with an irate husband or two, but financially he had yet to achieve adequate results.

He watched the Colonel closely, and after a week or two came to the conclusion that he still had access to some substantial funds, and that his objective of reaching the coast and finding a ship matched his own. He reviewed his present situation.

His 'business' was based in Mukibundu, a small town in the dusty central plains north of Kukukraali. He was not only bored with life in that tiny insular community, but had run out of drinking partners, women and funds. Being engaged by Ivor Pyle on his present duties had come just in time to rescue him from trouble brewing in several directions including the local bank manager, and also his wife. He could think of no good reason to go back, and plenty of reasons not to.

The current situation offered several encouraging possibilities. True, the Colonel was not the ideal companion at any time but he felt he could cope with that for a bit if the prospects made it worthwhile. There would be a touch of adventure in making a break from the lifestyle he now found so boring, and there was the added attraction of Miss Millicent Martini, who not only looked good but seemed very approachable, and above all, appeared to have her own source of revenue.

Clearly, she needed to be separated from her aunt and uncle, and if possible from some of her funds as well.

Percy Underwood laid his plans.

It was a serious shortage of bourbon that ultimately brought about an urgent determination to reach civilisation as quickly as possible. The need for it was the one issue on which there was widespread agreement, the only dissentients from this viewpoint being the four bearers on whose backs these stocks were normally transported – and even they were not totally disinterested. Stock losses, or 'leakage', a common enough problem in the supermarkets of today, was not entirely unknown in the heart of Africa.

Leaving the rhinos and other attractive targets in the area to fight amongst themselves, the hunting party set their minds firmly on the most direct route to the coast, and in due course picked up the trails and then the tracks that led them into the busy port of Mombasa. There they enjoyed the rare pleasure of a well-stocked bar, bedrooms and baths in the best hotel.

As Miss Millicent Martini lay in soak, much relieved after what had been for her the most exhausting and the most tedious few months of her life, she too decided it was time to review the situation.

The opportunity to go on a hunting safari in Africa with her rich uncle Ivor had at the time seemed like a dream come true – a chance to get away from the restrictions of home, to 'see the world' and maybe let rip a bit. Momma and Pa had provided her with a limited kitty, and also, unfortunately, limited scope as well under the eagle eye of Aunt Donna.

'Oh for some freedom and a chance to commit a sin or two,' were the unladylike thoughts that were passing through her mind as she lathered her shapely legs.

She was of course well aware of the interest being shown by Percy Underwood. She had made a fairly accurate assessment of his type and his intentions, and could see that there were some advantages to be gained by a flirtation with the hand of experience. She was not beyond planning an encounter which she could at once enjoy and also manipulate, and she was in some measure responsible for creating the impression in his eyes of having substantial funds of her own.

Such are the machinations and frailties of human nature, even in someone as attractively innocent as Miss Millicent Martini.

The Bull was also laying his plans. A visit to the docks had established that the liner *Trumpeter* was due in the following day from Durban, and heading north through the Suez Canal. That sounded perfect to him, and he booked a berth to England straight away and told the others of his plans.

The Pyles had it in mind to do something similar, but certainly not on the same ship as the Bull. Given the choice, they would not even be on the same continent. It suited Donna anyway to have more time to recover from the trauma of the safari and the uninvited guest, and she informed her niece of their decision.

Percy decided it was time to make a positive move. He had no intention or capacity to afford the cost of the cruise, even with the fee due from Ivor Pyle, and even if he forgot to pay the bearers, which was very likely indeed. He knocked on the door of Miss Martini's room and was invited in.

'Thought we might have a little chat, Millie – last night together and all that. Fancy a little farewell drink?'

He produced a flask of whiskey and she found the glasses.

'Where are you going then?... I expected you to be around for a while after a journey like that.'

She gave him an encouraging smile.

'Yes, pity,' he said, 'but I fancy to take some time off from my business and cruise up to the Med... It's been nice knowing you though... pity we couldn't have time to get to know each other a little better.'

He topped up her glass.

'Sounds wonderful... always wanted to cruise the Mediterranean. Maybe I'll get there with Uncle Ivor.'

She wrinkled her nose.

'They wouldn't let you go on ahead, I suppose?'

He moved onto the settee beside her.

'Not a chance.' A long pause. 'Not if they knew about it, that is.'

Both glasses were now empty and Percy applied the *coup de grâce*, emptying the flask into their glasses and closing the gap between them in the process.

'You could leave a note,' he suggested, 'tell them you'll be in the care of the Colonel as far as Port Said.'

265

Some care that would be, thought Millie, who had already noted the gleam in that worthy's eyes whenever their paths had crossed in the course of the trip.

'The trouble is,' went on Percy, 'I don't have the necessary cash immediately on hand, and we would need to move quickly – if you're on, that is.'

By this time his arm was around her waist, resistance – thanks to the bourbon – was falling and the temperature was rising.

She fell. 'I can manage that, and it would be rather fun.'

There followed further developments of a more personal nature into which no reader would wish to pry.

GUM-GUM

4

Gum-Gum

The river gunboat *Lady Luck* and her skipper Rusty McGinty, who figured so regularly in the dreams of the Bull, made slow progress on their return journey downstream towards the Mediterranean. Apart from occasional stops to barter for food from villagers or to collect timber for the ship's boiler, there was a tedious monotony to the daily routine that soon began to break down the high spirits brought about by the absence of the Colonel.

Chalky White, his ex-batman, was so affected on one or two occasions as to miss the commotion he had become accustomed to, and was even heard once to express some sympathy for that gentleman, especially when he was shown a photograph of his wife, Lady Buckmaster, which Gloria Bumpkin had found amongst his 'things', and he imagined going home to that. It was probably the first time such a sentiment had ever been

267

attributable to consideration of the Bull. Such is the debilitating effect of tedium.

The native porters lived a sort of separate existence on the foredeck, taking their turn on the wheel when required and playing their own form of ludo the rest of the time, punctuated by periodical fights and a little jocular blood-letting. It was never allowed to become too serious and no more than two ears and three or four fingers were lost in the entire voyage.

Rusty McGinty, his crew Charlie Perkins, and Chalky White passed a lot of the time playing cards. At first they tried to involve Gloria Bumpkin, but they soon discovered that thinking was not a strong element in her make-up, and she seemed to find it difficult to concentrate on a hand of cards for longer than two minutes at a time, even when she was holding four aces. Perhaps her weakness in matters of such importance had contributed to the obvious cooling off of her romance with the skipper, which in turn might explain why she found herself spending a lot more time in the galley. At such times she could feel so low as to remember the Colonel with a slight twinge of conscience.

The trouble with playing poker for any length of time is the need to have some form of currency with which to bet. Without it the game loses its purpose, and in a very short space of time this problem became paramount. Having started by playing for all the Bull's possessions, which now belonged to Charlie Perkins, they had played for the ship's dinghy, which now belonged to Chalky White, and then for the ship, which Charlie won with three jacks.

So it came about that Gloria Bumpkin became the 'kitty' on a night-by-night basis, and the game livened up again.

The outcome of the game was two weeks with Chalky

CHALKY WHITE   RUSTY McGINTY   CHARLIE PERKINS

White and six weeks with Charlie Perkins, and the problem to be faced at the conclusion was how to explain the situation to Miss Bumpkin. To their surprise they discovered this would not be necessary. Evidently you could hear far more from the galley than they supposed, especially if you stopped cooking, and they were treated not only to an earful of abuse from the 'kitty' but no meal either.

It transpired that what she found particularly upsetting was the six weeks with Charlie Perkins being won with nothing more than a pair of tens.

More might have followed had they not been interrupted by a change in the 'thump thump thump' of the engine, in favour of a 'ger-thump ger-thump ger-thump' followed by an ominous grinding sound and then... silence.

It is in a crisis like this that the professional expertise of the Captain comes into play, or should do. In this particular case, however, that expertise was not immediately available, due to the Captain's indisposition. This condition had been brought about by an extra-large intake of the Colonel's gin, which Rusty had hidden away as 'Captain's perks' and now thought to be appropriate to use in celebration of losing Gloria Bumpkin. He was flat out.

Charlie went below to check on the engine and was able to confirm that it was still there, and that it was not working. That was about the full extent of his technical ability beyond pouring in water for the boiler and stoking up the fire, and it substantially upstaged Chalky White in that department.

The vessel drifted on gently with the tide, turning and twisting as the mood took it, having no steerage way. It was Gloria who was the first to notice they were heading directly for some shallows, and announced it with a fit of screaming followed by a flood of tears, with the result that one of the porters found it impossible to concentrate on his game of ludo. He stood up, picked up the anchor he had been sitting on, threw it over the side, made the line fast and returned to his game.

Had Gloria not stopped screaming, she might well have suffered a similar fate.

Rusty McGinty woke up the next morning with a bad head and bad news. He established that the engine had seized up due to overheating, due to lack of coolant flow, due to a blocked inlet. Somebody would have to go over the side, dive under, and clear the blockage. So much for the technical bit – next came the human factor, and he started by asking for a volunteer.

Sadly, there was no response even when one of his precious bottles of gin was put up as a reward. This lack of community spirit in face of such a generous offer was probably connected with the intermittent bellowing of the hippopotamus family nearby and the regular sightings of one particularly ugly-looking crocodile who seemed to think this was his, or her, territory. (Nobody present was prepared to establish the sex of the animal.)

His sex was in fact of no great interest or importance to the crocodile either, as he was getting on in years and was known by the local tribe as 'Gum-Gum'. His teeth were not what they used to be, and he had become a bit of a loner, living on similarly aging fish and a few scraps thrown to him by the villagers now and then. He was curious about the arrival of the *Lady Luck* on his patch, but was glad of some company and not disposed to be unfriendly. He hoped they might even learn to throw him a few fish heads or something. He tried giving them a winning smile and wagging his tail but gave up after a day or two and lost interest, until he saw a complete body being lowered over the side and decided to go over and introduce himself.

The body was that of Captain Rusty McGinty, and his predicament came about by sheer incompetence at the card table.

It had taken three days of haggling before all on board agreed to take their chance on the turn of a card. All, that is, with the exception of Gloria, on the grounds that once she was over the side there was no certainty that anyone would pull her back, on top of which the job would certainly not get done.

For Rusty to have drawn the dreaded joker from his own pack of cards was considered very careless, and he got his deserts. At least Rusty knew the whereabouts of the offending inlet hole and what to do about it, and without wasting any time once he had been lowered over, he took a deep breath and dived down to it.

Gum-Gum made for the last known sighting, and all on board watched with grim fascination, hoping that if the worst happened it would be after Rusty had cleared the obstruction and not before.

271

It was Charlie Perkins who felt he should try to do something for the skipper he had learnt to live with and endure. He remembered the remains of Gloria's latest efforts in the galley, which nobody had felt able to eat or dispose of. He dashed below and came back with a bowlful, and tossed it over the side in the hope of distracting the crocodile.

Of course it worked perfectly. Gum-Gum, with his aging senses, could hardly be expected to know from that distance that the food had been prepared by Gloria or he might have had second thoughts. To her credit, he did actually eat it with evident pleasure. Well done Gloria!

With the job completed, Rusty was brought back on board, and when he learned the full story he went so far as to present Charlie with the bottle of gin, and give Gloria freedom from the galley for two weeks, which gave pleasure all round. He even had a smile for Gum-Gum, who gave him a big smile back. It was unfortunately completely misunderstood.

The engine sprang into life, the anchor was weighed, and the routine restored, as they continued on their course for Port Said, leaving Gum-Gum puzzled and a little sad.

5

A Points Victory

Lt. Col. Sir Ferdinand Buckmaster, OBE (retired), boarded the liner *Trumpeter* soon after it docked. There was no dockside party to see him off, but there were one or two quiet thanksgiving celebrations in the hotel rooms.

Percy Underwood and Millicent Martini delayed until the last minute before boarding, and a note indicating that she would be in the care of the Colonel was left for the Pyles. They were surprised but not too bothered, having been provided with a suitable story to relay to her parents back home. They would take their time and follow on the next boat to meet her at Port Said. Donna Pyle's view was that anyone who chose to be in the company of the Bull for a moment longer than they had to be, must have been badly affected by the sun.

Ivor Pyle, on the other hand, could understand that Milicent's preference for a period of relief from his

273

beloved wife's chatter, even at the expense of being on the same ship as the Bull, had its attractions.

The sudden disappearance of Percy Underwood he put down to the demands of the porters for payment, and he much regretted having cleared his debt with the hunter so promptly. The hullabaloo they made outside their hotel was such an embarrassment that he had to pacify them with an *ex-gratia* settlement that he considered to be a loan until such time as he caught up with 'Mr Underhand', as he called him. He was not aware that he would be at the back of a very long queue.

The Colonel was shown to his cabin, where he took a quiet siesta before turning his attention to the bar and later to the dining room for dinner. It was a very hot evening and he took his jacket off and hung it on the back of his chair, as he noticed all the seasoned passengers from Durban were doing. From his seat in the corner he could watch the other diners, and having a natural nosiness and nothing better to do, he did so.

His first surprise was to see Miss Millicent Martini enter on the arm of a gentleman who looked vaguely familiar but he couldn't place. This was because Percy had shaved off his beard, had a short haircut, and was wearing respectable clothes. Millicent had been expecting to find the Colonel here and came straight over, leaving her escort to find a table as far away as possible. The Bull sprang to his feet and asked her to join him, which she did.

As the Bull made signals to the waiter, he noticed with increasing interest the activities of that familiar figure, her escort, so far unidentified, touching the jackets in passing, until his hand slid expertly into the inside pocket of one and transferred a sizeable wallet and passports into his own. He continued to a table on the far side of the room and made himself comfortable.

Millicent was busily explaining how she was going on

ahead of the Pyles with the intention of meeting up again at Port Said.

'Who did you say your partner was?' asked the Bull.

'Why, that's Percy Underwood. I discovered this afternoon that he was on board as well for a trip to the Med. Quite a coincidence.'

The Bull, who was now missing his Gloria Bumpkin rather badly, was well aware that this is the kind of coincidence that is never left to chance.

He smiled. 'I'll tell the waiter to ask him over to our table then.'

Percy seemed strangely sheepish when he arrived at the table.

'Didn't know you without the beard,' said the Bull, 'but I recognised the technique. Remember you from the Royal Hussars – didn't last long though, did you? A few strange shortages in the mess, I seem to remember.'

Percy began to fidget.

'Nothing strange in your pocket at the moment, I suppose,' went on the Colonel, 'no strange wallets or passports or anything like that?'

The waiter arrived and Millicent said she would like a large gin and tonic. The Colonel had the same and glanced at Percy, who seemed to have withered and lost his tongue. He didn't look at all well.

At this point the Bull, in a rare moment of diplomacy, made a most uncharacteristic offer, with the chivalrous intention of causing the minimum embarrassment to Millicent.

'Hand 'em over and I'll see that they are returned to the owners. And I warn you, Underwood, one more incident and the Captain will be informed.'

It was an offer that Percy could not refuse, and after obeying the order, he made himself as scarce as possible as soon as possible.

275

BASIL
BLENKINSOP

THE CARSTAIRS'

'You see all sorts in the regiment,' said the Bull. It was Millicent's opinion that even out of uniform you are not immune. The twinkle in the eye of the Colonel was further confirmation.

He was now busy glancing through the passports.

'Roger Carstairs.' Interesting.

'Sybil Carstairs. Née Featherstone-Phipps.'

The Colonel's presence in Africa had been solely for the purpose of tracking down the owner of that name, the Reverend Bruce Featherstone-Phipps, so he could be forgiven for an oath and a sharp intake of breath – several, in fact.

By training and instinct he was a man of action.

'Millie,' he said, 'come over to that table and extend your knowledge of human nature even further. It's that kind of day.'

They picked up their drinks and moved over to the table from which he had watched the pickpocketing take place. Before the couple could express their surprise, the Bull approached the gentleman, put out his hand and said, 'Roger Carstairs, I presume?' and sat down.

'Ever been to Kukukraali, Carstairs?'

If, instead, the Colonel had reached over and planted a fist between the gentleman's eyes, the effect would have been much the same. His expression was like that of Percy Underwood a few moments before, only worse. He hedged.

'No,' he said.

The Bull knew better; his target was in his sights and he was in full attack mode.

'Met a lady called Amelia there. She said your supper is getting cold and young Henry wants his pocket money.'

Before Carstairs could reply the Bull turned to his companion.

'Heard that after you left him, your Reverend husband

277

got into a bit of a stew.' (The Bull was rather proud of that one!) 'Boiled by the N'Chuyus, they tell me.'

Up to that moment he was quite enjoying himself, but it was not to last. Suddenly he felt a hand being placed firmly on his shoulder.

'We've just had a tip-off about you,' stated the owner of the hand, a tall, powerful-looking man in the uniform of a First Officer. 'Con man and pickpocket artist, eh? It just shows you never can tell. I believe you have this gentleman's wallet and passports. May I have them please?'

The Colonel's normally ruddy complexion paled, then deepened to a dangerous shade of purple.

He spluttered and choked as he reached into his pocket and took out the items in question. Momentarily he was speechless and Millicent too had been struck dumb.

Carstairs could hardly believe his luck, but he was quick to take advantage of it.

'Thank you officer, I'd no idea they had gone. Clever operators, these two, but I must say the gentleman was becoming rather tiresome... you won't let him loose for the rest of the journey, I hope?'

The Bull could stand no more. Underwood had pulled a really fast one and it was obvious that explanations were useless at this stage – his extreme frustration could only find relief in action. Shoving the officer to one side, he reached over to Carstairs and dealt the very blow between the eyes that has already been described.

In the first-class dining saloon of the liner *Trumpeter* a civilised tranquillity and decorum was the norm, enhanced by the quiet efficiency of the stewards and waiters. One could normally rely on the gentle buzz of conversation broken only by the intermittent popping of corks and the gurgle of flowing wine.

Unfortunately, tonight was to be an extreme exception.

No sooner had Carstairs been projected through the diners behind him and into their untouched prawn cocktails than the officer, one Basil Blenkinsop, in trying to restrain the Bull, collided with a loaded waiter and into the adjoining table, joining the three lady diners on the floor together with a tureenful of vichyssoise.

Without excusing himself, Basil left the ladies and swept straight back into the attack. The Bull, who was by now berserk with fury and bellowing louder than his namesake, demolished the tables and diners around him and prepared for the challenge.

The ship's log records a points victory for Basil, but that may have been somewhat biased. Certainly, the Bull was a credit to his regimental background, and it was only with the help of many crew and staff members that the raging knight was ultimately put to rest in a lock-up. The same would have happened to Millicent Martini had she not used the full range of her seductive charms on the battered and bewildered Basil.

Coffee was served in the lounge.

6

A Case for the Bull

By the time *Trumpeter* berthed at Port Said Millicent had convinced the ship's Captain that an injustice had been done. The Captain felt it necessary to point out that a lot of damage had also been done, not only to the dining saloon but to a ship's officer as well.

The ship's officer's suffering, which was soon no more than a bruised ego, had brought with it substantial compensation in the shapely form of Miss Martini, whose generous attention to restoring his morale was welcomed with enthusiasm.

Since the occasion of Percy Underwood's allegations to the Captain concerning the Colonel, nothing had been seen of him – a very wise decision on his part, especially once the Bull had been set free. To understand the Bull's mood as he stood on the stern deck watching the docking procedure, it would be helpful to visualise the

arrival of his namesake in a bullring, dazed and venge-
ful, pawing at the ground and trying to focus on any
worthwhile target.

And there it was, moored innocently to a nearby quay!
The *Lady Luck*.

In the bullring it is normal practice for the bull to
be distracted and stimulated by the attentions of the
picador. It was Percy Underwood who fulfilled this
role and provided the diversion. The Bull spotted him
moving rather stealthily down the gangplank carrying a
large suitcase.

The Bull's blood pressure was now at boiling point
and his adrenalin was overflowing. He moved like a
sprinter off the blocks, and although he lacked the horns
of his namesake, his snorting was certainly on a par and
so was the murderous gleam in his eye. He was not
built for sprinting, so it is greatly to his credit that he
was soon close enough to Percy for his presence to be
felt and his snorts to become audible. One glance over
his shoulder convinced Percy that desperate measures
were called for, so as his pursuer closed on him he let
go of his suitcase, which not only gave him a much
needed burst of speed but also sent the Bull sprawling
in the dust.

As in the bullring, the bull was now dazed and confused but well and truly roused. Having lost one target,
he was mindful that he might be in danger of losing the
more important one, so dusting himself down, he grabbed
the suitcase and headed back for the docks to find the
Lady Luck before that too could make another getaway.

He was long overdue for a bit of luck, and it came
when he discovered that the chase had brought him
almost onto the quay where he could see the *Lady Luck*
at her moorings. Still carrying the case, he went aboard
what appeared to be an empty vessel, and took a look

below decks, where he found his batman, Chalky White, and the other member of his original party, Miss Gloria Bumpkin, in a very friendly situation indeed.

His exclamation of 'What d'you think you're doing?' was not very likely to receive an honest answer but it served to break the silence and give them time to pull themselves together, or in this case, apart. Chalky then had to set his mind to the problem of how to explain that there were only two days left of his winning fortnight with Miss Bumpkin, and that she was then due to Charlie Perkins for six weeks as a result of a pair of tens.

He didn't get a chance.

'Where are the rest of them?' demanded the furious Bull.

'Ashore,' replied Chalky as he adjusted his dress, and Gloria said how pleased she was to see the Colonel again and asked after his health, whilst doing the same. Thanks to his sudden infusion of adrenalin, the Bull was thinking fast.

'Start the engine,' he ordered, and from long experience Chalky knew better than to disobey. The *Lady Luck* was in fact already prepared for the off, and awaited only the return of the shore party with victuals. Without further ado the Bull went on deck and cast off.

'Full speed ahead,' he shouted, taking the wheel and making for the open water.

Further along the quay Captain Rusty McGinty and Charlie Perkins, on their way back loaded with stores, watched with horror as the boat moved away and they could distinctly make out the familiar figure of Lt. Col. Sir Ferdinand Buckmaster, OBE (retired), at the wheel.

McGinty moved fast. A large Arab dhow was moored on a temporary line close at hand, and ordering Charlie to follow, he jumped on board, complete with stores, and cast off, setting the lanteen sail and heading in the

direction taken by *Lady Luck*. This act of piracy was witnessed by the owner of the dhow sitting with his friends nearby and up to that moment enjoying a quiet hookah with them. He made it plain that he was unhappy with what he saw by leaping into the air and uttering phrases in Arabic which would be understandable in any language. His fellow fishermen offered to help, and after suitable negotiations regarding the cost, they all piled into another dhow and set off in pursuit.

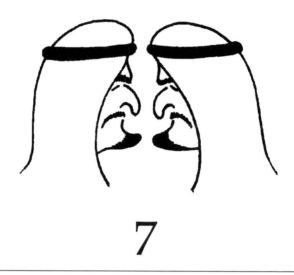

7

Follow that Dhow

Aboard *Trumpeter* the Captain was addressing a large assembly of disgruntled passengers from whose cabins a selection of wallets, cash and jewellery had been taken, and not returned. This must have happened overnight and complaints had been building up since before break-fast, and increasing as passengers went back to their own cabins from wherever they had spent the night.

He was now able to inform them that there was a good chance of recovery thanks to the alertness of the officer on morning watch. He had distinctly seen the Colonel, so recently released from custody, running along the nearby quay carrying a large suitcase, leaping aboard a small river gun-boat and heading out to sea. A ship's tender was being lowered at that moment, and a party under the command of First Officer Basil Blenkinsop would be sent in pursuit.

The ship was docked against the port side, from which the ship's tender was normally launched, so the vessel they lowered on the starboard side was not the one in regular use. This was bad luck on its inhabitants, Mr and Mrs Roger Carstairs, who had taken up residence in it at Durban and had successfully stowed away this far, enjoying first-class meals to boot. When the cover was removed and they splashed down into the harbour, their privacy was suddenly rudely invaded by several members of the ship's crew who started up the engine and set out to sea without a word of apology.

The Carstairs thought it advisable not to complain and packed up their comfortable little home, folded the camp bed and prepared their luggage for disembarkation at the first opportunity. Had they known that they were now desperately chasing after the Bull, they might well have jumped for it there and then.

Their pinnace was a good deal faster than the aging *Lady Luck*. It soon overtook a dhow in which they saw a group of unusually animated Arabs dancing about the deck and making threatening gesticulations, and then another, sailed to their surprise by a wild-eyed red-headed helmsman and a white crew member in the bow acting as look-out and pointing excitedly at a small ship on the horizon. The *Lady Luck* appeared to be a very popular attraction.

Half-an-hour later they were in hailing distance, but the messages they exchanged once the Bull and Basil recognised each other are best not recorded. When the pinnace drew level and the Bull could also make out Roger Carstairs and Sybil amongst the pursuers, his rage knew no bounds, and if the ancient river gun-boat had still been capable of its original function, another full-scale naval action would have been added to the colourful history of Port Said.

285

Fortunately, Chalky White could see the futility of the prolonged exchange of insults and he cut the engine. With only a few light casualties, the boarding party overcame the Bull and on the orders of the First Officer the suitcase was brought up on deck and thrown open.

Percy Underwood was not the most fastidious of men, and his dirty washing was by no means attractive either to gaze upon or to smell. Its prime use seemed to be as protective wrapping for a quantity of gin and whisky bottles, and the only other objects of any interest in the case were several packs of marked playing cards. Gradually it dawned on Basil that the unlikely story the Colonel was now blasting at them might be true, and it was certainly clear that the Bull could never have got into any of the clothes in the case he had been carrying.

It was Chalky White who came up with the best suggestion so far.

'Why don't we check out one or two of the bottles, just to see if it is the genuine article?'

There was a general murmur of agreement, especially from Miss Bumpkin. Glasses were produced, a truce was declared, a party spirit developed and bonhomie took over, with the inclusion of a tired, mollified and thirsty Colonel, but the exclusion of the Carstairs. They were strangely subdued, and it was the first time on record that Roger Carstairs had left any drink in any bottle.

When the first of the dhows arrived, the party was well under way and they scarcely noticed the bumping as it tied up alongside. They soon became aware of Rusty McGinty, however, who had plenty to say about his ship being stolen, until the Bull became roused again and started to square up and bring to the surface all the pent-up fury he had felt since being abandoned in the depths of Africa.

To the disappointment of all on board, who were

looking forward to a first-class Bull fight, they were interrupted at that point by the arrival of the second dhow, followed by a boarding party of irate Arabs. Without ceremony they grabbed Rusty and Charlie and threw them straight over the side and then looked around for any objectors. To their surprise and disappointment there weren't any. Everybody, with just two exceptions, was clearly in the mood to enjoy entertainment of that kind, and they were even more surprised to be offered a drink by a very mellow First Officer to celebrate their timely arrival.

It was a very sober and bedraggled McGinty and Charlie Perkins who were climbing back on board when they noticed the furtive activities of Roger Carstairs, who had remained with his wife in the pinnace. He appeared to be pulling out from under the thwart some kind of a hold-all. It was evidently heavy, and he was lugging it to the side with the clear intention of throwing it over, which he did.

Strangely, there was no splash.

Only then did he realise that one of the dhows was tied alongside at that point. McGinty and Charlie climbed into it and a remarkable sight met their eyes. They let out a cry that brought everybody to the rail of *Lady Luck*, unfortunately causing many of them to spill their drinks.

The bag had burst open and sprayed over the floor of the dhow was a fortune in cash and jewellery. The owner of the dhow, being a quick thinker, said what a pleasure the visit had been and jumped into it to take his leave. His friends also remembered urgent appointments and jumped aboard, followed very closely by Basil and his men. They became heavily engaged.

Captain McGinty and Charlie Perkins clambered onto *Lady Luck* and took stock of the situation. The pinnace containing its helmsman and the Carstairs was still tied alongside, and attached to it were the two dhows rocking violently under a squabbling mass of ship's crew and Arabs. The Bull was below, flat out, and Chalky White was closing in on Gloria in a romantic haze of unfinished business and obviously having in mind the proximity of the hand-over date.

It seemed like the right moment to cast off the pinnace and all its attachments and to set a course for the open sea.

So that's what they did.

8

Treasure Island

Now with her familiar Captain at the controls, the *Lady Luck* chugged happily out into the Mediterranean. McGinty's normal area of operations was this coastal strip and the Nile, and he set his present course only for the purpose of leaving trouble behind, rather than planning to go anywhere in particular.

They had managed to get their stores on board before leaving, and McGinty was comforted, in purely financial terms, also by the thought that he had the Colonel back on board with access to funds from the Limpet family solicitor, Eustace Pratt. He might have taken a different approach to things had he known that that particular source of revenue had been sealed off long ago, and it is highly probable that at this moment the Bull would have found himself seated in one of the dhows back in the harbour.

The Mediterranean is a moody sea. For much of its time the sun pours down on a surface as calm as a lake, but just like Gloria Bumpkin when she heard about Charlie's winning pair of tens and all it implied, the mood can change rapidly and become very black indeed. The clouds gathered, early darkness fell, and so did the rain, in ever increasing intensity. A heavy storm drove them further and further out to sea in a direction known only to the gods – certainly not to McGinty.

As the *Lady Luck* rode out the mountainous seas she regularly lifted her tail out of the water and the propeller roared in the freedom of the open air, until anyone listening would have heard a loud, ominous 'clunk', and it stopped.

But nobody on board was particularly interested at the time.

The Colonel on the saloon floor snored vigorously, Chalky White in his hammock slept with a smile on his face as he swung to and fro, while Gloria was too busy being ill to do what she desperately wanted to do – scream. Rusty and Charlie, far too sober for their liking after having missed out on most of the party, battened down everything so far as that was possible, crossed their fingers, and looked for the remaining dregs in the bottles as they rolled around the cabin floor.

If there was any way of knowing which direction was taken by the *Lady Luck* in that storm, the precise track would have been laid out on the detailed chart given

NOT TO SCALE

BUNKHAM-ON-OUSE

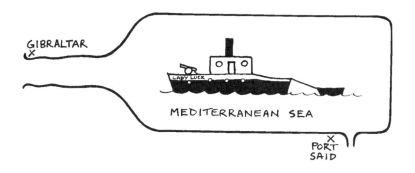

GIBRALTAR

LADY LUCK

MEDITERRANEAN SEA

PORT SAID

KUKUKRAALI ✗

above, for the reader's guidance. Unfortunately this information was never available.

A reference to the ship's log for that period provides only several pages of multi-coloured stains which still exude a whiff of alcohol, and what is presumed to be a contribution from Miss Bumpkin sealing the next two pages firmly together.

As to time, days and nights passed almost indistinguishably, and the ship's chronometer, normally set permanently at 18.00 hours (opening time), had jumped off the panelling and was now afloat on the saloon floor together with half-a-dozen empty bottles.

The Colonel had at some stage heaved himself onto a bunk to get clear of the water and was now preparing Daily Routine Orders. It had become a pleasant sunny morning, the sea was calm, bodies were stirring, and all were famished. Gloria was despatched to the galley

291

under the close supervision of Chalky White, while the skipper and his crew set about pumping out the bilges and trying to get under way.

'Where to?' was the question, and it was answered in part when Charlie gave a cry of 'Land ho' and pointed to it appearing slowly out of the morning haze.

There was a mountainous background to the tree-lined shore, and they gently drifted in a light breeze towards it. The engine still failed to respond, and after trying unsuccessfully everything that in the past had solved her problems, McGinty had to admit defeat. Paying no attention to the Daily Routine Orders presented to him by the Colonel, he concentrated instead on giving what guidance he could to the progress they were making and ordering Chalky to stand by with the anchor in case of need.

When they drifted into a little bay and the shallows could be seen, it was put to good use.

By this time the cooking smells from the galley had become so irresistible that despite Gloria's presence at the stove everything the least bit edible disappeared without trace – so ravenous was the ship's company. Only then did they take time to study their surroundings with any interest.

What they saw was a small wooden jetty, and near to it set in the trees a high vertical timber palisade enclosing a large hut. There was no sign of human activity.

A landing party was assembled consisting of the Colonel, inevitably, with Chalky White, his ex-NCO, having no choice, Charlie Perkins because he had once read *Treasure Island*, and Gloria, just to get her out of the way and on terra firma. The dinghy, which had survived the storm by being taken on board, was soon made ready, and they set off for the jetty, leaving Rusty to do battle with the engine. Once ashore they made for the stockade, peering through it and wandering round until they found a gate. From it hung a chain and a large padlock which appeared to have been prised open.

'I'll do a recce,' ordered the Colonel, 'stand guard and wait for me here.' He went through and they watched him enter the hut.

What happened next takes longer to tell than it did to occur. There were loud cries from inside the hut, the sounds of a scuffle, and several familiar bellows from the Bull. Unpleasantness was clearly afoot and judging from the number of voices, the Bull was sufficiently out-numbered to cast doubt on the wisdom of going to his aid. In an instant and with great presence of mind they all concluded this was a case where discretion should be the better part of valour, and they covered the distance to the dinghy so fast they had trouble pulling up and tumbled into it as one body. Somehow it stayed afloat, they cast off and rowed hard for the *Lady Luck* before daring to look back.

They saw the Bull being escorted out of the stockade by four very dishevelled uniformed men. The Bull him-self was less than immaculate and must have given a good account of himself, but now his hands were tied behind his back and a strip of his shirt had been used as a gag. The ship's company were sympathetic with his captors on this point.

They pointed to the *Lady Luck* and then, leaving a man with a rifle standing guard on the beach, set off on a small track and in time could be seen to disappear over the brow of a hill.

Rusty McGinty watched with the others and then went back to work on the engine with added zeal.

Nobody on board was in any doubt what they would have done next if the engine had been serviceable.

293

9

A Wee Gudgeon Pin

The next day, in the absence of any Daily Routine Orders, the skipper and crew concocted a plan of action. Gloria became a key figure in it and when it was put to her as a starring role there was no problem. While Rusty and Charlie worked on the engine Chalky took Gloria ashore, their purpose being to make contact with the guard, who was clearly bored, and try a little fraternising, a role for which Gloria was type cast. Their reception was not unfriendly and at the first opportunity Chalky excused himself to go off and collect wood for the boiler, leaving Gloria to 'overcome' the guard.

There was no contest, and as the pair disappeared into the undergrowth Chalky was able to sneak into the hut and examine the contents. He found himself in a sort of Aladdin's Cave made up of barrels and crates, caskets full of jewels and golden trinkets, an armoury of guns and ammunition, and...

He didn't stop to complete the inventory or to take more than just the one bottle of unidentified spirit before getting out and into the cover of the trees at top speed.

Back on board, Rusty announced to Charlie that the engine was useless due to what he described as 'a wee broken pin in the gudgeon', so they took 'a wee dram o' commissary water' up on deck and watched events on shore. They were just in time to experience two shocks in quick succession.

Coming down the path from the hills were the three soldiers who had taken away the Colonel, and he was trailing along behind, no longer tied up and unnaturally quiet. He had had a day and a night to discover that they could not understand a word he was bellowing and weren't interested anyway, and had tended to use the gag whenever it was necessary for peace and quiet. They had reached the conclusion that his profile did not fit that of any pirate or smuggler they ever been trained to deal with, and that being their purpose on the island, he was no more than a nuisance they could well do without. In this judgement they were not alone.

The second shock for Rusty and Charlie was the sound of another vessel motoring into the bay. They quickly took refuge below and watched developments through a porthole. The land party also saw the approaching craft and hurriedly found cover in the trees surrounding the stockade. This came as an unwelcome surprise to the guard and Gloria who, without the benefit of a common tongue or a formal introduction of any kind, were busily enjoying each other's company.

While the guard received a dressing down from his officer, Gloria dressed up and joined Chalky in the undergrowth bordering the sands. From there they watched as four unsavoury-looking characters came ashore from another craft similar in size to *Lady Luck* that had appeared at anchor close by. They looked very suspiciously at the small dinghy and then, brandishing wicked-looking knives, made for the entrance to the stockade and entered the hut.

With rifles cocked, the waiting soldiers followed them in. Wasting no time, Chalky and Gloria dashed for their dinghy, pushed off and paddled like mad for the *Lady Luck*. Whether or not they heard the shouts of the Bull as they did so we shall never know – either way it is probable that their actions would have been no different. The Bull certainly didn't take the hint if it was one, and released the second dinghy, scrambled in, and rowed for his life.

By the time he had splashed his way to the *Lady Luck* and clambered aboard, he was in time to see that Rusty and Charlie had taken the other dinghy across to the visitors' vessel and were busy in its engine room. Ashore he could see four uniformed figures jumping up and down, and four more who were quite incapable of doing so due to fatigue, injuries and handcuffs.

When Rusty and his crew returned from the pirates' ship, they had with them not only 'a wee gudgeon pin' but a few other useful spares, together with a dinghyful of victuals and a stock of hooch and wines to match, in volume rather than quality, the Colonel's original order from Harrods.

Some rifle fire from the shore stimulated Rusty to complete his work without delay, and celebrations only began in earnest when the engine burst into life, they waved farewell to the figures on the shore, and headed for the open sea.

10

Pyles of Flotsam

In the spring of 1907 the cruise liner SS *Colander, en route* from Port Said to Southampton, sank in the eastern Mediterranean. The news, when it reached them the following day, caused Lloyds to ring their bell and *The Times* newspaper to give it a few inches of space where they ran short of copy at the bottom of page 17. For the passengers the event was of more immediate importance, particularly for a pair of American tourists and their niece who was in their care.

The Pyles had boarded the ill-fated ship at Port Said, after finding Millicent Martini there and enforcing a separation, deemed to be temporary, from her new heart-throb, First Officer Basil Blenkinsop. The promised voyage through the Mediterranean was only a few days old when the ship foundered on rocks which the navigator was confident he had laid a course to easily clear.

First Officer Thomas Alcock, who was at the helm at the time, made the excuse that his attention had been distracted for much of his watch by a young American lady seeming to be specially interested in First Officers, but his story was judged to be no more than a fantasy. The fact that a young lady fitting her description had occupied the same lifeboat as him and was later rescued from the same nearby island was not allowed to cloud their judgement.

When the collision took place and the stricken ship came to a juddering halt, it happened that the Pyles had been leaning on the rail at the bow. Donna Pyle was busy explaining to her husband how she proposed to build extensions onto their 'little place back home' to accommodate the new carpets she had purchased from a very friendly little man in the Egyptian market at what he had assured her were 'give away' prices. And all that furniture too.

They shot straight over the bows so fast that Donna's mouth was still open when she hit the water. The unusual silence bothered Ivor Pyle, but after splashing around and struggling to keep his head above water he found her clinging to a large roll of carpets – part of the flotsam escaping through the gaping hole in the ship's side. He was pleased to notice that it had her name on it, and it was also on the large wooden cocktail cabinet which he clung onto.

While the rest of the passengers were being rescued and carefully shepherded into the ship's lifeboats and taken to the nearby dry land, the Pyles, having been projected clear of them all, found themselves drifting away and could do nothing about it, with Ivor still gurgling and Donna momentarily silenced. By the time she was back to normal in that department, they had drifted out of sight of the sinking ship, the roll of carpets was sinking fast and the cocktail cabinet was not much better. Their loss of value, possible total, caused Ivor to take a broader, more overall view of his finances and what his death duties would amount to, hoping he would be shown to be worth a lot more than his neighbours, the Oppenheimers, who had always managed to go one up on his automobiles.

Donna's thoughts were on their obituary notices – how many and which papers they would go into. She was concerned too about what would happen to her new mink wrap, and hoping it would not fall into the hands, or onto the shoulders, of that dreadful niece of hers in Boston.

She was in the throes of discussing these matters with her husband when she let out a scream and pointed to the smoke from a small ship bearing down on them, to be seen clearly only when they rose to the top of the swell. The closer it got, the louder she screamed.

On board the *Lady Luck* the skipper had already noticed the flotsam and had slowed down to look for anything useful. Although the Pyles did not qualify under that heading and despite the warning given by the Colonel, who could not fail to recognise that voice, they went over to see what was the problem. The ship's rope ladder was put over the side and the Pyles were invited aboard. They in turn pointed out that the carpets and cocktail cabinet were their purchases for back home and asked how they could be expected to get them up a rope ladder.

Rusty thought for a moment then said if they would wait there, he would go below and consult his price-list for cargo of such value, depending of course on where they would like it delivered. Meanwhile he poured himself a large tot of his native spirit.

They clambered on board. The Colonel snorted.

The Pyles saw him and fainted.

While the new passengers aboard *Lady Luck* were below decks recovering from their ordeal and mourning the loss of their bargain purchases, Rusty did some thinking. It was clear from a few of the more lucid comments made by the Colonel that the Pyles were American tourists on an extensive holiday, which suggested the presence of money. So did the mass of pearls, diamond brooches and rings worn by Donna Pyle. The money belt worn by Ivor Pyle confirmed it.

Rusty could sense his financial interest in the Bull withering away and a new source of income, with far more potential, in the process of development. As a result the Pyles were given the largest cabin and made as comfortable as the *Lady Luck* allowed, and a decree was issued that under no circumstances were they to be fed with anything cooked by Gloria. When they had sufficiently recovered, Rusty took a few bottles of the pirates' hooch into their cabin and started negotiations.

Ivor expressed his gratitude for the rescue at the same time as his wife said what a dinky little boat it was and suggested to Ivor that they must get one for the grandchildren to play with in the lake, when they got back home. She went on to apologise for having lost all the lovely photographs of all the family she always carried with her for the entertainment of her friends, and reassured him that there were lots of copies back home that she would be able to send him. She described how they included some sweet studio studies of her daughter Mary Lou from the age of two right up to her wedding and beyond.

Rusty said how nice that would be, and gave her the Colonel's address.

While she was still drawing breath, Rusty quickly enquired where he could take them and Ivor expressed the wish to get to any port where they might pick up another liner. The *Lady Luck*'s present position being nowhere in particular, Rusty decided to aim west for Gibraltar, which he knew to be a long way away but at the narrow end of the Mediterranean and therefore theoretically unmissable. Cash in advance resulted in a substantial transfer of dollars from the money belt into Rusty's safe keeping.

For the first day or two of the voyage the Colonel was strangely withdrawn and subdued. This was attributable to an early encounter between himself and Donna Pyle, when she had cornered him in his cabin to discuss her little place back home, her family, her daughter Mary Lou and her lovely grandchildren, and other similar subjects of general interest.

This time when the moment came for her to draw breath the Colonel took over with an expression of his views on Americans in general and the Pyles, their home, their daughter Mary Lou and her lovely grandchildren in particular. It seems he had then been struck on the head by one of Gloria's handbags, borrowed and wielded with surprising power and accuracy by Donna, who strongly objected to being interrupted.

In the period of peace and calm that followed, both Gloria and Donna were encouraged to learn how to steer the ship and stoke the boiler, thus freeing the Captain, Charlie Perkins and Chalky White to get the cards out again, and they made the mistake of inviting Ivor Pyle to join them, though it seemed like a good idea at the time. Since the only money on board was now in 'safe keeping' and Rusty had no intention of putting it at risk against nothing better than 'markers', they fell back on playing for the 'kitty' as before.

To their surprise Ivor cleaned up, finally winning six weeks with Gloria with a magnificent full house, kings on queens. (Gloria quite liked the sound of that.)

'If you don't mind, fellas,' Ivor murmured, 'I'd like to take a rain-check on that.'

When on the following day Rusty, Charlie and Chalky found they had each won two weeks with Donna Pyle, they began to realise that they were in the hands of a very sharp operator, and rather carelessly allowed the cards to blow away.

By the third day a strong tail wind was blowing and the Captain had the idea of setting a sail on the signalling mast. Sheets were tied together to form a makeshift spinnaker and immediately produced a very noticeable acceleration. In celebration they went below and liberated another barrel of the pirates' hooch.

It is a measure of its proof value that within the hour they had become, under the baton of Ivor Pyle, a fiercely vociferous barbershop quartet, making up in enthusiasm what might possibly be lacking in harmony. Goodwill broke out to such an extent that when the Bull started to hammer on his cabin partition he was invited to join them, and after a few trial shots of the hooch, he too fell under its spell and flabbergasted the ship's company by contributing several regimental choruses rarely heard outside the Mess.

Taking turns at the wheel of *Lady Luck*, Gloria and Donna failed to enjoy this uninhibited entertainment as much as the choir would have expected, although Gloria did find some relief in Donna's inability to compete with it. It was during this extraordinary night of hilarity that Gloria noticed with passing interest some lights on land, first on one side of the boat and then on the other, but they were gone before anybody surfaced in the morning and she thought nothing more of it.

It took several days for the ship's quintet to recover, and when they finally took food and went on deck they found little to interest them. The tail wind seemed to have strengthened, the seas had built up, and the horizon was empty, so they lashed the helm, put the women back on duty and went below for a 'hair of the dog'. In this way the days passed unnoticed, uncounted and unlogged, until over two weeks later a crisis caused Captain Rusty to take stock of the situation.

The crisis was the dire depletion of stocks of hooch. They were in fact draining the last dregs from the last barrel. Due to the ship's motion, the women had taken the minimum of concern for the galley or its contents, and when Rusty checked on the victuals he discovered they were down to their last dry biscuit. As for fuel, the last of the logs had already gone and they would have to start on the furniture and the barrels.

A few days more, now on starvation diet, they began to look at each other and visualise who would be the first sacrifice and make a worthwhile meal, while Rusty, still a little hazy, pondered the surprising length of the Mediterranean. Even to a strictly Nile navigator it was pretty clear that they should have seen land before now, and he was upset to think that he had substantially undercharged Ivor Pyle for the voyage. Just as he was wondering how to go about re-negotiating the deal there was a loud cry from Charlie.

'Land ho!'

The entire ship's company crowded onto the foredeck,

full of excitement for their first view of the famous Rock of Gibraltar. The *Lady Luck* threaded her way past a couple of small islands, and they found themselves heading for the harbour of a sizeable town.

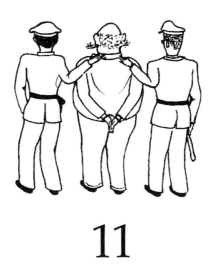

11

Have a Nice Day

Miami, that beautiful American city in sunny Florida inhabited by a happy community, was renowned for giving a warm welcome to the many strange visitors arriving on its shores. The harbourmaster was nevertheless at a loss when hailed by a large fierce red-faced gentleman on the bows of a visiting river gun-boat who demanded to know what they had done with the Rock and the apes.

The *Lady Luck* was by then tied up to the quay, and the Colonel went on to ask for a copy of *The Times*, when would the next liner to Blighty be in, and why didn't the man pull himself together, smarten up and give some answers instead of standing there like some sort of dumb freak?

The answer was only a few minutes arriving and took the form of a small squad of harbour police. They

305

handcuffed the Colonel and led him down the gang-plank and away, as he went on to make heated enquiries about 'What the hell are you damned yanks doing here anyway?' Within an hour, for the sake of peace and quiet at the station, he was returned to the ship with a strong recommendation that they have him put away. Charlie immediately asked for directions to the nearest asylum, but a plea from Gloria saved the day. It was Rusty's suggestion that perhaps they should invite Lady Buckmaster to join them and take charge that success-fully silenced him, and they had no further trouble from the Bull, who made for the nearest bar.

When customs officers visited the ship they were quickly convinced there was very little to inspect, and they wasted no time in leaving when the liquor crisis became apparent and Donna began giving them the full details of their safari holiday, starting with the planning stages back in little old New York, USA.

While the ship's company went off in search of food, Ivor Pyle sought the mail office and sent an urgent cable.

To Pyle and Peabody Pyle Tower New York stop Safari and cruise holiday over stop Not recom-mended stop Send Arbuckle here immediately with ample cash stop Pyle Gibraltar stop Collect stop

He then relaxed and joined the party at the bar/restaurant.

In New York, his butler was roused from his boredom and given the instructions, and his beady eyes lit up as he foresaw the opportunity for travel and adventure he had always yearned for. He packed a small bag of per-sonal effects and a large bag of money, and caught the liner *Bolognaise*, first stop Gibraltar.

On arrival six days later, Arbuckle made enquiries for Mr Pyle at the shipping office and received only a blank

ARBUCKLE

look, but he was pleasantly surprised to get an immediate response from a gentleman standing nearby.

It is an accepted fact that bad pennies have a habit of 'turning up', and the several extraordinary coincidences about to be experienced by Arbuckle serve only to illustrate how fickle is the finger of fate.

Percy Underwood had just arrived by 'stowaway steerage' from Port Said and beyond. To him the name 'Pyle' was synonymous with 'money' and he steered Arbuckle to the nearest bar for a chat. They took less than two bottles of Rioja to discover that they had a lot in common, and that Arbuckle had with him in cash the key to a beautiful friendship and a bright future.

And so it might have been, but for that fickle finger of fate.

They started well enough, booking a passage on the *Arcadia*, calling first at Port Said. Percy found Arbuckle, who proved to be no slouch with a pack of cards, very quick to learn the art of partnering him at the table, and also a great asset with his ability to insinuate himself into the confidence of wealthy schools of gamblers. After a few days they began building very successfully on the small fortune that had come their way.

Their evident wealth and development of it did not go unnoticed by a couple who, these days, made it their business to take an interest in such matters. The couple's accommodation was their customary lifeboat, stowing away having become a necessary lifestyle in the reduced circumstances of Roger and Sybil Carstairs, but they were tiring of it rapidly.

The Carstairs had decided they would be better off returning to Roger's old way of life in central Africa if he could just clear his debts there. When they disembarked at Port Said, they ensured that this would be possible by carrying with them that well-travelled, well-endowed suitcase they had taken, without asking, from the cabin of Mr Arbuckle.

In exchange they did leave Percy and Arbuckle a pack of marked cards with which to start again from scratch, and rumour has it that they boarded a river steamer and headed for Kukukraali.

AMBROSE + BELLE
NICKLEGRUBBER

12

P and P

Pyle and Peabody's Prescriptions were, of course, known throughout the USA and so was their ever expanding chain of drugstores, which included soda bars and a wide range of merchandise. Elmer Peabody was the accountant, his correct title being 'Financial Vice President'.

The arrangement was that Ivor, the President, made the money, Elmer counted it, and Donna and Pearl, Elmer's wife, spent it. So far, Ivor and Elmer had stayed ahead by several millions no matter how hard their wives tried to maintain a balance. It was Donna, going straight for the shopping area from the restaurant, who spotted a Pyle and Peabody Drugstore, and it was Ambrose Nicklegrubber, the manager, who recognised her as one of his company's Vice Presidents. All their pictures were framed on the wall in the back store.

'It sure is lovely to find a dear old P and P so far

310

from home,' she said. 'Didn't know we'd gotten into Europe.'

The manager didn't know that either and asked where.

'Why, in Gibraltar of course, that's what I mean,' replied Donna. 'It's in Europe, isn't it?'

'I guess it sure is, Ma'am.'

Ambrose knew now that this was some kind of new-fangled check-up or general knowledge test, and feared his job might well be on the line. Better tread carefully.

'What's happened to the Rock I've heard so much about?' asked Donna. 'It's the first thing you expect to see here.'

Ambrose thought fast.

'When it's on display it shifts very quickly...'

It was Donna's turn to be perplexed.

'Can't see any monkeys either. I thought they were supposed to be always on show?'

Ambrose decided it must be a new brand name.

'Clean out of stock, Ma'am,' he said, 'very popular with the tourists you know. They can't get enough of 'em to take back home.'

At that moment his wife Belle came through from the back store. Ambrose made the introductions.

'Long way from home for you, Mrs Nicklegrubber,' said Donna. 'Do you get back there to see your folks much?'

Ambrose sensed a trick question here and came in quickly with 'Only at night time, never during the day.'

'Scared of pirates around the coast, I suppose. Be careful how you go or you'll finish up on the rocks,' went on Donna. 'We nearly did ourselves not long ago, but that was due to sheer lack of control on the part of the man in charge. Luckily we got out in time but we lost all our carpets and furniture, and a lot of people went under. Elmer was up to his neck in it, and we were

311

lucky to survive... So do watch out – I must get back now and I'll tell Ivor about our little chat.'

She left behind her a very worried store manager, who was quick to have his wife clean the place up 'in case she brings old Pyle himself back here'.

'Better find out about those monkeys,' he muttered as he took a few slugs of P and P bourbon.

THE PEABODYS

While Donna was busy creating a headache for the Nicklegrubbers, McGinty had found a fellow-country-man serving behind the local bar.

'And where woo'd ye be from then?' he was asked, once the first couple of drinks had touched the sides.

'Port Said,' replied McGinty, 'and a long hard trip it was, to be sure, for the worst part of the time.'

'Don't know the place personally,' said Pat the bar-man, 'somewhere along the coast woo'd it be then?'

'Close to the Nile,' said McGinty. 'You must know that, to be sure.'

Not to be outdone, Pat said of course he did, and a fine little joint it was too, so it was.

'Hell of a lot of Americans about,' remarked McGinty. 'Do any of 'em live here?'

'About one hundred and fifty tousand I tink it is.' The barman winked. 'Blame me for t'ree o' dem at least. My wife does.'

McGinty tried to make some sense out of this. He downed his drink and repeated the order.

'What happened to the British then?'

'Got rid o' dem ages ago,' said Pat. 'Like to do dat back home too, eh?... See dem all down here... Why, just before you came in we had a big fat crackpot Englishman in here calling us all "bloody Yanks" – thought he was in Gibraltar! Tried to pay for his drink with an English half-crown. Too bloody bumptious he was – we bumped him alright, straight across the sidewalk.'

McGinty choked a little as he downed his bourbon in one sling and offered the barman a couple of the dollar bills he'd got from Ivor Pyle. He received his change in cents and made for the door, picking up from the table as he went an old copy of the *Miami Daily News*.

13

Pyle Tower

In the presidential offices of Pyle and Peabody on the twentieth floor of Pyle Tower, New York, Elmer Peabody was reading another cable from the company President.

> Stop Arbuckle stop Arriving Grand Central Station midday Tuesday with Donna and five shipmates stop Collect stop Pyle stop Collect stop

There was no time to lose. He ordered two of the company's limousines to await him, and gave instructions to all staff to prepare for the arrival of the President's wife and also the President, and to take all appropriate action.

When he returned in the afternoon with the seven intrepid adventurers, a full reception party had been arranged, complete with a band, bunting and paper chains, paper hats, and balloons. The common bond of

314

survival, excitement and bourbon had created an atmosphere of tolerance between them, to the point that it was not long before the Colonel, mindful too of the threat to invite Lady Buckmaster, could be seen sitting next to Donna Pyle, looking at her family photograph album and appearing to listen.

When the party was well under way, Gloria, wearing a paper hat inviting the most intimate attention and very little else, took to circulating amongst all the men of the party and reminding them of their successes at poker and the resultant unfinished business.

Enquiries about this from Donna Pyle only produced a faraway look from the Bull.

Late in the night Ivor Pyle climbed onto a table, supported by Vice President Peabody, spat out his cigar, called for attention and made a speech.

'My dear friends and buddies and also my wife. Thish is a very auspishus occash... moment and to commemor—'

'Three cheers for the Pylsh!' shouted Chalky.

'Up the Yanks!' came from Charlie, and a resounding belch from the Bull.

'Pyle and Peabody Inc. wish to show their appreshish— thanks, by creating some new positions in the development of the company and making the following appointments.

'At board level, Vish President (second class), Sir Ferdinand Buckmaster, on condition that his name can appear on our letterheading and that on no account will he appear at board meetings should we ever hold any.

'Duties – stores security and pursuit of outstanding accounts. Personal assistant, Mr Chalky White.'

He was steadily sobering up.

'Vice President (second class) – Captain Rusty McGinty. Duties – overseas trade and development, assisted by Mr Charlie Perkins.

'They will be allocated offices on the eighteenth floor.

'Miss Gloria Bumpkin, Vice...'

'First class,' shouted Chalky.

'Vice President (first class) ... duties – public relations and business entertainment ... office on the nineteenth floor.'

Whereupon he collapsed on the table alongside Vice President Rusty McGinty.

It is a great pleasure to report that thereafter, Wall Street recorded a steady growth in the fortunes of Pyle and Peabody Inc., with expansion extending far overseas, especially in Ireland and the United Kingdom.

The milk-bar and store in the High Street of Bunkham-on-Ouse was particularly popular with the young Hon. Pascal Limpet and his N'Chuyu friends. There was also a prosperous new store in Gibraltar. This plum appointment went to an applicant by the name of Ambrose Nicklegrubber and his wife, on a strong recommendation from Vice President Donna Pyle.

Whilst the turnover worldwide increased by leaps and bounds year by year, the profits did not always keep the same pace. Vice President Peabody judged that this might be attributable to the expenditure incurred by Vice President Bumpkin in the course of her duties (though nothing was ever said or done about it), and to the tireless efforts put in by Vice Presidents Donna and Pearl, together with stock deficiencies in the liquor department wherever Vice President McGinty and his personal assistant were at work.

Of all the fresh lines introduced into the food stores by the senior management, the surprise best seller by far was Bumpkin Pie.

AWAY WITH DEARLOVE

ERNEST
GOODBODY

It could be that the long doom-laden shadow of Ernest Goodbody that so influenced the affairs and fortunes of the Little Winkletonians and the Bunkham-on-Ouseites, also had a lasting effect on his creator.

Certainly a number of his characteristics are recognisable in Dearlove and Co., and it is to be hoped that a rumour recently reported in *The Bunkham and District Crier* is pure fiction.

This was to the effect that for their next holiday the Dearloves are considering taking a houseboat on the river Ouse, and it was followed by a graphic prophesy of widespread disaster and the inevitable confrontation with the new Town Clerk – Jasper Clawhammer's son Albert, and his equally formidable fiancée, Miss Victoria Buckmaster...

1

Mr Denzil Dearlove was a round man. Round, that is, as distinct from angular or flat or square. He was by profession an electrician, or, to be more precise, had been. He measured 5 feet 6 inches in height, plus at the present time a further half inch for the large bulbous bump on the top of his head, caused by a falling fluorescent light fitting at the time the measurement was taken in the clinic.

Nurse Merryweather, who was also injured, recovered consciousness within a few hours of being taken into intensive care.

The incident was considered to be nobody's fault, or in the jargon of the insurance company, an Act of God, though had the doctor in charge known that the light fitting had been installed by Mr Dearlove himself under an earlier contract, he might have presumed God's innocence. It might also have thrown some light, almost literally, on the mysterious electrocution of old Mrs

Wellworthy when she had attended the clinic on a rainy day the week before and poked it with her wet umbrella.

Mr Dearlove weighed 13 stones approximately – approximately because there had not been time to add the last few ounce weights onto the balance arm of the weighing machine before it collapsed. Mr Dearlove fervently denied that the adjustments he had dealt with while waiting for attention had anything to do with it, and if it had been anybody except Mr Dearlove, they might have believed him.

The unfortunate thing about it all was the damage done to his glasses, his very last spare set that he badly needed at home in his constant search for the last three pairs supplied to him by the DHSS. In this occupation he could rely on the assistance of his devoted wife, Annabelle, who, in the course of their long married life together, had spent a large part of it crawling round the floor with him in search of his or her own spectacles, as the case may be.

Mr Dearlove's sight was, to put it mildly, below average – with his spectacles on, that is. His hearing could be classified as about the same standard, providing you addressed him on his right hand side, his best ear. He was in all other respects a reasonably fit and healthy man, if you forget about his breathing problems, and he was very good at that ... forgetting.

Close friends of the Dearloves were the Butterworths who lived in the flat next door. The Butterworths were also in their late sixties, with faculties which were not quite up to the quality of their neighbours'. They could be distinguished from the Dearloves by a difference in height of some eight inches more, and in weight of about three stones less, and by a dark blue bruise which was invariably prominent on each of their foreheads.

Charlie and Flo Butterworth could empathise with the

Dearloves over the spectacles problem as they suffered much the same, with the result that they had more than once been known to bump into each other on hands and knees in the corridor, and on occasions to finish up by spending the evening in each other's homes by mistake. Luckily, this always became apparent to the Butterworths when they got into the wrong bed and found their feet clearing the end of it by nearly a foot, or you might say, four feet.

Charlie Butterworth had been retired from his job as a driving instructor for several years now. The precise occasion on which the final decision was made was deeply engraved on his memory. It had put a severe strain on their neighbourly friendship, and was, by no coincidence, the last occasion on which Denzil Dearlove had tried to learn to drive.

Full details of that fateful encounter are best left to the imagination. There should be little difficulty, having regard to the participants, in visualising how the instruction car, a couple of small saloon cars, a motorcyclist, a Rolls-Royce, a bus and two telephone boxes all suffered varying degrees of damage, from indentation to complete write-off.

Their friendship survived mainly because Charlie had already begun to recognise the onset of some limitations, and the suspicions of his employers were becoming aroused by the increasing number of new cars he needed for an increasingly limited number of pupils taking increasingly longer to achieve test failures.

He did, however, manage to retain his driving licence, which was a great help to them when all four went on their first caravan holiday. As it turned out, it was also their last.

That particular holiday registered strongly in all their memories, bad as they were.

2

The holiday had been planned with great care, right from the moment when Flo had suggested that they might go away together.

Charlie had agreed that it was awful weather and perhaps they should take a holiday somewhere, maybe as a foursome by the sea.

Flo said she didn't know the place, but if it was on the east coast, she would prefer to go west, maybe across to the Isle of Man.

Denzil asked, 'What caravan? I didn't know you had one.'

Charlie replied that it would be fine if he could lay his hands on one, and Flo thought it was nearer to quarter past two.

Annabelle agreed that's what they should do, but not to Japan, as she didn't fancy raw fish, and suggested they might try a caravan holiday, if they could hire one.

'It would save such a lot on hotel bills,' she said, and

Charlie agreed that the hills in the West Country were pretty steep, but they were worse in Wales.

Flo said she did not want to go west if it was as windy as all that, so why not just make merry and leave it to chance.

Which is more or less how they came to take the ferry across the Channel to France.

The planning and preparation stages, the packaging and stowage of the victuals in the car, the car boot and the caravan, were all miraculously achieved in a period of four weeks. Miraculous is no exaggeration, when you include long periods of spectacles hunting into brand new territory, and a tendency on the part of all concerned to get confused between the car doors, the caravan door and the entrance to the flats, with the result that most of the items were carried to and fro many times before finally coming to rest somewhere.

As navigator and map reader, Denzil thought it advisable to get three more pairs of glasses, together with a large magnifying glass, and he put them in a safe place, where they remained perfectly safe from everybody, including Denzil himself. His offers to improve the lighting in the caravan were resisted by the others, especially Annabelle who was still finding time to pay visits to Nurse Merryweather during her recovery in hospital, and to the bus-driver and the motorcyclist, who were now doing well in a rehabilitation centre.

They planned to cross to France via Dover, but when they arrived by chance at Newhaven instead, they decided it would do very well anyway.

Denzil and Annabelle were put in charge of language and money because of their overseas experience – they had been abroad before on a seven-day package deal to the Costa Brava, many years ago. So whilst awaiting the ferry, Annabelle sought out the bureau de change, and, flourishing a twenty-pound note, requested some pesetas.

The nice little man behind the counter asked if she really needed francs, and she replied that she always was, and hoped the French were too. He explained that pesetas were the currency of Spain and a fascinating conversation ensued about the weather. Annabelle had expected sunshine all the way, and asked several people in the queue that was building up if they also were expecting rain.

One opinion was given that he hoped lightning would strike as soon as possible and near at hand, and had it not been for a loud blast on the ferry's hooter heralding its departure, a lot more similar views might have been expressed. As it was, the nice little man pulled down the shutters with a huge sigh, and Annabelle went back and got in the car empty-handed. By this time all the vehicles were going aboard, and when they were all packed in, the ship's doors were slammed closed and off went the ferry.

Denzil and Charlie were very busy navigating their way into the ferry, so it was Flo who first noticed the absence of Annabelle. When they were finally parked (to the great relief of three officials and many nearby drivers), they looked inside the caravan without success, and a hurried discussion followed. It was decided that Denzil should report the problem to the Captain, whilst the other two took a look round.

With the benefit of hindsight, it would certainly have been better to do neither.

Charlie and Flo set off in different directions in the semi-darkness of the car deck, opening every car door they could find (it being against the company's safety rules to lock them), and calling out 'Annabelle' at regular intervals.

As for Annabelle, she had found herself in the back of a large limousine in the company of two magnificent St Bernard dogs and a chic little French poodle, and all three had set about giving her a thorough wash with no opportunity at all to say anything. As soon as possible after the car had been parked on board she burst out of the door, closely followed by her new companions, and then by the occupants of the front seats – a large man in a loud check suit and a shapely lady elegantly attired in a close-fitting mini suit. They both seemed a little *malheureuse*.

There had been a build-up of confusion throughout the car deck. Car doors were open everywhere, making it necessary to pass through many of them just to make any progress at all. The dogs found this immensely exciting, barking and yapping their way in pursuit of Annabelle, with their owners hard on their heels.

Finding the Captain was not such an easy matter as Denzil had expected. He lost count of the number of decks he visited, the number of cabin doors he opened, and the number of irate occupants he disturbed. By the time he did find the Captain he was accompanied by a sizeable delegation of very unhappy passengers, some in their night attire, wishing to register complaints or be directed to the lifeboats.

At the same time reports were coming through to the Captain of mayhem on the car deck, where it appeared that vandals and wild animals were running amok. Hearing this report, Denzil thought of the danger such a situation posed for all three of his companions, always presuming that Annabelle was on board somewhere. He registered the strongest possible complaint and asked that armed protection should be provided without delay.

News of the problems on the car deck spread through the ship like wildfire, and everybody headed back down there to protect their possessions. The resultant pandemonium everywhere can be better imagined than described, and even then is likely to be underrated.

It is a fact that the ship's log of that particular voyage has since become classified as essential reading for all aspiring cross-Channel skippers before obtaining their ticket, and the Captain, who took early retirement immediately afterwards, has written a best seller on the subject, entitled *Sea Dogs – SOS!'*

Arrival at the docks in Dieppe was luckily just in time to save the Captain and many of the crew from complete delirium and mental breakdown, and the sight of the receding rear-lights of the Butterworth caravan sent up a small cheer from those capable of witnessing it. Blissfully unaware of such matters, the four friends, now happily reunited, set off in the early light of dawn to give Normandy the benefit of their company.

Quite soon Charlie noticed that a number of oncoming motorists were driving quite dangerously on the wrong side of the road, and remarked on this to Denzil. Sounding the horn seemed to make no impression on them and, indeed, had the effect of getting a raucous response and some insolent gestures, until Charlie finally pulled in onto the verge to avoid a particularly dangerous lorry, and they stopped to get their breath back. It was Annabelle who pointed out that in Spain she had noticed a lot of vehicles doing the same sort of thing, and she reminded them that in America everybody did it, as they had all seen on the films.

Flo said she didn't realise they had been on the films, but it would be exciting to watch, and where were the cameras?

Charlie told her they were in the boot, and did she want them now? Flo replied that she couldn't think why, and was quite comfortable in the shoes she was wearing.

Meanwhile they all watched the traffic, and Charlie

decided to try it their way, which was certainly one of the best decisions they made throughout the holiday – possibly the only one that was successfully put into practice.

It was an idyllic morning in June, fresh and warming in the glorious sunshine, and they settled down to enjoy the vista of the flat open countryside, and all the novelty of being 'abroad'.

It had been a tiring night and before long the ladies began to doze. In a flash of brilliance Denzil remembered the caravan; they pulled in to the side, made the ladies comfortable in the caravan beds, and went on their way.

3

The owners of the dogs were Herbert Smart and Rosie Green, and it took them the entire voyage to recover their St Bernards, Max and Marlene, and to come to terms with the car owners involved.

Apart from a dozen or so broken windows, much of the coachwork damage caused by the swinging car doors was, in the opinion of Herbert Smart, superficial, but the owners did not see eye to eye with him on this. Lists of names and addresses and car numbers were being exchanged like some new party game, and the Kennel Club would have been very unhappy to hear some of the views being expressed on the subject of dogs in general and owners in particular.

Claims against the shipping line were being fielded by the Captain in respect of the car-door rule in face of roaming wild animals, and he found this particularly hard to take while for most of the time being lovingly licked clean by those very same beasts.

Herbert's temper was not improved either by the loss of Chloe, Rosie's poodle, and of the night in the double berth with Rosie he had specially booked for the occasion. A small black cloud hovered above his Jaguar as he drove off the ferry and up the ramp, and his only comfort was the knowledge that the contents of his car boot had come through customs undisturbed. He drove off at breakneck speed, overtaking everything in sight, including an ancient British Ford containing four ancient British people and towing a caravan. A little further on however, he was unable to resist Rosie's demand for a 'pit-stop' in the aptly named Rendezvous Café.

Several cars behind came a Hertz hire car, a white Opel containing the Oppenheimers, Elmer and Goldie, from Massachusetts, USA, who had just 'done' Great Britain and were about to 'do' Europe. An impressive array of photographic and video equipment filled most of the back seat, and the rest of it was now occupied without their knowledge or consent by a French poodle, who had taken up residence during the earlier pandemonium and was comfortably asleep in the corner. The chaos on the car deck was now just a bad memory as they set course to follow the detailed route map for 'Europe in ten days', charted for them by their travel agent back home.

The passing trade was good for the Rendezvous Café that day – quite a lot didn't pass. These included the Dearlove party, and in due time the Oppenheimers as well.

Leaving the ladies asleep in the caravan, Charlie and Denzil went into the café for relief and for 'elevenses'. Finding they had stopped, Flo in the caravan felt the same need for relief; it is a surprising fact that she found the *Mesdames* at first attempt, but not at all surprising that she was unable to sustain such a success rate on her

333

return. Still a little dozy, she settled into the back seat of the Jaguar, where she was given the standard warm and wet welcome by Max and Marlene.

In the warmth of their welcome she fell asleep again.

When Flo failed to return to the caravan, Annabelle got worried and went in search of her in the *Mesdames*, where she took the opportunity to powder her nose. Had she left her nose shiny, things might have worked out very differently, for in that precise time the Jaguar drove off, followed by the Ford followed by the caravan.

Pressure was building up in the Jaguar. Much as Herbert wanted to press on to Paris, with a boot-load of reasons, he was faced with opposition of the most formidable kind. Female. Rosie was mourning the loss of her beloved Chloe, and very forcibly expressed her conviction that the further and faster they left the vicinity, the less chance there was of finding her. Furthermore, she was tired, and could find little sympathy and no stimulation from the black niggly mood of her escort.

'Two single rooms at the next hotel,' she stated, quite categorically. The token resistance offered by Herbert was a waste of time, and when on the outskirts of a small village she spotted an attractive little hotel, Herbert gave in and they pulled into the car park. Opening the rear door to let out the dogs, he was less than delighted to find Flo tumbling out with them, still in a daze.

'Who the hell are you?' shouted Herbert.

'Very well thank you,' said Flo, 'but what have you done with Annabelle?'

'Who's Annabelle? And what are you doing here?' asked Herbert.

'I don't believe you,' answered Flo, 'she couldn't just disappear. And what have you done with our caravan?'

By this time Rosie had joined them and while Herbert

struggled to find patience, she helped Flo to her feet, dusted her down and did some thinking.

'You're from the car with the caravan, aren't you? You lost Annabelle on the boat, didn't you?'

Flo bristled. 'Certainly not. She bought it herself and I think she looks very nice in it too. I hope she's got it on now, she might need it this evening if she's got lost. Perhaps we should call the police.'

Herbert seemed to be strongly against that idea, so much so that he softened noticeably and suggested they all go inside for a nice cup of tea and a chat.

'Will your dogs be alright with a cat?' asked Flo, and at the mention of dogs Rosie dissolved into tears.

'You must try to be nicer to your lovely wife,' scolded Flo. 'I have an idea. Let's go into the restaurant and have a nice cup of tea.'

'Good idea,' said Herbert.

4

Denzil and Charlie were making good progress. They chatted away happily to each other along the way without any chance of actually conversing, which, in contrast to the United Nations, where the same procedure is used, resulted in complete harmony.

On the outskirts of Rouen they came upon a caravan site and drove in. Once parked, they relaxed after their busy day, and then went back to the caravan for a beverage. The ladies had disappeared, presumably to the toilet, so they settled down with a can of lager apiece to wait for them.

A six-pack of lager later, they realised that the ladies were missing and went in search. They finished up in the site manager's office, and were greeted with a shrill cry of

'*Que voulez-vous? Que voulez-vous?* Wipe your feet then, wipe your feet then!'

There was a large cage hanging by the window in which sat their colourful interrogator.

'*Attendez* Jacques, *attendez* Jacques!' screeched the parrot, whereupon through a door at the back of the room, Jacques appeared.

Without removing his cigarette he said, '*Bonjour Messieurs, cent francs s'il vous plaît.*'

'*Où est les Mesdames?*' enquired Denzil, digging deep into far off school days, rather well, he thought.

He got a funny look from Jacques.

'What's the trouble, mate?' he said. 'Won't the Gents do for you?', and at that moment the parrot found it necessary to come out with

'Who's a pretty boy then, who's a pretty boy then?'

Greatly relieved that the language problem was solved, Charlie explained, 'We've lost our wives.'

'Write down how you did it,' came the reply. 'It'll be a best seller.'

Jacques, being not long ago Jack from the Old Kent Road, had a heart of gold very well camouflaged under his scruffy tee shirt advertising a local bordello. Below this and partially covered by his overhanging belly were the remains of a pair of paint-stained jeans, and above it his crinkled unshaven face, framed by some tangled grey hair, could best be described as 'lived in'. He listened to their story.

'Funny things 'appen around 'ere,' he said. 'I don't want to worry you like, but you'd never believe what goes on. Papers are full of it. Still, never mind, I'm sure some of it's hexaggerated – must be. Just couldn't be true. Still, you never know, they might still be quite all right.'

'Stick 'em up, stick 'em up!' cried the parrot. 'Call a copper, call a copper!'

'Good idea, Archimedes,' said Jack. 'It's a job for the Old Bill right enough. Let's order up a gendarme,' and he promptly got on the phone.

337

While they waited, he dealt with their traveller's cheques at what he described as a favourable rate, without being specific about who it favoured.

The gendarmerie arrived within the hour, represented by Messieurs Lourenne *et* Ardille (Laurel and Hardy to Denzil and Charlie). They took what information there was from Jacques, said it was too late to do anything today, and promised to come back in the morning, if by then the gentlemen still wanted to have their wives found, and if they could think of something to do about it.

Elmer and Goldie Oppenheimer, touring in their white Opel, had no such worries. They were enjoying Europe, now that they had done twenty miles of it, and had successfully negotiated a pot of coffee and a mountain of assorted patisserie by direct reference to their phrasebook, at the Rendezvous Café. They watched with amusement, which gradually became concern, the curious activities of a little English lady who seemed to be darting hither and thither, chattering to herself and to anyone else she came upon, which sometimes included the hatstand.

Annabelle was in difficulties. She knew the caravan had to be out there somewhere but she could not find it. Neither could she find anybody to ask about it. Those replies she did get were just as useless to her as the response from the hatstand. She could only make out the odd word and that was in French, usually from drivers who held strong, not very sympathetic, views on caravans, especially English caravans.

She bumped into most of the tables in her travels, and luckily these included that of the Oppenheimers, where she saved herself by planting her hand in a plate of meringues while repeating miserably '*Où est la caravan? Où est la caravan?*'

Elmer sat her down, Goldie wiped her hand, and they both offered her coffee.

'What's your problem, ma'am?' asked Elmer.

'So have I,' said Annabelle. 'I've lost my caravan'.

'With me, it's usually my handbag, isn't it, Elmer,' said Goldie. 'Or my glasses.'

Annabelle sighed.

'No, I've got my glasses, somewhere, but I don't really need them to find the caravan. It's quite big, you know, big enough for four of us.'

'How kind of you to offer,' said Goldie, 'but we've got our own car. It's an Opel, you know.'

'Yes, you can get so attached to them, can't you,' replied Annabelle, by which time Elmer decided to intervene.

Introductions were made, *l'addition* was dealt with, and they all went outside to look for Annabelle's caravan, without success. Time was getting on, so the Oppenheimers decided that the best plan would be for Annabelle to travel with them to the next hotel and stay the night while they sought local help.

Elmer let Annabelle into the back of the car, where she was greeted enthusiastically for the second time that day by Chloe.

'How nice, just like one of the dogs I made friends with this morning. What's her name?'

Elmer was confused. 'Don't know,' he said.

'What a bad memory you've got,' chided Annabelle. 'Perhaps your wife knows.'

'Perhaps she does at that. You never know what next with Goldie.' He glared across the car. 'Where d'you pick up this damn thing, Goldie? D'you have to buy every goddam thing you set eyes on?'

'Oh Elmer, darling, it was just a little bargain I caught sight of on the ferry – just what I was looking for. I thought I put it in the boot.'

339

'I'm against dogs in boots,' said Annabelle, 'though I know they can make an awful mess in bad weather. Does she wear one of those pretty little doggie jackets as well? Do tell me her name.'

'It's not a dog, it's a dolly, and it's for our little grandson, Spencer.' At that moment Goldie became aware of Chloe.

'Elmer,' she demanded, 'what's that dog doing there?'

Before Elmer could think of anything to say without further complication, Chloe decided to give him some concentrated attention by leaping onto the back of his seat and washing his face.

'OK. Let's go for a walk and do some thinking,' he said, leaving the ladies to continue their respective conversations.

Elmer needed the break, and so did Chloe. They got along fine, and by the time Elmer had found some food and drink for his new, wonderfully quiet, companion, they had become firm friends. They returned to the car, where a friendship of a quite contrasting nature based on the simultaneous exchange of ideas had blossomed, and they drove off contentedly, everybody deeply absorbed in their own thoughts.

They began looking for accommodation for the night and when they came upon a small hotel on the outskirts of a pretty little village, Goldie decided they should stay there and Elmer decided to agree. Most of their decisions were arrived at by that process.

Their rooms on the second floor were eminently French in decor and attention to detail, and very comfortable. They prepared themselves for a pleasant, relaxed evening meal and overnight stay after a long, busy, bewildering day.

5

The Hotel de la Ville on the approach to the village of
Beauchamps is owned and run by M and Mme Baron.
To be more exact, the Hotel de la Ville, the village of
Beauchamps and M Baron are run by Mme Baron.

Known locally as 'Madame La Général', Matilde Baron
is in stature on the petite side, but in *prestance*, formidable.
In these two characteristics, as in many others, Georges
Baron is precisely the opposite. The hotel staff consists of
seventeen-year-old Claudine Baron (the evidence of some
momentary matrimonial accord), and the aging husband
and wife team of Jean and Marie Bertrande, whose duties
include whatever needs to be done.

They would all always remember that night in June
which began when in the late afternoon, a Jaguar drew
into the car park and discharged a large check-suited
unmistakably English man, two huge St Bernard dogs, a
smart young lady in a bad temper, and after a short
delay, an older lady, taller and sweeter, but rather

befuddled. After the dogs had been exercised they were shut up in the car and the trio came into the hotel and ordered tea.

It was while the tea was being served by Marie in the restaurant at the back of the hotel that an Opel pulled in and rooms were provided on the second floor for the nice American couple and for the little English lady with the affectionate little poodle. Business was looking up, especially when the English trio from the Jaguar asked for accommodation – three single rooms. These were provided on the first floor.

Within half-an-hour of being shown to his room, the Englishman, Mr Herbert Smart, reappeared downstairs still quite obviously in a black mood, looking for the bar, where he settled down to some very serious drinking. His lady friend Rosie, claiming to be suffering from a headache, ordered a meal in her room.

On the floor above, Annabelle made for the toilet which was at the end of the corridor. Much to her credit, she found it successfully at the first attempt, but in doing so, allowed Chloe to roam free. Chloe drifted down onto the first floor, then picked up a familiar scent, which she followed down the next flight of stairs and into the bar, where she joined Herbert. When Annabelle noticed the absence of Chloe, for whom she now felt a strong affection and some responsibility, she went down to the next floor and began her search along the corridor, calling gently as she went. Thus it was that Flo, who was at that moment also navigating the same corridor after satisfying a similar need, suddenly found herself in a pair of arms which to her delight turned out to belong to her best friend.

They retired to Flo's room.

'Thank goodness I've found you, Annabelle,' she said, with a huge sigh of relief. 'Where are the men?'

'It's a man and a woman, actually,' replied Annabelle, 'but never mind them – what have you done with Denzil and Charlie?'

There followed a five-minute exchange of unanswered questions before it became clear that Denzil, Charlie, and a poodle named Chloe with a record of reappearances, were all unaccounted for. They decided to ask the management to telephone the gendarmerie for help. The request reached the ears of Mme Baron, and a call from her was quite sufficient to ensure prompt action from the local force.

It was bad luck on Messieurs Lourenne *et* Ardille that the attractions of the latest female recruit in their offices had caused them to linger a moment too long in the gendarmerie. The obvious connection between the demand from Mme Baron and their recent report from the caravan park meant their day's work was far from over.

First, they telephoned the 'successful results of their intensive enquiries' to Jacques at the caravan park. Then they made off with police car siren at full blast in the direction of the Hotel de la Ville at Beauchamps, arriving there as darkness fell, just after ten. The blaring sirens brought Annabelle and Flo from dozing in the lounge to the reception desk, where the introductions were made by Mme Baron.

The urgent clamour of the siren together with the headlights flashing across the windows aroused the interest of everybody in the hotel, not least Herbert Smart, and Chloe, in the bar. Even under the benign influence of a bottle of Johnnie Walker, the alarm bells in his befuddled head began to ring loudly, and he let go an irritable kick at Chloe as she began yapping at the top of her squeaky voice. Herbert grabbed her and tried to shut her up by folding his coat over her head, as he made a dash for the front door and out to his car.

'Chloe! Chloe!' cried Annabelle, dashing off in the direction of the bar, followed by Flo and by 'Laurel and Hardy'. The familiar sound of Chloe was also music to the ears of her mistress, Rosie, who had already ventured outside her room to see what all the commotion was about, and whose headache now quickly disappeared. Dressed only in the most inadequate chemise, she dashed down the stairs, giving vent to the same cry, 'Chloe! Chloe!' She was followed down to the hall by the Oppenheimers and by the Bertrandes and Claudine, all in various stages of undress, enquiring where the fire was.

The confusion was momentarily compounded by a loss of concentration on the part of Laurel and Hardy as they caught sight of Rosie descending the stairs, during which time Herbert made it to his car and started up. The stifled yaps of Chloe had not, however, escaped Rosie's ears.

'He's stealing my Chloe,' she cried at the gendarmes. '*Il est un voleur. Ma pauvre chien, ma pauvre Chloe!*'

Needing only the slightest excuse, the bold gendarmes hustled Rosie into their car and took off in pursuit of the Jaguar, siren blaring as they sent the gravel flying in their wake.

6

Denzil and Charlie, with the help of Jacques, had reached the last of the third six-pack of lager when he answered the telephone and gave them the news that their wives had been found. It was now pitch dark, and the prospect of driving back to the hotel was distinctly unattractive.

Whether it was the bravado brought on by the lager, or an act of unselfish true love that persuaded them to do it must remain a mystery, but it was certainly not the result of any recommendation from Jacques. He could see any number of reasons and excuses for waiting until the morning – the prospect of a plentiful supply of English beer being one of the foremost. But the die was cast.

Assisted again by Jacques, they managed to detach the caravan. Jacques drove the car as far as the exit gate, and the pair set course for the Hotel de la Ville, Beauchamps. There was little or no traffic on the road, and in view of their natural limitations, compounded by their present condition, this was a stroke of very good luck for all those fortunate Frenchmen who were home safely in bed that night.

Weaving gently from side to side down the road, they were somehow dodged by the few cars coming the other way, except for one. Well, to be exact, two.

The first of them was also following a weaving pattern, at considerably greater speed than they were capable of, and their respective zig-zag paths very nearly matched. Indeed, if Herbert Smart had not lost his nerve at the last moment and swerved wildly, no contact at all would have been made, and who knows how matters would have developed. But he did, catching Charlie's Ford a glancing blow that was sufficient to deposit the Jaguar in a ditch beside the road, in a highly undignified attitude. There were no complaints from Herbert, who was unconscious at the wheel, but there were from Chloe, who leapt out of the window through a gap that was too small for Max and Marlene, yapping her head off.

While Charlie and Denzil were discussing what strange things people do, and whether they should complain about the extraordinary behaviour of the vehicles in France, particularly the one they had just passed, another one appeared, this time clearly, even to them, a police car, with blue light flashing and siren sounding. They drew to one side to allow it to pass, but unfortunately chose the same side as the police car. There followed a screeching of brakes, another glancing encounter, and clouds of dust as the Renault veered off the road, through a fence, and was conveniently slowed down in a duck pond.

As Laurel and Hardy stepped out into the muddy water, there followed *un bataille de chivalrie* between these worthy Frenchman for the privilege of lifting their attractively lightly clad passenger to the safety of dry land.

346

The skirmish was won by M Ardille, but not greatly appreciated by Rosie when he slipped in the oozing slime when on the verge of success, with the inevitable result. M Lourenne might be forgiven for a poorly concealed smirk as he paddled to the rescue of both.

As they stood surveying the scene, they became aware that sheep were exploring the hole in the fence and drifting onto the road, and then heard Chloe yapping her way towards the escaping flock of sheep. To their great credit they still remembered the purpose of their excursion, even in this chaotic, uncomfortable and highly undignified scenario. They called her by name, and she immediately came over to them with a friendly smile and much tail-wagging.

By virtue of their highly skilled technical training they were able to deduce that if Chloe was loose, the car in which she had been travelling could not be far away, so they squelched their way down the road and were soon in sight of the Jaguar – the back end of it anyway, which was angled up, with the boot gaping, the lid having sprung open. They examined Herbert, who was still unconscious at the wheel, and satisfied themselves and Rosie that he was still alive and apparently not seriously injured. It was noticeable that she seemed strangely unconcerned.

Charlie and Denzil's progress was by comparison completely uneventful, and deep in their respective personal conversations on the subject of French drivers, they arrived at the Hotel de la Ville, Beauchamps, and were surprised to find the front door still unlocked at one o'clock in the morning and lights on in the lounge. There, to their great relief, they found their wives and also several other faces they recognised from their recent travels. Over cups of coffee, they had a typical conversation with their wives, from which nobody learned very much, and it was left to Elmer Oppenheimer to step in and bring Charlie and Denzil up to date on the events of the evening at the Hotel de la Ville. After a suitable rearrangement of the rooms, they all turned in and tried to calm down and get a little sleep before dawn.

Back at the caravan park, Jacques was worried. He had watched with nervous apprehension as Denzil and Charlie weaved their way out of his gate and down the road, and as an incurable betting man, assessed their odds of a safe journey to the hotel at no better than evens. His conscience, an organ which had caused him very little bother over the years, asserted itself for once on behalf of these dear old souls whose simple innocence and trust, and lager, had given him an unusual sense of responsibility. He telephoned the hotel a couple of times to see if they had arrived safely, seriously under-estimating the speed at which they travelled and getting a negative reply.

In the end he had to satisfy himself that he had done the best he could by getting out his battered old Citroën 2 C/V and setting off to check on their progress, at least for a few miles. He had not been out more than a quarter of an hour before he saw a torch being waved at him from the middle of the road, and came to a halt at the request of a mud spattered figure who claimed to be a gendarme, and was accompanied by a young lady wearing a khaki gendarme's jacket over a very inadequate khaki night-dress. They appeared to be survivors from a Jaguar he could see with its nose in the ditch.

When they tried to explain that a third member of their party had gone back on foot to the nearest duck pond to make a telephone call, he began to wonder if his command of the language was all that it should be, and was glad to find that the shivering young lady spoke his native tongue. Even so, he had a problem with the story

348

she had to tell, until, that is, he took a look in the driver's seat of the car.

'Well I'll be damned, will wonders never cease,' he exploded. 'Never thought to see Herbie Smart again, not outside, anyway!'

'Outside of what?' asked Rosie, and got the answer she half expected.

'Wandsworth. I was a guest of Her Majesty there for a short spell. Shared a cell with Herbie – he was in for a while longer. Strong on jewellery, he was. Reckoned he'd got a bit stowed away for when he finished his time. Wanted my help, he did, but I'd 'ad enough, especially of 'im… Hope he's not a friend of yours?'

'No, not any more.'

Jacques began to feel very sorry for the girl. She was a muddy picture of misery, her teeth were chattering, and she had clearly had a nasty shock, not only from some sort of accident, but also from him.

'You'd better hop in, girl. I'll take you back to my place and find you something warm to put on… Don't look so worried, Laurel and Hardy here will tell you I'm OK.'

She didn't wait for any translations. Shaking herself clear of M Ardille, whose ardour was by now at a very low ebb, and grabbing up Chloe, whose affection included enthusiastically licking the mud off her face, she jumped into Jacques' car, snuggled down, and said, 'Let's go!'

The gendarme started off up the road to see how his mate was progressing, and Jacques, who rarely missed a trick and had noticed that the boot of the Jaguar had sprung open, took the opportunity to take a peep inside it. It was spacious and appeared almost empty, as the couple's suitcases were still at the hotel, and what remained had been thrown to the back of the boot.

This consisted of several large packets of dog biscuits,

but tucked away behind them he could just make out the handle and top of a sizeable leather holdall. This he quickly transferred to the back seat of his car before moving into the driver's seat and turning the car round.

As they set course back in the direction of Rouen and the caravan park, they were passed by two police cars and an ambulance, lights flashing and sirens blaring, heading for the Jaguar in response to the radio call from Gendarme Lourenne.

Police cars with flashing lights and sirens had unpleasant associations for Jacques, or 'Jack', as he had been when his experience with them had been most vivid. Knowing Herbie Smart as he did, he felt sure that whatever was on the back seat of his car would almost certainly be of interest to them, and, perish the thought, might even be why they were on his track.

In a mood rapidly approaching desperation, it occurred to him that the gendarmes might already be aware of what was in the boot of the Jaguar. What then!

On arrival at the caravan park, he lost no time in taking Rosie and Chloe into his own large caravan and putting the kettle on, before excusing himself for a moment. Regrettably he would have to get rid of that bag – with his record he could not afford to take any chances. He had a flash of inspiration. Snatching it from the back seat of his car, he crossed to the caravan that had so recently and conveniently arrived, Denzil and Charlie's, and found the perfect sanctuary in the ladies' clothes closet.

7

When the Dearloves and the Butterworths set off at about ten o'clock the next morning to collect their caravan, they were once again in a contented holiday mood. It was a warm sunny day, they were happily together again after their extraordinary adventures, and in their adversity had made some good friends in the Oppenheimers. Goldie's pressing invitation to them to 'drop in any time you're over', confirmed with rather less enthusiasm by Elmer, had been especially well received by the ladies, who made a detailed note of their New York address.

'We'll definitely come,' promised Annabelle, 'just love to see that Grand Canyon and Hollywood and every-thing. We'll bring the caravan for a week or two.'

Elmer had shuddered, opened his mouth, then looking at Goldie, closed it again.

'Funny thing,' said Annabelle after they had travelled a few miles on the road to Rouen, 'the way the French let their sheep drift about all over the road. And did you see that car in the duck pond – dreadful drivers over here – going too fast I suppose, and trying to avoid the animals.'

'Of course I shall, that's why I'm slowing down,' said Charlie.

Soon after passing an irate farmer who seemed to be trying to drive the sheep back up the road, they came upon a breakdown lorry struggling to heave a Jaguar out of the roadside ditch.

'If it's all going to be like this, I think we'd certainly be much safer in America,' said Flo, 'even with all those gangsters about... That car's just like the one I travelled in with those two great big dogs.'

On arrival at the caravan park, they all trooped into Jacques' office.

'Stick 'em up, stick 'em up!' came the greeting from Archimedes. 'Call a copper, call a copper!'

Jacques appeared, followed by a surprise for the visitors – Rosie and Chloe. Flo introduced Rosie to her friends, and Annabelle did the same thing for Chloe. Jacques, completely flummoxed by all this, was then introduced to the ladies.

'Wipe your feet then, wipe your feet then!' came from the corner.

'Nice to find someone who speaks English so clearly,' said Annabelle, and headed off in that direction to say hallo.

Over more cups of tea, Flo asked Rosie, 'Whatever happened to your husband?'

'Please,' said Rosie, 'don't call that dreadful man my husband! This was to have been our first holiday together – thanks to Jack here I now know a lot more about him and begin to have a better idea of what this trip was all about – hardly the romantic ideal I thought it was.

'I run a small business offering kennel accommodation

352

– a cats' and dogs' home if you like, and it includes an official quarantine for animals entering the country. I met Herbert Smart when he came looking for a pair of large dogs – I often find myself with strays I am pleased to find a home for at cheap prices, and he found just what he wanted in Max and Marlene. He invited me out, and wasted no time before asking me to accompany him on a trip down to a cottage he's buying in the Dordogne. I couldn't resist, it all sounded so nice, and I could take Chloe, he seemed keen on that idea, as I could easily cope with the quarantine problem on my return.

'I must say I was beginning to regret my hasty decision soon after we started, and Jack here has filled in some background that settles it.'

Annabelle said goodbye to the parrot and rejoined the group.

'I've been wondering,' she said, 'whatever happened to your husband, Rosie?'

Rosie swallowed.

'Jack has found out for me that Mr Smart is now in a hospital in Rouen with a few broken ribs and is in no danger. It seems he swerved to avoid an oncoming car driving on the wrong side of the road and that's how he finished up in the ditch.'

'How careless!' said Annabelle. 'He might have hurt his dogs or caused an accident. Where are the poor dears?'

'Max and Marlene are OK and safely in police care. So are the remains of the Jaguar, for some reason...' She hesitated. 'I don't really want to see him again if I can help it. I'll drop a line to him and then go home, but my things are still at the hotel...' She tailed off, and looked ready to weep. The gallant Jacques came to the rescue, and arrangements were made for her to stay for a night, though not on the terms he had in mind, after which he would run her back to the Hotel de la Ville.

The caravanners did the same, to recover from all the excitement.

'These foreign drivers,' said Charlie, as he kissed Flo goodnight, 'if only they would take more care. Denzil and I had some pretty close shaves ourselves last night.'

Flo snuggled up.

'Fancy that! Is that just because they've got more hair? Anyway, you can't expect them all to drive like you dear – they simply haven't got the experience, and, well, they're only foreigners, remember.'

8

An unrelenting fate was not smiling on those worthy Gendarmes Lourenne and Ardille these days. Ever since those *anglais* had appeared on the scene it had been giving them a tough time, and they had only a few hours' sleep that night before they were once again called in urgently to the gendarmerie. A notice for immediate attention, circulated by Interpol, had reached the eyes of their chief, and a possible connection with their activities of the night before was obvious.

It was strongly suspected that the diamonds and other stones resulting from a number of jewel robberies in England had been smuggled across the Channel within the last few days and were destined for fences in Paris or Amsterdam. Any suspicious persons or circumstances were to be subjected to close scrutiny. The remains of the Jaguar, now in their custody, had already been examined, and Lourenne and Ardille were to examine the suitcases, which were not in the car, and interview the lady passenger.

In a replacement car, their first call was at the caravan park, where they knew they would find Rosie. There they learned from her that the suitcases belonging to the couple were still at the hotel, and being well aware of the speed of Herbert Smart's departure, that came as no surprise. Lourenne's offer to take Rosie and collect the cases was gratefully accepted, and they left M Ardille to interview the four English people with the caravan.

Jacques seemed strangely reluctant when he was invited to act as interpreter, but he had little choice. The parrot was no help to him either, with outbursts of *'Que voulez-vous? Que voulez-vous?'* and 'Stick 'em up... Call a copper! Call a copper!' at regular intervals.

After a short conversation in French between Ardille and Jacques, he tried his best to explain in English to the four of them what it was all about, though it was quite clear that he was not comfortable in the role of interpreter, or well cast to represent a law enforcement officer.

He cleared his throat.

'Well folks, it seems they're on the look-out for some missing loot, and they want to know if you can help them. They seem to have their eye specially on Rosie and her mate with the Jaguar, but they have to talk to everyone they can, to what they call eliminate 'em from their enquiries like.'

'Oh Denzil, what a nice young man,' said Annabelle. 'Is he still looking for that nice little doggie for Rosie? I think we should tell him about that car we saw in the duck pond yesterday, and the car in the ditch too. Perhaps he could do something about all those sheep before some other crazy driver does the same thing.'

There followed a long discussion on the dangers of

356

driving in France, whether to go any further, what other kinds of animals and drivers they might encounter, also touching on the weather, Denzil's arthritic shoulder, the low battery in Flo's hearing aid, a corn on Charlie's small toe, and other matters of similar interest. Three-quarters of an hour went by, during which time M. Ardille had fallen asleep in his chair and Jacques began to feel a bit dozy.

'Perhaps I could help with mending the fences or something,' offered Denzil, 'maybe electrify them even. If only I had my tools with me.'

This had the effect of silencing the other three for a moment, but then a few words from Annabelle brought Jacques to the edge of his chair.

'While the nice young policeman is here, I'd like him to take that funny case I found in the cupboard last night and hand it in to lost property. It's got a name on it I couldn't read without my glasses, and I seem to have mislaid them. Perhaps he would help me look for them, with those sharp young eyes of his. Ask him, Jack, please, while I go and get it.'

But Jacques, for some reason, seemed to be tongue-tied, and could only manage a gurgle.

It was at this critical moment that a squeal of brakes outside the office heralded the return of M Lourenne, Rosie and Chloe. They came into the office as Annabelle left for the caravan.

'Les bagages des mesdames – j'ai les trouver – il y a ici. J'ai les examiné et ils sont pas de problem.'

'Ici, nous avons un problem nouveau, très interessant,' said his partner, who had followed enough of Annabelle's last remarks to get the general idea, and was finding Jacques' obvious discomfiture of additional interest.

Annabelle came in with the large expensive looking holdall.

'I wonder how this could have found its way into my wardrobe,' she said. 'I'm sure it wasn't there the night before.'

The same question was exercising Gendarme Ardille's mind. Rosie was staring at it, and took it from Annabelle.

'That's Herbert's,' she said. 'I'm sure I've seen it in the boot of his car. What on earth is it doing here? I suppose they'll want to examine it like the rest of my luggage.'

'*Excusez-moi,*' said Lourenne, and grabbed it.

They all gathered round to see what all the trouble was about, with the exception of Jacques, who seemed anxious to stay as far away from it as possible.

It was unlocked, and Lourenne flicked it open, tipping its contents onto the floor. It stank a bit, the dirty washing, especially the underwear, and even more as they turned it over and over.

A pair of very despondent gendarmes returned to their station. They had that feeling they had been on the right track, there was the smell of something highly suspicious about the whole thing – Herbert's wild dash from the hotel needed more explanation, and the odd reactions of Jacques and his obvious relief when they left empty handed didn't seem to add up.

Herbert's dogs were barking their heads off as they entered the building, so relieving their frustration with a moment of compassion, they opened the bags of dog biscuits and threw handfuls into the kennel.

The broken biscuits scattered across the floor, and some of them sparkled.

As the truth dawned on them, the brilliance of the diamonds was reflected in the triumphant eyes of two delirious gendarmes.

Their delirium was sadly to be short-lived as the hungry dogs pounced on the 'evidence' with relish and without regard for the consequences, licked the platter clean and wagged their tails for more.

'*Merde!*' cried the pair in unison, which neatly summed up their detection duties for the next two days.

9

The first thing both couples did on their return from France three weeks later, after resting for twenty-four hours, that is, was to take their films of the holiday in for developing. Two days later Annabelle and Flo collected them with their shopping and they all got together in Flo's flat to look at them.

Their spectacles were needed, and not surprisingly, a search had to be put in hand for two pairs. In this instance it was Charlie's and Flo's, and they were in the familiar process of crawling around the floor when the door chimes announced a visitor. Charlie went to the door.

To his surprise and concern, on opening the door he found himself confronted by an officer of the law.

'Good afternoon, sir, I am PC Blossom from the local constabulary. May I ask if I am addressing Mr C. Butterworth?'

Charlie was tongue-tied. He nodded.

'Might I please have a word with your good self and your wife ... particularly your wife, Mrs Florence Butterworth?'

'You'd better c-come in, officer,' Charlie stammered.

Annabelle was the first to get up off the floor.

'I don't know what you're looking for, young man, but if it means undressing my friend Flo, I shall insist on being present ... and the men must go into the other room. Anyway, before you start whatever it is, perhaps you will help as an expert to locate two pairs of missing glasses. And mind where you tread with those great boots of yours.'

The warning was well-advised but a fraction too late. Constable Blossom felt and heard the crunch of glass and frame as he advanced across the room, neither of which registered with the others present, but became apparent to two of them at least when he picked up and carefully examined the twisted remains. Blossom flushed.

'Don't bother helping to find the other pair,' said Denzil with a hint of sarcasm. 'Is there some way we can help you?'

'If it's to do with the problems on the ferry back from France, we shall be pleased to explain what happened,' offered Charlie. 'We tried to explain to the Captain – he came down to see us but as soon as he did, he cried out "Oh no!", turned round and ran up the stairway.'

'Same rude man we had trouble with on the way out,' said Denzil. 'Anyway, I still don't think those ramps are wide enough for caravans, and we certainly would never have tried reversing down it if they hadn't kept shouting *"Au revoir"*. It's an easy mistake to make, you know. Good job the hitch broke or we'd be suing for the car as well.'

'Thank goodness Rosie and the dogs got out of it all right,' added Flo. 'And when Max and Marlene and

Chloe went for those men bringing Rosie ashore, well, what do you expect?'

PC Blossom took out his notebook and held up his hand.

'My notes don't include anything on that subject, but if you wish to make a statement on the matter, I can inform my superior, who I am sure will be pleased to deal with it at the station.'

He said it with a wicked smile. His sergeant was going to love that.

'Is he the man we should make our claim to for the spectacles?' asked Flo. An innocent enough question, but not a popular one with PC Blossom, whose smile quickly disappeared.

'May I enquire, ladies, which of you is Mrs Florence Butterworth?'

'Does it make any difference?' asked Denzil. 'We all went on holiday together.'

Annabelle started to cry. 'Of course it makes a difference,' she whimpered. 'After all these years too, fancy saying that, Denzil.'

She got up off the floor, where she had still been looking for the other pair of spectacles, and promptly found them as her foot moved under a chair and crunched them into the carpet.

'There!' she said. 'That's all your horrible fault, Denzil Dearlove,' and strutted towards the door. Unfortunately, with tears in her eyes instead of glasses, it was the cupboard door she found, stumbled into, and had to crawl out of.

Half-an-hour later, after delicate negotiations and an abject apology from Denzil with lengthy explanations, all was calm once again and they were seated round the table, drinking tea.

A very confused officer of the law decided to try just

once more to carry out his mission. He consulted his notebook again.

'Is it correct, Mrs Butterworth, that during your recent travels to France, you rode in the back of a Jaguar motor vehicle driven by a Mr Herbert Smart with two large dogs?'

'Oh no,' said Flo, 'Mr Smart was with his lady friend, Miss Rosie. I was in the back with the two large dogs ... such friendly animals, and nice and warm ... Max and Marlene...'

'Thank you, ma'am,' cut in Blossom. 'It seems that the case of Rex versus Mr Smart will take place in due time, and your presence will be required to give evidence.'

'I'm sorry officer, but it was Max, not Rex, like I said, and I deny giving him any presents. Didn't much like the man, but Rosie was all right, and the dogs were lovely.'

PC Blossom completed his duty by handing Flo an official notice from the court. He breathed a sigh of relief.

'Can we all come along and watch?' asked Annabelle. 'Maybe we can help.'

PC Blossom gave this offer some thought, and could be excused for falling back on a well-worn cliché.

'Don't ring us, madam,' he quoted, 'we'll ring you.'

'That's very kind, officer, but there's no need to send a car. Charlie will bring us, won't you, Charlie?'

As he said it, Denzil was peering everywhere for the constable, but PC Blossom had quietly let himself out.

One enthusiastic reader kindly enquired if *Five Times as Funny* is based on Bernard's true life experience. Sadly, he has since been committed. The reader, that is!

But ... there is such a thing. With his wife Mary, Bernard did sail around the world in the 38ft ketch *Mameena*, a true story of a year's adventurous ocean sailing, covering 17,000 miles, culminating in truly dramatic fashion.

The book is titled *Whatever Happened to Thursday?* and the tale is told in his typically light-hearted pacey prose. A pleasant, fascinating read, it is available in hardback through The Book Guild, price £12.